ANGEL BURNS

SOUL FORGE BOOK SIX

LESLIE CLAIRE WALKER

sfp

**My Name is Night Sanchez. Every choice leads me to the darkest
road.**

iii

It's been months since I became one with the Angel of Death, and I've
barely begun to understand my transformation. My found family isn't
sure how to deal with the new me.

I need them more than ever when the Angel reveals a catastrophic
secret. We're all that stands between the world and the Angel's apocalyptic endgame.

No matter how brave we are, we don't have enough power to
defeat him.

But surrender is not in my nature. I'll walk the darkest road with
my family united at my side.

I'll hold onto hope even if my soul burns. And then I'll find a way
to triumph.

ALSO BY LESLIE CLAIRE WALKER

THE AWAKENED MAGIC SAGA

THE SOUL FORGE

(The Complete Series)

Angel Hunts

Angel Rises

Angel Falls

Angel Strikes

Angel Roars

Angel Burns

THE FAERY CHRONICLES

(The Complete Series)

Faery Novice

Faery Prophet

Faery Sovereign

SHORT STORY COLLECTIONS

Ink & Blood

Ink & Stars

Ink & Sword

CHAPTER 1

THE FULL MOON stared down from a spring sky awash in stars and wisps of cloud. A cool gust from the east lifted the long dark hair from our shoulders, caressing our skin like a lover. Its temperature was warmer than our chilled skin. Its perfume tasted of pink and white cherry blossoms and the musk of the Willamette River that cut Portland in half, east from west.

Our family—my family—I no longer knew how to think of myself now that I'd become two people wrapped into a single human body—rested snugly in their beds at Addie's house on the east side, trapped in the smothering arms of their dreams. The Angel of Death and I preferred the west side these days. I perched several stories above SW 5th Avenue, the downtown streets deserted below.

My family and I were still unsure of each other. They wanted me to reassure them that enough of the Night Sanchez they'd known remained after the last fight, when the Angel and I had finally merged into one being. We wanted them to understand the ways in which we'd changed and what that meant, even if we didn't understand it all ourselves.

It was normal. Human.

I sighed, the movement undulating from lungs and heart to the crown of my very human head and down over the black wings folded along my back. It'd been three months. We'd done our best to understand and integrate our new normal. But we had obligations bigger than family, more important than love. How long before those responsibilities took us away?

How long before end of the world?

If I was one-hundred-percent honest, my restlessness came from more than that. I wanted the freedom. I wanted to be who and what I'd become without feeling like I had to hide it. Or apologize for it.

Without the Angel, the battle would've been lost. Without the Angel, humanity would have no defense against the forces of disintegration and dissolution that wanted to end the world. Everything we'd done, we'd done to save lives. To save all the worlds.

A swift intake of breath and the deliberate crunch of gravel told us we weren't alone a heartbeat before the air filled with the scents that spoke of home: grass and earth.

Red knelt beside me, salt—and—pepper hair floating with the breeze. The bright green and rich brown of his halo—the manifestation of his life force and flavor of his magic—deepened. He reached up to smooth his mustache, the barest touch of southeast Texas in his voice. "Here again?"

"We like it here."

"The view?"

"It's spectacular." Every line and curve of his face, the breadth of his chest beneath the unzipped heather—gray hoodie and black T—shirt, the muscular thighs inside his faded jeans. I wanted him here and now.

I always wanted him, but the strength of it, the insistent heat low in my belly, was new and seductive and slightly alarming in its lack of inhibition.

He grinned. "I haven't been the one keeping you company all night."

The company in question crouched across the street, above the green tile entrance to the Portland Building. Portlandia, thirty—four feet of copper woman in classical clothes, trident in her left hand, right hand, reached down in benediction. To others, she was a statue. To the Angel and I, she was a goddess frozen in space, the protector of the city. Her eyes gave nothing away. She seemed inert. But we knew better.

She was alive, like we were alive. We could smell her, the copper of her forging reminding us of blood. The world didn't see her clearly. They saw what they'd been taught to see.

"She have anything new to say?" Red asked.

My lips curved. "Not yet. Everything all right at home? No Horsemen of the Apocalypse on the stoop? No one tied up in the basement? No attacking hordes of possessed people?"

"None of those. Not even an archangel."

I felt a little sad about that, although I wasn't sure why. Michael showed up when he wanted to rather than when we needed him, constrained by rules I didn't understand and frankly didn't care about. But he'd finally come through. I had to respect that, even if I couldn't count on it happening again.

Michael's absence should've felt reassuring. Instead, if felt like—

I met Red's green gaze. "It's the calm before the storm."

"The moment before the other shoe drops. That's why you're really here."

To be alone with the protector of the city. To figure out who and what we'd become. To work our magic as it manifested for us now. To be ready to fight at full power when the battle came.

I nodded.

"Michael said we'd have some time—for you to get used to being Death, for the other side to figure out their next step. But I can already feel it coming, whatever it is."

It could be the End again, the enemy who'd been there before the beginning of creation and who sought to destroy all the worlds, to return everything and everyone to the void. It could be the remnants of the Order of the Blood Moon, the magical assassins to whom I'd once belonged. Or the eldest Watchers, who'd roamed the earth from the beginning of time, keeping a weather eye on magical beings, preserving the human order, and enforcing magical law.

But I didn't think so.

Three Horsemen had already manifested in the human world, possessing human vessels. Once the last of us appeared, the Apocalypse would follow.

"The fourth Horseman," I said. "The one called War."

"We can't stop that, can we?"

We couldn't stop Famine from joining forces with the End. We hadn't been able to stop our own change or the transformation of our friend Luna into the Horseman Pestilence. Destiny seemed to want what it wanted, the rest of us be damned. "The odds aren't good."

"What do you want to do?"

"Look for her."

He raised a brow. "You're assuming it'll be a woman."

"The rest of us are."

He inclined his head, giving me the point. "You gettin' on that right this minute?"

"At three—thirty in the morning, with no clue yet where to go?"

"Come on home, then."

"Is that why you came? To bring me home?"

"Why else?"

I sighed. "Where'd you park?"

"Stacy sent me."

He hadn't driven at all. Our witch had teleported him. Previously, that kind of magic had been reserved for emergencies. For battle. Were the Angel and I an emergency now?

Red furrowed his brow, reaching out to cup the side of our face. "I can see what you're thinking. Answer's no."

He could more than read my expression. He could feel every emotion that coursed through us via the heart link we shared. For a moment, the sacred heart tattoo on his chest flared, the fabric of his shirt unable to conceal its glow.

Lines etched at the corners of his mouth seemed starker than they'd been a minute ago, as if the depth of feeling in his heart hurt him.

The last battle had done Red considerable damage. He hadn't come clean about what had happened at the house after it had been invaded by the souls of the dead, their touch colder than the grave and just as fatal.

I'd seen only a small part of his fight. Spirits rising through the basement floor, busting through the protections and taking down Stacy—and with her, almost closing off the magical connections we'd used as a lifeline, to help each other, to survive.

Red had saved Stacy. I still didn't know how. He'd refused to tell me, and the others who'd been with him kept mum as well.

At first, I'd thought he didn't want to burden me during my own healing, but as the days had passed and he'd avoided the subject, I understood he was hiding it—maybe hiding from it.

I raised a hand to cover his, to press his palm to my skin. "What do you need?"

"You." He leaned over to brush his lips across ours.

I caught his bottom lip with my teeth as he pulled away, drawing him in, deepening the kiss. I fisted a hand in the fabric of his shirt.

He laughed, his breath warm and inviting.

"Home is overpopulated," I said.

"I'll grant you that, but none of the houseguests are sleeping in our room."

I glanced away, eyes drawn again to Portlandia. She hadn't moved an inch, her copper body frozen by the hands of the sculptor who'd crafted her. Maybe it was my imagination that muscles moved beneath the metal, that a voice issued forth from her still mouth. That she called my name.

I rose on steady legs, an inhuman silhouette in the dark, wings unfurling to full width.

Red whistled. "You're something, you know that?"

I did. "We can fly you home."

He shook his head. "No need. Stacy gave me a return ticket. You can be my passenger. Where's your backpack?"

The backpack meant to conceal the wings. "We didn't bring it."

"Night, you're gonna get yourself caught. Seen."

"By who? The Portland Police Bureau is out in the streets looking for angels?"

"Bullets might not kill you, but they'll fuck you up," he said. "Sort of like what'll happen if the normals on the ground catch a glimpse of a woman with white fire in her eyes and giant wings. This is Portland, and people don't bat an eye at the unusual, but when you take off flying, they're gonna figure out you're not wearing a costume."

He was right. The Angel and I knew better. But we also wanted to feel free.

The Angel didn't care much about human concerns, but the human part of us put them first. It was stupid to give in to the desire for complete freedom. If there was anything I'd learned over the years, that kind of freedom was as much an illusion as safety.

I folded our wings down to their most compact, a foot's worth of feather and muscle and cartilage. "Better?"

"Grab onto me," he said, rising to his feet. "Don't let go."

I wrapped my arms around his waist and held his gaze as the night began to spin in a blur of moon and stars and clouds and copper goddess. Concrete and glass and steel. A single houseless human, all his worldly belongings in a green trash bag, settling down for the night on the sidewalk beneath us.

The air exploded in sulfur and heat. The sensation of being violently yanked through space dragged my heart into my throat. Then, the power pulled us across the city, the lights of the freeways and their reflection on the river a streak of light.

A heartbeat later, our feet settled on the front porch of Addie's buttercream yellow house in the glow of the overhead light, boards creaking underfoot. The big tuxedo tomcat who called the wide porch rail home had gone hunting for the night. Or fled from the predator in the rocker beside the door.

He smelled of ancient paper and millennia, his silence so thick, it took on a life of its own. He had no halo—not a halo full of emptiness, like the End, but no halo at all. He pushed to his feet, his white shirt bright in the dark. The black leather duster he wore skimmed his black leather pants, billowing around the soles of his motorcycle boots. He wore power as if he'd always had it, as if he didn't need to prove himself to anyone else.

That was true freedom—the power to make your own choices, to own them, to live with them.

If the consequences of what Malek had done from his creation as the serpent in the Garden of Eden through this moment tore him up inside, he didn't show it. If he wanted to scream to all the heavens and all the hells with the pain of it, he never would. The End had taken away his voice, the voice of temptation, forever.

Forever was Malek's reality. Now, it was the Angel's and mine, too.

Fear took root in my heart for the first moment since the time just after our transformation. We slowed our breathing, drawing out our exhalation to a six—count, inhaling for four, calming our nervous system so we could focus.

The serpent hadn't planted himself in that rocking chair to meditate or ruminate. He'd been waiting for us.

Malek raised his hands and signed.

We need to talk.

CHAPTER 2

MALEK LED THE WAY inside, kicking off his boots as soon as he entered, just like everyone else welcomed into Addie's house. The house spirit took his measure as it did everyone's and let him pass, but the tension in the air reflected its displeasure at being required to do so.

Malek come to our aid and Addie had invited him in. He had free run of the place, but no one wanted him here—not even his apprentice, who needed his help to recover after her latest resurrection.

Red and I followed him to the kitchen, threading through the rarely—used dining room on the left and the living area on the right with its facing sofas and dark fireplace, family photos crowding the mantle. The silence of our sock feet on the oak gave us a momentary sense of the house as it should be in the middle of the night: filled with beloved people whose slowed breathing gave the air a sense of deep stillness, their worries overtaken by dreams.

No intruders. No feeling of imminent attack. Clear sight lines to the back of the house. Protections, whole and strong.

Malek had brewed a fresh pot of coffee and set out mugs in the center of the well—loved oak table. He grabbed a white bag from its throne on the counter, the mouth—watering scent of eggs and bacon grease wafting through the paper.

We sat. He poured. When he finished, he doled out breakfast sandwiches wrapped in wax paper and oblong hashbrowns in black cardboard sleeves.

Red folded his arms across his chest, foregoing breakfast while I dug in with gusto. English muffin, bacon, eggs, avocado. It tasted like heaven and I was hungry. These days, I were always hungry.

Malek signed. *Beth's in trouble.*

"Beth can barely stand up and walk around the house," Red said. "What kind of trouble could she have gotten up to in that condition?"

She asked me to leave.

"Leave Portland?"

Malek nodded.

"When's your flight?"

Malek stared at him as if he were a child. An insufferable child.

I swallowed a mouthful of salty, crispy hash brown. "He's not going."

Malek shrugged. *I haven't decided yet. I'm not sure what's best for her.*

Rich, coming from him. "You ordered her to lie to us. She refused to keep your secret. She knows you're going to punish her—it's just a matter of time."

I won't hurt her.

A few months ago, I'd have believed him. Now, I understood the difference between what he wanted and what he might be forced to do. All Elders, including Malek, operated by their own rules. Those rules weren't guidelines. They weren't up for debate. The letter of the law could be bent, but not broken.

"You don't want to hurt her," I said. "But you will. You extract a price for your services. For lies told to you. For betrayal. That's what you do. It's part of who you are. What do you usually do to people who betray you?"

He didn't answer, but he didn't need to. He made an example of people who did that to him. They died bloody and screaming.

"You can't let her off the hook," Red said. "How does that work out for her?"

An eavesdropper cleared her throat in the doorway. "Standing right here."

Beth's black—frame glasses had slid down her nose. She pushed them back into place with a shaky but purposeful middle finger. Her orange—and—black halo was still two shades lighter than it should've been and perspiration sheened her forehead. Her bird's nest of braids looked more exuberant than usual, owing to the joys of hot, then cold, then hot sweats and too much time lying flat. She'd pulled on a pair of faded jeans with frayed knees to compliment her pink—and—black kitty pajama top, and wriggled her toes inside mismatched wool socks.

Red pushed to his feet. "You shouldn't be out of bed."

"I shouldn't have crawled up the basement stairs, either, but I had to know what was going on up here. The suspense will kill me—or, you know, you will."

She'd aimed that barb at Malek. He absorbed the strike with a blank expression.

"Night," she said by way of hello. "Felt you and the Angel come home."

That was a new thing. Beth had never "felt" me do anything before the transformation. Now, she could tag my location if she focused. She seemed perplexed as to why, but I thought it was because she'd died twice, and she was still very close to the second death in time and magic.

"Hey, Red," she said. "Are you going to eat that sandwich or let it congeal? Inquiring hungry people want to know."

He stood, offering her his chair with one hand while he grabbed his mug with the other.

She took a handful of unsteady steps and collapsed in the seat. "Jesus, will this ever end? It's like it's worse, going through a second resurrection. Why won't anyone let me stay dead?"

You know why.

Beth rolled her eyes. She looked at me. "So, what's the plan?"

I swallowed the last of my breakfast sandwich and washed it down with a gulp of coffee. "You need to rest."

"It only took me half an hour to make it to the kitchen. In a couple of days, I'll be ready to take on the world. I can promise I'll be there when you call, and then I can die all over again."

I leaned back in my chair. "Did you come here to fight?"

She wiped her damp brow with her sleeve. "I'm not mad at you, Night."

"You are," I said.

"It wasn't your fault, what happened." She pulled a slice of bacon from the middle of her sandwich. "It was my fault. Or, actually, it was nobody's. The choices were fight or don't fight, and no way was I about to turn tail and run and leave you in the lurch. Also, I hate Famine. You want to know what else I hate? Secrets. Unnecessary secrets."

Malek started to sign.

Beth waved him off. "Just stop, please. I'm not going to give away secrets that are about you, boss man. But the information Night needs to fight the good fight? Holding onto it for leverage is a dick move."

Red choked on his coffee.

Beth had just called one of the most powerful beings in all the worlds—the one to whom she owed her life—a dick.

Malek met her gaze. *That's why I was waiting for them. To tell them what they need to know.*

Beth blinked at him. "Oh."

You should go back to bed.

"Not until I finish the bacon and you tell me what the price is for disobedience."

You already know.

"You planning to wait until I recover to kill me? That seems, I don't know, mean."

I held up a hand to referee the back—and—forth. "It's his nature."

"It's yours, too, now," she said.

"Now?"

I'd killed my Order mentor, Lily. She'd taken me in and given me a place to belong. Turned me into a soulless killing machine. Come to me for help and tried to kill me. She was dead, and I wasn't sorry. Lily was the least of my sins.

Beth shrugged. "You were an assassin, so okay."

And she was Malek's apprentice.

He'd instructed Beth to save the lives of our people at a critical time with magical ink that also served as a tool of surveillance. He'd watched us without our knowledge or permission. He would've kept watching for powers—knew—how—long if Beth hadn't blurted the entire plan.

The question wasn't *what did Beth deserve?* It was *what did Malek deserve?*

He'd acted like an ally, a friend. Friends didn't spy and they didn't lie about it.

Malek didn't fear us. He also didn't make excuses. He read my thoughts because I made them plain on my face.

What do you want from me, Night?

He wanted to balance the scales? Fine. "Consider Beth's price paid."

He shook his head. *Make another choice.*

"You can owe us, the Angel and me."

After a moment, he nodded.

"They'll collect," Beth said.

Counting on it.

That didn't feel disconcerting at all.

"That's my cue." Beth took a deep breath, blew it out long and slow, then gripped the table's edge.

Red swooped in beside her and circled her waist with a strong arm. "Lean on me if you need to. Tell me if you need to stop. Or if I need to carry you."

She didn't give him any shit about babying her. She simply nodded and let him lead her out.

Malek waited to speak again until their footfalls faded, until we heard the basement door open on whining hinges and close again.

I don't want her to hate me.

On the surface, that was ludicrous. Any grown man uttering those words would deserve an ass—kicking, much less a goddamn god who'd just made it crystal clear that he held her life in his hands. Dig a little deeper, though, and I could see much more.

She doesn't think the rules should apply to her.

"She's not just just an extension of you, Malek. She's her own person."

She's my apprentice.

"She's your daughter, the same way that Faith is mine."

I've never had kin.

That was the problem. "How are the rules different when it concerns your child? Are they different?"

He closed his eyes for a moment, as if to hide from the question. When he opened them again, I saw the millennia of his life reflected in their depths.

It doesn't get easier.

"What's that?"

The decision—making. Experience with Beth has taught me that every situation is new. No one has ever....

"Loved you before?"

He cracked a genuine smile that faded as quickly as it arrived.

"This is what you really wanted to talk to Red and me about?"

Malek nodded.

It seemed so unimportant in the grand scheme of all the worlds. We were in the middle of a cosmic fight. What was one relationship in the midst of that? On the other hand, what the fight did to each of us was intensely personal, and Malek truly seemed perplexed.

I knew what it meant to be human, but could something like that be taught to a being who'd never been fragile or vulnerable?

"You want my help with Beth? You can have it," I said. "Under one condition. That you're not holding on to any more information we need to know."

I told Beth I was here to tell you things.

I waited.

He raised his hands to sign, then dropped them in his lap. After a moment, he tried again. *I'm not above lying to get what I want. And, in this case, I wanted her to let go of the bone she's got her teeth clamped around. To rest. To heal. That's all.*

"There's nothing else?"

He shook his head.

He'd just told us that he wasn't above lying, and he was lying now. Why? I started to ask. He held up a hand to forestall the question and shook his head.

Why wouldn't he tell us? Not the right time? Not the right place? Did he fear the consequences? Malek didn't strike us as afraid of anything or anyone—except Beth.

The Angel and I reached out, our consciousness brushing against the house spirit's, looking for anything out of the ordinary. Someone watching. Some threat it might have sensed that we hadn't. We felt no one and nothing out of place. The only thing out of the ordinary was a quiet so deep, we could hear the creak of boards and the sighing of the house itself as it settled, the ticking of the kitchen clock a heartbeat.

In all the time I'd lived here, I'd never heard it so still.

Can you feel it? Malek asked. *The fourth Horseman is arriving.*

I sucked in a breath and blew it out slowly, leaning back into my chair. Things that had seemed unrelated drifted toward each other and began to lock into place, like pieces of a jigsaw puzzle. My restlessness. The compulsion to figure out what I'd become that manifested in nights spent with Portlandia.

I wanted to know for myself. To wrap my mind around the new me. But it wasn't—couldn't—be just about me.

Discovering how my magic had changed and learning the nuances and limits of the Angel's and my power could mean the difference between life and death for the people I loved, not to mention the cosmic fight about to go down and what that could mean for all living beings in all the worlds. I had to get right with all.

Malek's fingers flashed. *You thought you had time.*

"I was wrong." The end of the world was now. "Do you know who the fourth Horseman is?"

He looked as if I'd punched him in the gut. *It's not confirmed.*

He hadn't exactly dodged the question, but he hadn't answered it either. "Who?"

She's a kid.

Now I felt as if I'd been hit. My daughter Faith's face bloomed in my mind. Hard enough that she'd been born with magic that allowed her to talk with gods, worse that she served as the human host for the god of magic.

"How young?" I asked.

Eighteen.

Faith was seventeen. So was Beth. I got why Malek's fear of and for Beth felt like more—because it *was* more.

Even as the words tumbled from my mouth, I knew how stupid they sounded. "It's not fair."

Cosmic powers didn't care whether you were forty—seven or seventeen. They didn't care whether you had plans or goals or scholarships, whether you were loved or abused as a child, whether you needed years of therapy or whether you could afford financially or mentally or spiritually or physically to join the fight. They cared only whether you had the magic and the potential to do the work.

You think they shouldn't have to carry the weight because we love them.

My mouth curved into a sad smile. "If only."

He looked away for a moment. When he met my gaze again, he'd wiped all trace of a father's love and worry from his face. *We should know by morning.*

"You've got someone working on this."

You remember what I told you about the Horsemen?

The curse that took his voice had been cast by the last incarnation of the four Horsemen. He guarded that secret as if it were buried treasure. United, the Horsemen had enough power to hurt him. He couldn't allow us all to become embodied in the human world.

"You're gonna to try to take out this kid?"

Self—defense.

"Only if she's a direct threat. If danger is imminent."

You expect me to wait for the inevitable?

He was like everyone else—he'd do what was in his best interests. Problem was, at his level of power and influence, I didn't always understand enough to mark his best interests. That made him hard to trust.

"Why are you telling me all this?"

Same reason I told you about my curse in the first place.

He wanted my help. "I won't kill the girl for you."

You'll protect her with your life.

That truth hung heavy in the air. I held his gaze.

I'm counting on you.

"To stand between you and the girl?"

To save us all.

"What do you need saving from?"

Myself.

"Understood."

Not just an acknowledgment of his request, but an admission that I knew how it felt to need that kind of saving. That everything I'd done from the moment I made the decision to abort the mission to assassinate Faith, to take her and run, had been about redeeming myself.

I knew what it meant to need saving from myself.

He nodded, pushing back from the table and rising. He didn't once look over his shoulder as he made his silent way toward the back door. He unhooked the chain and flicked the deadbolt with the pad of his thumb, hesitating for a heartbeat before stepping into the dark.

He didn't bother pulling the door closed. Chill and damp blew into the kitchen on blustery wind. I took a deep breath and got up, every pop and crack of my joints and every thud of my steps and creak of the floor a reminder that, no matter how much magic the Angel and I wielded, there were beings more powerful. We might not be enough.

I shuddered, a wave of fear rolling through me, sticking to my skin and lodging in my gut as I locked up behind the serpent.

In the morning, everything would change. The identity of the fourth Horseman would be revealed. Malek would go from a some-time friend to a full—time enemy. The Angel and I needed to be ready.

The question was, how?

CHAPTER 3

I SLIPPED INSIDE the room I shared with Red as wind gusted outside. The rattle of window glass and the whip and clack of branches against the side of the house zinged the the fine hairs on my arms. I paused mid—step to listen, half—expecting another threat to materialize. But I felt only the strong beat of my heart and heard only the gentle exhale of my breath. I rolled my neck, willing the tension to leave.

Red hadn't yet made it back from the basement. Not surprising. He didn't have it in him to leave Beth agitated, not if he could do or say something to calm her. If words alone didn't do the trick, he'd lace them with his heart's magic so she'd feel heard and understood. So she'd feel safe.

The night light in the bathroom glowed like a beacon. I stripped as I headed toward it, the muscles in my back working more than they ought in order to be rid of my shirt, sparking frustration that wanted to fire into anger. My clothes felt like a burden. My skin, too. I wanted to be free. I wanted to let go of the perilous future for one goddamn minute. Beyond a shadow of a doubt, if I flicked on the light and caught my reflection in the mirror, I'd be able to see the weight on my shoulders, the pressure against my skin, the worry lines around my eyes.

Malek was going to be a problem. At least he had enough self—awareness to know it. To ask for help. But whether I could handle him was another story. No one in the history of the world had ever been able to beat him, not even the curse that took his voice. Now that the end of the world loomed and the only real threat to him rose, he would be more dangerous than ever.

If Malek had correctly guessed the identity of the fourth Horseman, then we were dealing with a kid my daughter's age. That was going to be a problem, too. Not just because her circumstances reminded me of Faith's—following my thoughts down that dark road cut deep—but because eighteen was old enough to know enough about the world, but young enough to believe you knew everything. On one hand, making sure she sided with the Angel and I, with Luna and Pestilence, mattered more than anything. On the other hand, she was just a girl, a priceless human being who hadn't asked to be drawn into this fight. Hosting a Horseman could obliterate her. Twist her into something unrecognizable. Kill her soul. It was my job to fight her if I had to. It was also my job to fight for her.

The fall of water from the shower head bounced off the tight muscles and rolled off my feathers. It took a long moment for the steam to ease my breathing, for the tension in my shoulders and low back to let go.

My mind would turn over possibilities and probabilities whether or not I focused on them. The Order had trained me to do that, to search for the flaw in the plan, the monkey in the wrench. To lessen the chance of failure.

Without more information, all the mental and intuitive gymnastics in the world wouldn't mean much. I'd just be telling myself stories that might turn out to be so much smoke. So I breathed out for a count of six, in for a count of four, until my nervous system calmed. Until I could simply be right here, right now.

I felt Red before I saw him. The magic that connected our hearts pulsed, letting me know he was close, letting me know what he felt.

My frustration and vigilance softened around the edges as his feelings flooded in. Physical and emotional exhaustion. A well of compassion in need of filling. Raw nerves.

The shower curtain crinkled as he joined me under the spray. His grass and earth scent infused the steam, magnified by the heat. He bent to rest his forehead against mine, the heart link between us pulsing again. The worlds and all the other people in them and the impending Apocalypse and all the fear and uncertainty fell away.

He looked like I felt. He felt like unleashed lightning.

"Everything all right downstairs?" I asked.

His lips curved into a half—smile. "She takes it out of me."

On the downtown roof, he'd been playful and rested, his life force strong. Now, he was on the edge. "Must've been some conversation."

He sighed. "It's not just her. I thought we'd have more time before the shit hit the fan."

"We have until morning."

He drew back and met my gaze. "A handful of hours?"

"When you put it like that, it sounds like nothing." I framed his face with my hands, pulling his mouth to meet mine.

He eased in to my kiss, the tension he carried transforming as I opened my mouth, drawing him deeper. His nerves still sparked, but the raw frustration shifted to raw need. He traced a hand down the length of my spine, sending shivers across my skin. He fisted the other hand in the hair at the nape of my neck. He tugged gently at first, then tightened the pressure until my head fell back, baring my throat, lips wandering the curve of my neck.

"A handful of hours with you is everything," he whispered.

It would be what we made it.

His mouth was so close. When I tried to chase it, he pulled my hair again. This time, an impulse to let go of control, to surrender, bloomed in my chest.

"I want," I said.

"You want what?"

My magic rose, slipping past the edges of my skin, winding around his body, sliding into his mind. It happened faster than a heartbeat, easier than a breath. He saw what I wanted him to see, felt what I wanted him to feel. A kiss so deep, it devoured us both as he entered me.

He met my gaze. "Careful."

Because I wasn't supposed to enter his mind without permission. Because his free will trumped my magic except in case of emergency.

I didn't have complete control and I would never take it. I only wanted him to see, to understand.

He let go of my hair. I stood tall, no pressure, no demands. I didn't look away. I didn't so much as blink. The intimacy of that long gaze, the intensity of watching emotions play across his face, was overwhelming. There were no walls. No shields.

He stepped toward me, more than closing the distance, backing me against the wall. The sacred heart tattooed on his chest flared with light as he lifted me.

"Hold on to me," he said.

I wrapped my legs around him as the heart link flared, opening the door between us wide, spilling his emotions into us and ours into him, desire and love, joy and sorrow, fear and hope spiraling together. He drove into me, sealing the connection: heart, soul, and body. In that moment, there was no one else in the world. No time but now. His fire to my ice. Life and Death. His pleasure cascading into me, and mine into him.

I reached for his mouth once more with mine, but he pulled away, gaze focused on my face, watching the emotions that raced behind my eyes, listening for every catch of my breath and every sound. For a moment, I wondered what he saw. Then all I could do was feel—the cool wall behind me, Red's hands on me, his cock inside me. He moved slowly, deliberately. Every stroke unmoored me from the world around us, until he was all I could see.

He took my breath away.

He claimed my mouth, finally giving me the taste of him I craved. I lost all hold on space and time, diving into him as he braced me tighter against the wall. His rhythm quickened, his strokes growing harder, fiercer, driving me on the crest of a wave that reached impossibly high, impossibly fast.

I couldn't think. I couldn't breathe. I cried out his name, mind to mind, as I shattered into a thousand shards of lust and love. He pushed harder, faster, and the first orgasm bloomed into a second and then a third before he followed me, the wave crashing over and through us.

Slowly and carefully, the world re—entered my senses. I could hear the blood rushing in my head, my panting breath. Feel the water and sweat slicking our skin. Smell the musk of our sex. Taste the salt on his skin as I kissed his forehead. The sacred heart on his chest glowed with his light.

If I were ever lost, that would be the light that guided me back home. I felt that with ever cell in my body, a singular truth greater than any other.

He whispered, breath warm against my throat. "Set you down now."

I nodded.

He lowered me gently to stand on legs that might as well have been made from rubber. It took a minute before they decided to hold me upright.

Red threaded his fingers through my hair. "Damn."

"Damn," I echoed.

He cupped a hand beneath my chin, tilting my face to meet his gaze. "This just gets better."

"Every day."

He searched my face. "No fear."

I nodded.

"Say it, Night."

"No fear." I wanted that to be as true as his light. For a moment, imagining made it so.

We'd made the decision together after the transformation, in the early days after he'd brought me home with the Angel firmly embedded in my DNA. We'd spent so much time afraid of what would happen if—when—human and angel became one. Once the thing we feared more than anything else came to pass, we had nothing left to be scared of except living.

Living could be fucking terrifying.

By the time we dried off and climbed under the covers, the sky outside had begun to lighten, the first rays of dawn creeping through around the edges of the window blinds. We spooned in fleeting darkness, breathing beginning to deepen, the siren song of sleep calling.

I closed my eyes, secure in the cradle of Red's arms, and let go of consciousness. The Angel and I needed less sleep now than before. We could get by on the couple of hours' shut—eye we'd had before heading out last night now that we'd mostly finished processing the transformation. Still, sleep felt like heaven, and we felt perfectly willing to let it steal us away.

A tap on the window startled me awake.

CHAPTER 4

RED TIGHTENED HIS ARM around my waist. "What?"

I slipped out of his embrace, kicked off the weighted blanket, and padded to the window, parting the blinds with my fingers to catch a glimpse of an enormous crow perched on the ledge. "Bird."

I gave him an ample dose of side—eye. What were the odds?

The crow's big black gaze locked on mine. It looked like any other big, fat crow in Portland, but seeking out our gaze and remaining this close to us, even with the protection of the window glass, marked it as a messenger from the realm of Faery.

Our friend, Kevin the Faery King, favored this method of communication. Smart phones didn't work so well in his realm, and even if he could manage to send a text or make a call from a more in between place, those could be intercepted. The crow couldn't be compelled to divulge a message to anyone other than its intended target, and acted as a conduit for conversation as much as an information repository.

"What's it want?" Red rolled onto his back and sat up, shoving off the weighted blanket and sheets, giving me a glorious view of his body.

Lust kindled in my belly, its call a siren song I could follow into deep water until I was over my head. I could drown in it and be grateful for that. I swallowed hard and gritted my teeth. I needed to focus. To listen.

Red braced his hands on the mattress, fingertips digging into the pillow top. He expected bad news. It was the only kind we ever received by crow messenger.

I looked at the bird, reading the intelligence in its eyes.

It stood straighter. Taller. *Come now.*

Now meant the need was urgent. *Does Kevin need us?*

Luna.

Once upon a time, Luna been a normal, a bartender in downtown Portland. Few friends and little money, but she'd come here to build a life that she could call her own and she was doing it, goddammit. Until the night the archangel Gabriel swept her into the fight by marking her as a potential asset, dosing her with magic that she might be able to handle. If she assimilated the power, then she'd live. If not, she'd die a terrible death, body and soul.

If she hadn't come to us, and if we hadn't intervened, she'd have disintegrated for good and that would've been that. But she did, and we did, and she'd lived. The price of her life had been possession by the Horseman Pestilence. She and her Horseman had taken our side. The side of life.

They'd stayed with Kevin and his people in Faery. Luna and Pestilence had to learn how to live with each other. How to live with their magic, with what they'd become. Kevin provided safe space to do both.

Anything else?

The crow launched itself from the ledge and winged away, its black—feathered body melding with the gloaming before it vanished altogether. Returning to Faery, or going on to live its crow life until Kevin called it again? I still didn't understand how it all worked.

"It's Luna," I said aloud.

Red swung his legs to the side, planting his feet on the floor. "Trouble."

Trouble was inevitable. Trouble was like breathing.

"You coming back to bed, or you want to go now?"

I walked over to sit beside him.

"So...now?"

I nodded.

"Want company?"

"You should sleep. At least, one of us should."

He sighed.

"I'll be back soon."

"Be sure you are."

I kissed him goodbye. He took his time kissing me back, fanning the flame I tried to ignore. The heart link bloomed with new light and life, and I felt his exhaustion and the promise of desire.

He pulled away. "Later."

"I'll hold you to it."

He settled into bed again, watching me through heavy—lidded eyes before exhaustion took him. He snored softly as I dug clean clothes from the dresser in the closet, slipping into them and nicking the door shut behind me.

The hall was empty. Down the way, the kitchen lights glowed at full strength, the clang of pots and pans evidence that a breakfast—maker had awakened. Addie. Or Sunday.

I took the closest path to Faery—a few steps on the creaking hall floor and down the basement stairs into the underground chill, through the veil of protections that Addie had built, strengthened with all of our magic, into the ritual space. In the center of the circle of brightly colored pillows and atop the red jute rug, Beth slept on a camping cot, blanket pulled so high that only the tips of her wild braids showed.

I sent a breath of peace to her. She deserved to have ease. To heal. To find some solid ground to stand on before she made decisions she might regret.

Then, I stepped around the circle, toward the far end of the space, our power rising to kiss the edges of our skin, the temperature dropping around us, raising the fine hairs on my arms and legs to standing. Calling up the image of the magical door, keyed only to those of us with permission to pass, caused it to appear in the wall. No outline of light or silhouette of darkness, but a patch the color of twilight that beckoned.

As I moved into the gloaming, a flash of heat singed the ends of my hair, the stench of sulfur exploding into a yellow cloud of choking fumes—the In—Between, that place literally between the worlds. A second later, I hurtled out of it and into a different kind of stink: black rubber mats on concrete floors. Sweat. Bleach wipes. Lights off and doors closed, the air stale and thick with shadows.

Justice Gym, the first place I'd called home after we arrived in Portland. The place we'd found Red, and the kids who'd befriended Faith. It'd been too long since I'd come here.

The transformation hadn't leant itself to visiting any of my favorite haunts. Too much pain. Too much uncertainty. Getting used to the changes in my body and the novelty of sharing my patchwork soul with the Angel had taken all our will and focus.

Without an immediate threat, Red had spent plenty of time here. The floor had been reorganized, weights moved around and kettlebells and jump ropes stashed in a different spot. Walls painted a vibrant blue and not yet marred. He'd thrown a good bit of himself into work, getting back to taking in strays and making sure they learned their own worth. Seeing the best in them and reflecting it back.

And augmenting the protections we'd built around the gym. They were solid and whole. No one who wasn't supposed to be here would be able to get in without damage, no matter how powerful they might be. Nowhere would ever be one—hundred—percent safe, but that was no reason not to throw all his skill and elbow grease into the problem.

The thud of shoes to our left caught our attention. The short set of steps that led to the entry were empty, but the office at their feet was not.

Sunday Sloan walked through the office door, tucking her long, wet blond curls into a braid. She wore all black, from her denim jack at T—shirt to her pants and boots—her usual cross between Order operative and cat burglar. Her rose gold halo looked downright serene, and that was not usual at all.

I blinked at her. "What are you doing here?"

Her voice was a flow of water over smooth river rock. "What's it look like? Intercepting you."

At dawn. Sunday had never willingly been up this early in her entire life.

"I'm bored, Night. It's been three months since I've killed anything. Give me someone to fight."

"You fight four times a week."

"We're sparring, you and me. Not the same."

And, therefore, not real. "Not going to a fight."

"You hope not."

That was a major difference between us. I supposed it would always be that way. The Angel and I keyed ourselves to the next door, the one that led to Faery.

She sidled up beside me. "The Faery King has a war on his hands?"

"Not that I know of."

"An ancient evil has invaded Faery?"

"An ancient evil has invaded everywhere. Where have you been, Sunday?"

"The Order has sent another assassin after us," she said. "That's what it is."

"I don't know what it is, except that it's Luna."

"She's having trouble with the Horseman."

I rolled my eyes. "What part of *I don't know* don't you understand?"

"Jeez, Sanchez. Chill."

I stared at her.

She took a single step back.

Weird. "What?"

"It's uncanny. When I meet your gaze, I can see you in there, same as always. But I can see the Angel, too, and that still feels new."

"Creeps you out?"

"Gives me pause."

"What does that mean, exactly?"

She opened her mouth to answer, but all that came out at first was an exasperated huff. "I don't like him."

"You never have. But you tolerate him—"

"Because he helps us win."

He had. Every single fight. "That hasn't changed."

"Something has."

"You mean I have."

She folded her arms across her chest. "I'm not trying to smack you, Night. If I was, you'd know it. So, stop defending."

Was that what I was doing? Protecting myself against my best friend? I never wanted to do that. I never wanted to have to. I held up both hands in surrender.

Her face softened. "We can go on all day about how you're different, all the ways you're still Night and all the ways you're not. You know what? I don't give a shit about that. Nothing I say is news, and nothing I say is gonna change what's already done."

"The others have second thoughts. They don't trust me."

"You blame them?"

After everything I'd done and everything I'd given up to keep my family safe, to save magical children, to keep the city safe, to save the goddamn world—the way they looked at me when they thought I didn't see and the conversations I knew they held behind my back stung. "You think I shouldn't?"

"Does it matter?"

"Yes." What Sunday thought mattered deeply. No one else knew me as well as she did, in all my glory and at my screwed—up worst.

"It's normal to be pissed. That's what I think, so don't beat yourself up about it. But don't get on your high horse, either. It's normal for them to wonder where they stand with you because there's been an Angel—sized earthquake and everything has shifted. Is that so hard to understand?"

The muscles in my back suddenly felt like lumps of granite, and I realized my shoulders had climbed as high as my ears. I turned my attention to them, willing them to loosen up. "No."

Sunday cocked her head to the side, acknowledging my good sense. "What's different—besides you, and besides them—is me. My definition of winning."

"Really? How?"

"The price has to be right."

I furrowed my brow. "I'm afraid you're gonna have to spell that out for me."

"I'm not willing to sacrifice you."

"Not willing?"

"I won't."

Winning had only ever meant one thing to Sunday. Complete and utter annihilation of the enemy at all costs. We'd never talked like this. Not before any of the battles we'd fought since the Angel had come to town. Not back when we'd been lovers, when we'd been each other's lifeline in the midst of the hell that had been the Order of the Blood Moon.

"Why now?"

"Maybe I finally understand that the ends don't justify the means."

That shocked a laugh out of me. "Knock me over with a feather."

"It's not funny, Night."

The sound of my mirth echoed against the walls of the empty gym, then faded. "I guess not."

She let her hands fall to her sides. "I mean it. Every word."

I loved her, too. "If you want to come with me to Faery, keep your magic to yourself and keep your weapons in their proper places."

"It's not a social call."

No, it wasn't. "Just behave."

"I'll take that as a challenge."

"Bet you twenty you mess it up."

She flashed a wry grin. "Open the portal already, Sanchez. Take me to my doom."

The joke fell flat in my heart. The feathers inside my ribcage fluttered, marking the words as something more. As prophecy.

CHAPTER 5

I MET SUNDAY'S GAZE. She winked at me.

It was hard to stay irritated when she did that. When we'd been romantic partners, she'd used that sly wink to every advantage.

In front of us, the door to Faery opened with a blast of sulfur and heat. I moved through the In—Between and, a moment later, into air so fresh the only way to describe it was sweet. I stepped onto oak floors that shone, not with polish, but with life. Sentient stone walls rose close on either side, sconces set into silver frames alight with flames that seemed to be filled with watching eyes that marked mine —and Sunday's—presence in the corridor. The air filled with whispers that I heard with our ears and felt on our skin as they winged their way to the master of the place.

If we'd been uninvited and managed to find a way in, they'd have raised an alarm. But we belonged here, and like Addie's house spirit, the consciousness of the Faery King's home knew that.

The walls shifted around us, fading and reappearing at different angles, providing the path toward what, or whom, we sought. For a split—second, I felt disoriented, head filling with the kind of pressure that promised a headache. Then, the pressure eased and my sense of direction returned, good as new.

"I hate that," Sunday said.

"We don't make the rules here."

"Neither does the King. This place has a mind of its own. It has feelings and an agenda older than him. Freaks me out."

I was still getting used to the idea that the Angel was as old, if not older, than the royal home in Faery. That he took things like shifting corridors and ancient, sentient houses in stride.

The hall stretched like a rubber band or a vision in a funhouse mirror, adding another twenty feet at the far side and closing off to create a dead end. At the terminus, a door appeared. Not a portal between realms, just a regular door with a regular, brass knob. Not the kind of thing we'd seen in Faery before, but then we hadn't had much time to spend here.

"See what I mean?" Sunday asked. "It's like something out of a haunted house. Or a horror movie."

I took a step forward, then stopped suddenly as the knob turned, the door opening to the inside on creaking hinges, a shaft of light flowing into the hall.

Definitely horror—movie worthy.

"Am I right?" Sunday asked. "I'm all the way right."

The door continued on its inward arc, opening all the way to reveal a familiar face.

Eyes the color of a rain—drenched green field, fine lines etched at their corners testifying to the ordeal Luna had undergone. That she was still in the middle of, because powers knew it might never be over. Freckles dotted her cheeks and nose, her light brown complexion tinted a rusty gold, and not because she'd dusted on makeup. The coloring came from the inside. From the Horseman she carried.

She'd traded in her holey, faded jeans and gray hoodie for brown leather that looked soft as butter—boots, pants, and vest, no shirt. She wore her hair in a Mohawk of epic proportion, the ends dyed the same light green as the flecks in her black mirror of a halo.

"Hey," I said. "You rang?"

"If you call me Pestilence, I'm disinviting you."

"As long as you don't call her Death," Sunday said.

Luna moved aside to make way for us. "We can talk inside."

I started toward the door, but Sunday didn't follow—weird for someone who'd professed such a deep desire for action not five minutes ago. I glanced over my shoulder to find her holding her breath, rooted to the spot where she stood.

I knew that look. She'd seen something in Luna that she hadn't before. And judging by the quality of the tension Sunday held in her body, that something was desire.

I snapped my wings to get her attention.

She looked at me.

Smooth, we mouthed.

"Well, Luna said. "You coming?"

Sunday drew a ragged breath—though she covered it well—and stepped in front of me, taking the lead. It was all I could do not to laugh out loud when she gave Luna a not—very—subtle once—over on her way through the door, or when Luna responded by blushing six shades of red.

The room was simple: double bed in the center, a tall pine wardrobe and a full—length mirror against the far wall, an occupied rocking chair in the corner under the bright light of a floor lamp.

That was the only normal thing about it.

My hackles rose. Beside me, Sunday hissed.

The man in the rocker wore a long black leather trench, like Malek's, but there the resemblance ended. This one wore jeans rather than leather pants, and a black T—shirt instead of a tank. He had pale skin and cobalt blue eyes without pupils and a halo full of fleeting shadows.

Shadow. The first Watcher — the first child of angels and men. He held the power of both species within him, including the power to create and unravel life. He could speak a word or wave his hand at a human or any other living thing and unmake them on the spot, leaving nothing but the echo of a final heartbeat and a current of final breath. He led the rest of his kind on the side of the End in the apocalyptic fight. Maybe he didn't relish the destruction of all things—

maybe he even thought he could prevent it. But he wanted the power aligning himself with the End would give him. He wanted to be the only power.

We hadn't seen him since the night he'd ripped my body and soul apart in an attempt to get to the Angel, to take *La Muerte* for himself. He'd done it mercilessly. Joyfully.

The Angel had shredded him to unrecognizable pieces and scattered him to the winds.

"The fuck is going on here?"

I pushed past Luna, my magic rising, ready to pierce his mind.

Sunday's magic struck the first blow. The focus drained from his eyes. He blinked, trying to clear his sight.

"Blind," he said.

Sunday's voice flew over my shoulder, sharp as a spear. "Take him out, Night."

He raised his hands. "I'm not here to fight."

"Too bad," Sunday said. "I want blood. I want yours."

Shadow made no move to counter her magic. If anything, his halo shrank. He was deliberately not engaging.

I held up a hand. "Wait."

"What do you mean, wait?"

"She means stand the hell down," Luna said. "Do it."

I glanced back to see Luna braced at the threshold, blocking Sunday's access to the room, the flat of her hand pressed against Sunday's heart.

Sunday's halo burst into rose—gold flames.

"Back off," Luna said. "I didn't invite you here to kill. I didn't invite you here at all, Sunday. I asked for Night."

Sunday narrowed her eyes. "I watch her back."

"Then watch it."

"You have him on a leash?"

Luna nodded.

Sunday's gaze flicked over me, then to Shadow. A moment later, he blinked again, his sight clearing.

"Thank you," he said.

"Shove it up your ass." Sunday looked at Luna. "Take your hand off me."

Luna pulled back, stepping out of the way to allow Sunday inside.

She shut the door behind us. "We have about two minutes before we have company. You use offensive magic in this house, the King's going to demand a reason."

Sunday shrugged.

"Your funeral," Luna said. "I asked you here, Night, because Shadow is here. I thought you should know. I also thought you should know he's not the same.

"Not the same, how? He's not still the first Watcher? He's not still fucking evil?"

"*La Muerte* destroyed him. He's been reborn."

Shadow lowered his arms to his sides. "Something tells me Night understands what that means better than most."

So, he guessed—or saw—what had changed in me. "What does it mean to you?"

"A clean slate," he said. "The opportunity to make different choices."

"How many of these have you had?"

"I can count them on two hands."

"How many times have you chosen the side of life?"

"This is the first," he said.

Sunday leaned against the wall. "And we're just supposed to believe that?"

"Believe what you want," he said. "But this will go easier if you give me the benefit of the doubt."

"What will go easier?" she asked.

"We need him," Luna said. "Without him, we're probably screwed."

"Need him for what, Luna?" I asked.

"We know who the fourth Horseman is," Luna said.

"Malek told me as much—or, he told me that you weren't sure yet, but you would be by now."

"Malek." Luna sighed. "He's right."

The feathers around our heart fluttered. There it was—the other shoe, dropped. The first bands of rain as the storm lumbered ashore, the worst on the horizon.

"Did you go looking for her?" Sunday asked. "Did she come to you?"

Luna shook her head. "She doesn't know what she is. Not yet."

"She wouldn't believe it if we told her," Shadow said. "This has to be handled delicately."

"Back up," I said. "How do you know her?"

"I love her," Shadow said.

Sunday laughed, but as she watched his face, her mirth faded. "You're serious."

He held her gaze. "She means more to me than anyone or anything. Doubt that at your peril."

I heard no lie in his words.

He glanced at me. "Do you want to look? If you need confirmation, I'll allow you in."

I stared at him. He was actually offering a glimpse into his mind, no strings attached. "Yes."

"Go gently. I'm young yet, and I have neither the strength nor the control to ensure your safety should you trip my survival instinct."

He meant all of that exactly as he spoke it. His survival instinct would carry all of the power of the first Watcher. Even if I couldn't be killed, I could be hurt. He didn't want to harm me.

The Angel's and my magic rose to kiss my skin, flying forth with the slip and whisper of wings, piercing his mind, pinning him to the spot and seeking the information about the woman he professed to love. We caught a glimpse of sunlight shining on blue—black hair. Of changeable eyes filled with a seriousness that seemed out of character for someone so young—and she *was* young, like Malek said.

The landscape of Shadow's mind shifted, storm clouds pushing out the sun. A great hand closed into a fist around us, drawing me away from the woman and into darkness so total, it obscured all my senses. We saw nothing. Heard nothing. Until a scream sundered the silence, bristling and bloody.

A million pieces of Shadow's shattered being, scattered on the four winds, particulates hidden among the leaves of trees and the soil of the earth, floating on water and sunken among the sand and stone of river— and ocean—bottoms, flowing back together slowly and steadily. Drawn inexorably toward one another, no choice but to obey.

They fit together like pieces of a puzzle, magic soldering muscle and tendon and bone, sparking synapses, creating themselves anew.

He'd felt all of it. Every splinter of pain. Every wound, knitting. Every flash of lightning within his newly—constituting flesh. His rebirth had taken days, every microsecond brimming with agony. He'd awakened brand new, with no memory of who he was or what he'd done.

The first person who'd spoken to him was the woman with the blue—black hair and changeable eyes. He'd fallen in love at first sight.

He wanted me to know that. To feel it as viscerally as he did.

He released me, opening the way out and closing all other avenues.

Was he hiding something? Did he have a secret he didn't want us to know? He wouldn't be the first.

As my magic slid back into my mind, I met Shadow's gaze. "He's telling the truth."

Sunday sighed. "Don't think that makes you a good guy now."

"I'm under no illusion," he said.

"Who is it?" Sunday asked.

"I don't recognize her."

Luna answered for him. "She's under Malek's protection."

I knew only one woman—girl—under the serpent's protection. Beth. This girl wasn't Beth.

Voices sounded outside the door, and the thud of footfalls, drawing closer.

"That'll be the company we're expecting," Luna said.

Sunday raised a brow. "The law coming to take me away?"

"Just apologize if he asks." Luna tugged on the doorknob.

The oak swung inward, revealing two visitors.

The first, I knew. His halo was the color of forest loam after a rain. He wore brown leather in a shade that matched his brown hair and eyes, white wings folded thin as a knife's blade against his back. He carried the authority of royalty, which he was. He was also an eighteen—year—old kid who hadn't gotten the chance to finish high school and never would—at least, that was what he'd been once upon a time.

The woman with him had the same hair and eyes I'd seen in Shadow's mind. She wore black sneakers, faded jeans threadbare at the knees, and a black T—shirt with the sleeves cut off, the front emblazoned with white letters that read *Many Gods, No Masters.* Leather straps that reminded us of a backpack's—or a shoulder holster's— intersected in the center of her chest. It took a moment to marry the sight to the hilt of the sword sticking up behind her left shoulder, the blade sheathed at her back.

I hadn't seen a halo like hers before, the color of seaweed cradled in foaming waves. The magic was fae—flavored. Water fae.

"Still not amused, Kev," she said. "I might be fae now, but I don't belong to you or your girlfriend. Just because you're a king now doesn't make you the boss of me—a fact you seem to have conveniently forgotten."

"It's not convenient at all," he said, as his gaze brushed mine and froze. He beetled his brows.

"What?" Luna asked.

Kevin glanced at her. "You haven't looked at them?"

"Looked how?"

"Her eyes."

"Cool, right?"

"Beneath the starfire," Kevin said.

She shook her head.

Luna was still young in her magic. Of course she hadn't noticed how different I'd become. We could have that conversation later if we found the time.

We nodded at the water fae. The…mermaid. "Who's this?"

She cocked her head. "Who's asking?"

"The Angel of Death," Kevin said.

"Fuck."

Her magic rose, as did the Angel's and mine. Our collective power met in the space between us, weaving the familiar feeling that meant proximity to another Horseman of the Apocalypse. The finger on the heart. The knowledge that, somehow, we all belonged with each other. To each other.

I held my breath. Time slowed and stopped for the space of a heartbeat.

Her serious eyes mirrored the recognition we felt.

"Who are you?" she asked again, this time with a sense of wonder.

The Watcher stood, the lamp behind him casting his shadow over us all. "She's the only one who can keep you alive, Amy."

CHAPTER 6

AMY HELD SHADOW'S gaze. "I'm in danger?"

Kevin took a step back, positioning himself behind Amy, his wings unfurling without a sound to block the exit. "It's not the first time, I know. But this is different."

She glanced behind her, appraising Kevin's stance. "Are you the danger?"

He shook his head.

"Is she?" Amy pointed at me.

"Malek is," he said.

Words shot from her mouth like bullets. "Malek helped me when no one else would. He's the only one who didn't try to talk me out of doing what I had to do, the only one who helped me. He stood by me while the rest of you fucking left."

Kevin opened his mouth to reply, then slammed it shut. This wasn't the first time he'd taken fire from Amy about this. This was old business between them. Business we didn't have time for now.

I inclined my head toward the chair Shadow had vacated. "Sit, Amy."

"I don't taking orders from you," she snapped.

"It's an invitation."

She trained her gaze on Shadow again. He nodded.

Only then did she move for the rocker, risking the gauntlet between the bed and the dresser and taking careful stock of everyone she passed, checking for weapons and reading body language. She pulled the blade from its sheath on her back with crystalline ring and set it on her lap. Once she'd settled with her back to the wall and her lover by her side, her shoulders dropped a good inch below her ears, giving her enough space to listen. Good.

I couldn't give her my undivided attention—not yet. The blade commanded the Angel's and my focus with its deadly beauty. It had been crafted of silver, a metal too soft for such a thing, but it emanated strength and resolve. If we listened closely, we could just make out an undercurrent of voices flowing from it, whispers that Amy heard clearly, judging from the sudden, open expression on her face. The sword shone with its own halo, silver like its fae constitution and deepest red, like heart's blood. It was a living thing. It had a name, and the Angel and I knew what it was because he was old enough to have been alive when it was forged.

The blade was called War.

Luna made her way to Amy, crouching in front of her as if she were a child and Luna was trying to put herself on the same level. From that position, Luna seemed less threatening. Less like a Horseman and more like a friend.

"You trust me?" she asked.

Amy shrugged one shoulder. "I don't distrust you."

"That's all I get? I haven't given you any reason to doubt me."

"Sorry. That's the baseline."

A good way to keep herself from being hurt. A bad way to have to be in the world. I understood it all too well.

"I believe Malek did all of those things for you," Luna said. "I might believe that he did them when he didn't have to."

"I'm supposed to thank you for believing the truth?"

"I can even believe he did them because he cares about you. Like Shadow, he loves you."

Amy closed her eyes tightly for a moment. Shadow fidgeted where he stood.

He'd admitted to us that he loved her, but he hadn't yet told her. Awkward. And useful information to have in my back pocket about how Shadow and Amy danced with each other.

Luna set a hand on Amy's knee, drawing the girl out of herself and into the room again.

Amy zeroed in on Luna's hand. "You should move that."

Luna pushed to her feet. "Night, you want to take this?"

I folded my arms across our chest. "Malek may love you, but that doesn't change the fact that he is who he is. He's the serpent from the Garden of Eden and his relationship with humans is sketchy. He'll help humans he cares about and let the rest die in a fire if it comes to that. He'll hurt or kill anyone who crosses him, and anyone who makes promises to him that they can't or don't keep has it worst."

Amy nodded. "I know all of that. I just don't know what it has to do with me."

Luna sighed. "We think you're going to betray Malek. You won't have a choice. It's your fate."

"I don't believe in fate," Amy said. "Anyway, what do you know about Malek—besides the obvious?"

I'd sworn as much secrecy as I could to Malek when he'd revealed how his voice had been stolen. He'd been cursed by the End, and the vehicle for that curse had been the Four Horsemen. Malek put up a tough façade about what had happened. In telling us, he'd seemed very concerned, nothing more. But I understood it amounted to more than that. It wasn't about how Malek felt. It was about what he would do to ensure he never became that vulnerable again.

"You should let us finish," I said. "Then you'll get it."

Amy waited, the rude expression on her face equal turns skeptical and disdainful.

"We think you're a Horseman, like us."

"What?"

"You feel like a Horseman to me, and to the Angel of Death."

"And to me," Luna said. "And to Pestilence."

Amy looked from me to Luna, then glanced up at Shadow. "You believe this bullshit?"

He thinned his lips.

"That's a yes," she said.

His eyes softened. "I wish it wasn't so."

"Which one?" Amy asked. "Which one am I?"

Sunday shot her side—eye, as if she were stupid. There were only four, and three of them walked in the worlds.

The most well—known Horseman to Kevin's people was Famine, in all of her little girl—pigtails—tortoiseshell glasses glory. She'd planted herself firmly in the camp of those who wanted all the worlds destroyed.

That left Luna and me. We fought for the side of life as well—not the way normal humans commonly thought about it, as a hopeful defense against mortality, but the entire cycle of life. The pattern of birth, growth, decline, death, decay, and, for those of us who chose it, rebirth. Our enemies wanted total destruction. We would spend every molecule of magic and every ounce of physical energy not only thwarting them, but making sure that they never won, even if it meant fighting forever.

Three Horsemen down. One to go.

Amy whispered softly, the word she spoke barely audible. "Fuck."

"Can you all give us the room," I asked.

Sunday shook her head. "Not leaving you alone."

"I can't be killed."

She held my gaze. I knew every thought behind her blue eyes not because of magic, but because I'd known her for every formative year of our lives. We knew things about each other that we'd never told another soul.

Right now, Sunday was thinking that just because I couldn't be killed didn't mean I couldn't be hurt in any number of ways. She refused to let that happen if she could help it. She'd trusted me to take care of myself and begrudged *La Muerte* enough rope to hang himself, but wouldn't extend that level of trust to what we'd become together. We were something new.

I held her gaze.

After a moment, she nodded. "I'll be right outside."

She filed out, Kevin behind her. He stopped to hold the door for Luna, who looked at me with a mixture of angst and hope, and Shadow, who bent first to speak low into Amy's ear. He would also be outside the door. She needed only to call his name and he'd come running.

Once Kevin stepped out, silence settled between Amy and me. She studied my eyes, brown and laced with starfire. Her gaze glided over my skin, brown and at the same time pale from the cold the Angel and I generated. She lingered over the black—feathered wings, drawn against my back.

"You were human before," she said. "When did you get your magic? I mean, when did it show up for you? You're a natural, right? Born with it?"

"I was small. Five years old."

"And you were an assassin?"

I raised a brow. "Malek told you?"

She glanced at the sword on her lap. "Not him. The blade records and remembers fae conflict, and conflicts important to the fae. It remembers you."

"I've never been a part of a fae conflict." As far as I knew, I'd barely registered on fae radar.

"You're not Jane Doe, whose actions make a tiny ripple in the time-line," she said. "You're the Angel of Death. That makes you and your history worth the sword's time."

I granted her the point.

"Are you sure about me?"

"As sure as I can be."

"Is there, like, a big sign on my forehead? When you look up Horsemen of the Apocalypse, my picture's next to the definition?"

"No."

"Then there's a chance it's not true."

"A chance, yes. But I feel it, Amy. Don't you?"

"What I feel is none of your business. If it's all the same to you, I'm holding onto that chance." She seemed to search for a reason to hold on, as if she needed to explain. "I need some hope in this world."

Hope was in short supply for those of us born with magic. The way Amy had asked about my history marked her as something else. "When did you turn fae?"

"I don't like to talk about it."

"Regrets?"

She shook her head and mulled what to say. "My parents turned into monster cannibals. They...died. My boyfriend fell in love with another girl. A demon was on its way to destroy the world. All my friends had magic. All of them could help. I was a liability full of awkward, angry feelings. Malek gave me an outlet for them—a magical tattoo on my ankle. It gave me superpowers like my friends and a way to survive my mega—feelings. Didn't fix my life, though."

"That's a lot to say to someone you don't trust."

She chuckled. "You're here to interrogate me, right?"

"I'm asking questions you should expect, aren't I?"

"Before you force your way into my mind?"

I held her gaze.

She was the first to look away. "What else do you want to know?"

"Whose side you're on."

"Worried I want the world to end? I don't hate my life so much anymore."

"Because of Shadow?"

She nodded.

"He was a bad guy."

"He's a good guy now." The words were tinged with as much hope as genuine belief. "Every moment is a choice for him. He has to keep choosing over and over again to be good."

"That makes him the same as the rest of us," I said. "Except that he holds the power of the first Watcher. He can make and unmake people. He can make and unmake worlds."

She frowned. "No one should have that much power."

"And the people who want it—"

"Are the ones we should be worried about most," she said. "I'm not the fourth Horseman. I can't be."

"Luna says you are."

She sighed in resignation.

"How did you end up with the blade?" I asked.

"Short version is that Kevin's queen gave it to me. Said it was mine to wield."

"Big responsibility."

"It has no respect for what I want or need. Like, you know, sleep. Or food. Or sex. Everything's an emergency with this thing. Ah, shit." She turned her gaze inward, her eyes unfocused, and cocked her head. She listened to something we couldn't hear.

"Gotta go." She vaulted to her feet. "Now."

CHAPTER 7

"THERE'S A FIGHT AT MALEK'S." Amy dropped War into its sheath, rushed past us and out the door, and grabbed Kevin by the shoulders, turning him in the direction she wanted him to move. "Show me the way out, Kev. Trouble behind Malek's shop. The city's on fire again."

Kevin's voice cracked like a whip. "Hands off."

She let go. "Now. Please."

Kevin waved me forward. "C'mon, Night."

The second I left the room, he raised his hands and whispered a word in a language I didn't understand.

The door to Luna's room slammed shut with enough force to shake the frame. A deep blow glow bloomed behind the wood, light bursting through the seams. A heartbeat later, the shine dimmed. The door swung open again, hinges creaking. The stench of sulfur billowed into the hall, marking the portal Kevin's words had crafted. It would lead to the In—Between and then to Snake Bite Tattoo.

Amy barreled through the opening, Shadow hot on her heels.

I looked at Sunday. "You wanted a fight?"

She winked at me and leapt through the door.

I started after them.

Kevin laid a hand on my shoulder. "This is the Order."

"How—"

"They've been testing our borders. I meant to tell you."

"Better late than never."

"You shouldn't show yourself, Night. They don't know you're with us."

"They will as soon as they see Sunday."

He mulled that for a split—second. "There goes our advantage."

"We can talk strategy later. After the fight."

He nodded. "Sealing the portal behind you. No retreat."

He wasn't coming, and neither by the look of her was Luna. "Understood."

I stepped into the space between worlds, through a curtain of fire and sulfur, stomach dropping into the bowl of my belly and heat singing the ends of my hair. I landed on the asphalt in the alley behind Snake Bite Tattoo, back against the brick wall in what should have been the peaceful, pre—dawn hush. The first thing I heard was the skid of metal on metal.

Illuminated by the glow from a single security light, Amy parried a knife strike, closed her hand around the attacker's wrist, and pulled them into the point of her sword. War opened the enemy from navel to rib cage. Amy yanked the blade from their flesh with a howl that curled every hair on my body, then turned her back to go after the next operative. Her boots slip—slid on drenched pavement as rain fell like bullets.

There were eight from the Order, dressed in black from steel—toe boots to the watch caps on their heads. They moved so fast. Did I know any of them? Did it matter?

Sunday had her hands full with three, two of them blinded by her magic, but not down. Shadow took on two operatives, one that continued to circle him while he'd grab the other by the scruff of his shirt, his magic already reweaving the man's clothes into chains that reached for the ground, their iron links sentient, burrowing and anchoring themselves in the asphalt.

I moved toward the circling operative, but a woman jumped from the roof, landing in front of me, cutting me off.

This one, we recognized. Dark black skin and eyes that glowed with an inner fire, name of Jae. Sunday and I had worked with her on too many missions to count. Her magic could call electrical energy, contain or unleash it. Her halo curled with smoke, the scent of ozone rising.

Her hands crackled with the lightning. She let loose a bolt from each hand before she'd even caught her balance.

No time to dodge. The electrical charge hit me square in the chest, sparks arcing down my arms and up into my jaw. My heart stuttered. The water droplets on my skin exploded to steam. The rain in the air sizzled as it struck my halo and my mouth tasted of ashes.

Jae drew down more lightning, lunging close. Punched before I could react, striking my solar plexus. Another blast of electricity shot through me.

The blow should've dropped me. It should've killed me. It would have, before the Angel had invaded my mind and become part of me.

Jae's eyes widened.

The Angel and I struck—wings shooting out, turning to stone as the tips as they pierced her shoulders. We pinned her arms to her sides. Lifted her off the ground.

Power flashed behind her eyes. "The fuck are you still standing?"

I speared her with my magic, busting past the defenses she'd erected against me. I peeled open her mind as if it were ripe fruit and excavated the entire operation from her thoughts.

There was no one else on the roof. No traps waiting at either end of the alley. But there was a second team three blocks from here, closing in. They carried silver chains spelled to capture and hold Amy and a special sheath to not only contain her sword, but silence and hide it.

Jae and her team worked for what remained of the Order—small, loyal groups of operatives without headquarters. They set up base camp near their next target—and all their targets had been magical children, the same magical children the Order would normally sweep off the street and take in.

We'd never known Jae to be any different than Sunday, Miguel, or us. She'd done what she'd had to do in order to survive, but she hadn't been cruel. She'd calculated her odds of survival and acted accordingly. But things had changed. Jae had changed.

She and the rest of the ragtag Order were killing the magical kids they found. Burning it all down. The world. Magic.

Magic was a natural force—a natural law. It couldn't be destroyed unless the apocalyptic fight didn't go our way. Unless all the worlds were dissolved into nothing. Unless the End won.

Jae's voice bloomed in my mind. *It's not about the End. It's about the misery.*

It took me a moment to understand. To remember that, before the Order found me, my life had been a series of horrors as my magic grew and expressed itself in frightening ways.

Without the Order, there was no systematic, organized way to train magical children. The Order itself had seen to that, destroying rival systems, making sure that it was the only option. Jae and her people could've begun again. They could've crafted a new place. A better place.

Instead, they'd chosen to destroy the children themselves.

The good can never outweigh the evil. The joy can never outweigh the suffering.

I held her gaze. *Amy's not a magical child.*

Jade didn't reply, but she didn't need to. Amy was an inexhaustible power source, much like the Angel of Death had been at one time, before he escaped imprisonment inside the Order. Or she would be, once the Horseman inside her began to manifest.

If I killed Jade, someone else would take her place. The Order had always worked that way—and Jade and her operatives still did. If I let her live, she'd find a way to accomplish her mission no matter what it took. There would be no changing her mind, no bringing her over to our side. Her commitment felt total. No questions, no doubts.

I used my magic to force her to her knees. I could kill her the way

I'd done it as an operative, by digging until I found a primal fear or a heartbreaking memory and sealing her consciousness inside until she died in agony.

I never wanted to kill that way again.

The Angel and I punched one stone wing into the side of her head. She crumpled, breath shallow and shuddering for a heartbeat before her heart stilled.

I drew back my magic, focusing again on the fight around me—or what was left of it. The Order operatives lay on the asphalt like broken, bloodied dolls. No casualties on our side. The operatives had underestimated us.

Except the Order never underestimated. They erred on the side of overwhelming force.

Sunday looked at me, her mouth pressed into a thin line. Blood streaked her blond hair, a cut along her cheekbone welled red. "The fuck was that?"

Exactly. "That wasn't even hard."

Amy spat a mouthful of bright red and rubbed her jaw. Judging by the shape of the bruise already forming, someone had hit her with the hilt of a knife.

"What do you mean, easy?" she asked. "They keep coming back. Bigger numbers, better skills."

The Angel and I softened our wings, resting them against my back. "They're here for you."

Amy narrowed her eyes. "How could you know that?"

"Jade told me."

"Jade—is that the dead woman?"

I nodded.

"You were in her mind."

I nodded again. "How many times have them come after you?"

"They don't come after me so much as show up, and War lets me know where to go."

"You're the only one who meets them?"

"Usually. Sometimes Shadow's with me. But most of the time, it's just me."

I glanced at Sunday. "The operatives weren't expecting us."

She touched the cut on her cheek, inspecting the smear of blood on her fingers. "They sent all those people for you, Amy."

Amy whistled. "If you hadn't been here, they'd have taken me down."

"Not down." Sunday bent to clean her blade on Jade's shirt.

Amy squinted at her. "What?"

"None of them used their magic on you," Sunday said. "What does that tell you?"

"They didn't have magic."

Sunday shook her head. "All Order operatives have magic. Paralyzing or deadly magic—sometimes both. They didn't use it on you because they need you conscious, cooperative, and alive. They weren't coming to take you down. They were coming to take you."

Amy cocked her head. "Because they also think I'm the fourth Horseman."

Sunday arched a brow.

"So, what now? I come with you back to Portland? You promise to keep me safe? These operatives will just follow me there."

Sunday sighed. "If they do, they'll have to send an army. They'd have to go through us to get to you. Smarter to stage an operation here—threaten someone you care about and draw you out, especially if they do it while the rest of us are fighting on a different front."

"You've thought about this a lot," Amy said.

"It's who I was."

"Who you still are, judging by the way you fought and how much you enjoyed it."

Sunday shrugged. "Killing the bad guys isn't supposed to be a guilty pleasure. It's all of the pleasure, none of the guilt."

"Question remains," Amy said. "What now?"

"Now, the messengers come," I said.

"The who?"

As her question faded, balls of light the color of twilight filled the sky, one for each of the dead. They hovered over the hearts of their charges, singing a song so faint I could hardly hear it. The sound reminded me of bells—church bells, if churches smelled like a forest after a rain, fresh and new and wild.

Amy sucked in a breath, her eyes wide with wonder. "I've never seen them. Heard of them, but never set eyes on them before. I've seen people die. I've killed them. How can I see them now?"

Shadow cleared his throat. "Because of Night."

"Are they doing what I think they are?" Amy asked.

"They're here to take the souls of the dead."

Sunday's lips quirked. "I thought that was your job, Sanchez."

I flashed her a grin that began to fade as soon as it appeared. "It's more complicated than that."

"Always is. Can we get out of here now?"

The operatives who worked with those we'd killed would know by now that their friends were dead. They'd send backup if they hadn't already.

I met Amy's gaze. "You can't stay here. We know you can take care of yourself—if the odds are in your favor. You have two choices: Faery or Portland."

"Not Faery," she said. "I can't spend that kind of time with Kevin."

Shadow shifted his weight from one leg to another. He clearly had thoughts on the subject, but didn't voice them.

"Portland, then," Sunday said.

"Whatever." Amy pulled a phone from her back pocket. "I need to make a call."

"Who are you phoning?" Sunday asked.

"Rude."

The local magical law enforcement, Rude Davies. He needed to know that his only other magical teammate actively defending the city was about to take a trip.

I stepped back as she dialed, giving her space. Shadow moved closer to her, filling the place I'd vacated. They orbited each other, one instinctively moving to complement the other. If Amy lowered her gaze or stopped to think, Shadow took a defensive posture. He didn't let go of his guard for a second.

Sunday moved around them, closing the distance between us and leaning in close. "She's really the fourth?"

"Feels like it."

"Something's off with her. And not just because she's dating Shadow, although that makes me question her judgment in general. I don't know if it's the sword or her attitude. Or just how fucked up she is emotionally."

"What does any of that have to do with it?"

"She's not stable, Night. Not even a little bit."

"That makes her easy to knock off balance. It makes her a loose cannon. It makes her easier to manipulate. Doesn't mean she's not War."

Sunday frowned. "I can't explain it better than that."

"It's a gut feeling?"

She nodded.

We never ignored gut feelings. Pretending everything was all right while your survival instinct raised five alarms always ended badly.

"We'll keep an eye on her."

"At least two eyes."

Amy hung up and tucked the phone away. "He's a couple of blocks from here, grabbing coffee. He wants us to meet him inside the shop."

"Why?" Sunday asked.

"There's an emergency."

CHAPTER 8

RUDOLPH DIAMOND DAVIES III stepped inside Snake Bite Tattoo like a man on a mission. His orange buzz cut seemed to glow under the overhead fluorescents, and he'd traded his usual Hawaiian shirt for a plain black T—shirt and a pair of black jeans. His rainbow halo was subdued, as if he were trying to mute his natural brightness. His gaze swept the team. When he got to me, his eyes widened.

"Dude," he said. "I knew you'd changed, but I didn't *know*. Amy, lock up behind me?"

The question was delivered in a carefree manner, but that was just bravado.

I narrowed my eyes. "What's the emergency?"

"I was being followed."

"Not anymore?"

"I think I lost them," he said.

"You think?"

He ignored the question. "Every time I tried to get a casual glimpse, it vanished on me."

"It?"

"I couldn't exactly tell without confronting it, and it wouldn't let me." Rude paused. "It's more than that, though. Like, every magical sense I have started tingling, and then the tingling ratcheted up until all my nerves were screaming. I've never met anybody or anything that made me feel like that. Having backup seemed like a good plan."

The only beings I'd experienced as that powerful were archangels and Horsemen. "It wasn't Famine, was it?"

Rude looked at me as if I were stupid. Or as if I thought he was stupid.

"Did this guy have black hair and wear a shirt that says *Ride the Lightning?*"

"Like I said, I didn't get a look."

If Michael were following Rude—I couldn't think of a good reason for him to do that. Michael would make himself known. Gabriel didn't hide, either. He just barged in and did what he wanted. This had to be someone new. And new at this stage of the game could only mean trouble.

Amy asked Rude a question I didn't hear as I tuned their voices out, scanning the space. The lobby held two facing, black vinyl sofas and a glass coffee table between them. The counter was glass. Protections shone in the floor, ceiling, and walls.

For a split—second, my vision blurred and changed. The Angel moved inside me, viewing the world through my eyes and giving me a more complete glimpse into Malek's wards as the shop walls began to glow, and portions of its white walls darkened as magical symbols materialized. I didn't recognize the shadowy, writhing shapes, but the Angel did. They were protections set into the structure of the building, energized by years of feeding with Malek's blood. And something outside had activated them.

Behind us, the back room shone like the sun.

I interrupted the conversation. "Is there an entrance or exit in the back?"

Amy stopped mid—sentence and furrowed her brow. "No."

No back door meant no secondary way out, but it also meant no ambush from behind. I pointed to the back room. "Everyone in there, now. Sunday—"

"I'm with you," she said.

Amy tightened her grip on her sword. "The emergency is here now?"

The fine hairs on my arms stood at attention. "Almost."

Rude opened his mouth to object to my orders. Sunday shoved toward the back room, propelling him halfway there before he dug in his heels, sneakers squeaking on the tile.

"Not leaving you."

Amy planted her feet on the floor, sending magical roots into the foundation of the building. "Neither am I."

I glanced at Shadow. He shook his head. He wouldn't leave Amy.

"Stupid," Sunday said.

"Shadow, I need you to prepare a way out for us. Punch a hole through the wall. Open a portal."

He hesitated.

I speared his mind with my magic. He raised his defenses, but didn't deploy them against me.

I've got Amy. I won't let anything happen to her.

He held my gaze for the space of a breath, then turned on his heel and stalked into the back room.

There was no more time. The Angel's and my magic licked my skin, cold as the grave, frosting the air around me. Instinct borne of self—preservation made the others step back.

The front door rattled in its frame hard enough to tear its hinges. The protections woven into it flared. For a heartbeat, the violent motion stilled. Dust motes hung in the air, backlit by burning magic, flashing like fireflies. The sound of Amy's breathing, harsh and shallow, filled the space.

The deadbolt flicked open. The knob turned.

The Angel's consciousness flowed through my body, taking control of my arms and hands, curling my fingers into fists. From the corner of my eye, I caught a glimpse of Sunday's rose gold halo billowing like a mushroom cloud.

The door slammed open, smashing into the wall so hard, the knob thunked into the sheetrock. A six—foot tall column of blue fire burned at the threshold.

Sunday hissed. "Holy shit."

The flames flickered and began to die, revealing a human—shaped shadow within. It stepped forward, all three of its eyes trained on me —two in the usual places, and one in the center of its forehead. Its armor glittered like diamonds, the golden hilt of a sword rising from the sheath on its back. The room went absolutely still as a hush descended. I couldn't blink. I couldn't breathe.

In that moment, I caught a glimpse of road that had led me to hear. Every decision, every turning point, every path abandoned. I saw all the possible roads that branched from this point forward, all of them shrouded in mist, some of them darker than others.

Then time jump—started again, and I exhaled as the archangel stepped toward me—it had to be an archangel, because nothing else shone so brightly and broadcast enough power to bend the air around their body. The stillness that had descended over the room filled its halo, not coloring it, exactly, but flavoring it. It tasted like clear, cold mountain air. The kind of air you could see through with perfect clarity.

The archangel's majesty faded in mid—stride. As it approached, the flames of its hair became amber—brown waves that cascaded to the middle of its back. The third eye receded, its doe—eyed gaze laser —focused on my face. No, not *its. Hers.*

At least, I thought the archangel was female.

She wore a crisp white suit that fit her considerable curves like a glove. Her face was devoid of makeup except lipstick as red as fresh blood. Gold hoops glinted at her ears. Her long, slender fingers caught my eye. They were delicate and strong and even the smallest movement seemed to hypnotize.

I forced my gaze to rise, meeting hers. Her eyes had the same hypnotic effect. I wanted to lose myself in their depths. A grin tugged at her lips before she blinked, breaking the spell.

Her voice rolled like thunder. "Death."

My blood answered with flashes of lightning—her brother, Michael, was my ancestor. His blood flowed in my veins.

Some of the old stories claimed that Michael and Lucifer were enemies. That Lucifer had defied God and God had sent Michael to fight him, hurling him from Heaven. That Lucifer hated humanity. My experience told me that the old stories usually held a kernel of truth, but no more than that.

Which kernel was true?

The Angel answered my question. *All of them, at one time or another.*

Her thunder rolled again. "I'm here to take the girl under my protection."

"Why?" Amy asked.

Lucifer held her gaze. "Because you need protection."

"I can take care of myself."

"Can you fight the world, little girl? That's what's coming for you."

"Because I'm the Fourth Horseman."

Lucifer nodded.

"They want to kill me?"

"They want to convince you to do what they believe you should do. Everyone has an opinion, a course of action they believe is right. If you don't do what they want, the world will end in fiery destruction. That's what they'll say."

"No one can make me do anything I don't want to," Amy said.

"You're wrong." Lucifer pointed at me before sweeping her hand to include the others. "These fine people pretend to be your friends. They don't care what you want or what's best for you. They only want you to choose to their side. If you won't agree, you'd best believe they'll do whatever it takes to sway you. It wouldn't be the first time Night has done so, and it won't be the last."

Amy looked at me from the corner of her eye. "Is that true?"

"Yes."

Amy's eyes widened. She'd expected me to lie, or to at least gloss over the truth.

"I won't pretend to be someone I'm not," I said.

Lucifer raised a brow. "Do you know who you are, really? How can you, when you don't know the extent of yours and the Angel's power, or what it will cost you in the end?"

Her words sent a chill up my spine. I shook it off. "I'm not pretending to be Amy's friend. I am telling her the whole truth and nothing but the truth as I see it. She feels to me, reads to me, walks and talks as if she is the Horseman War. She doesn't yet know what that means."

Lucifer folded her arms across her chest. "And you do?"

Sunday took a step forward. "Night knows better than anyone because she's living it. Night and the Angel are powerful. With her – all of us – we can keep Amy safe."

"And if Amy decides to let the world crash and burn? What then? What will you do?"

"Stop talking about me and at me and around me." Amy looked Lucifer up and down. "Aren't you the fallen angel, the one they called the Devil? Isn't everyone in the world afraid of you? You show up here without being invited, barge into Malek's shop, and tell me you want to take me away from here and protect me or save me – and, what, this is out of the goodness of your heart? No one here is helping me out of the goodness of their heart. They all want something from me."

"I only want you to trust yourself. I want you to realize that, deep inside your heart, you already know what's best. I am offering you the space and time to uncover the truth inside you."

"And then?"

"Then I'll continue to offer you the protection you need to make your vision real."

"Why is this so important to you?"

"It's the only thing that matters. It's the only thing that has ever mattered, since the world was born."

Lucifer's words hit me like a gut punch. All my life – until the night I made the fateful choice to save the girl who would become my daughter and leave the Order – I had tried to fit into the molds other people wanted me to fit in. I tried to be what they wanted me to be because I needed them to love me, to put a roof over my head, to keep me safe and give me somewhere to belong. I did it with my parents, the Order, and even Sunday.

When I struck out on my own for the first time, every choice was mine, and mine alone. It was up to me to shape my life and to shape myself, to keep someone else safe, to wash the blood from from my hands as best I could. I'd done that ever since.

After the Angel came and the world began to march toward the end of all things, making those choices became harder because the stakes ratcheted up with each passing day. But I still tried. Some days, I did better than others. Even having the chance was a gift and a sacred obligation.

"You're talking about free will," I said.

Lucifer nodded. "You've been there. You know. But you've never hit bottom."

I'd hit so far down and so hard, it'd shattered me.

"No," she said. "Not yet."

Amy tightened her grip on the hilt of her sword. "You talk and talk but you're not saying anything I don't already know. You say that you want to preserve my choice. My free will. But you don't really care about me. This isn't about me at all. This is about your need to prove something."

In the space of a breath, the tension in the room grew so thick, I could hardly breathe. The pressure built until the Angel's and my magic flared in self—defense. I couldn't call it back. I couldn't control it at all.

CHAPTER 9

S MOKY TENDRILS SHOT from my skin, seeking purchase in Lucifer's. My vision blurred around the edges, turning everyone and everything into funhouse mirror versions of themselves. The tile underfoot tilted. I fought to hold my balance.

Our magic slipped through pin prick holes in Lucifer's defenses, sliding into her mind.

Stop, the Angel said.

But I couldn't, and neither could he, because the force that drew our magic forth refused to let go. It stuck to us like a spiderweb. Struggling against the pull only tangled our magic more deeply.

Lucifer's mind was dark and full of echoes, like an empty warehouse. Then pinpoints of light winked to life all around, and the empty room became a sea of stars. The ground underfoot — the foundation of Lucifer's mind — began to glow, gently at first. But then the glow became a shine became a blast of blinding light. Like the floor of the shop, the ground tilted, knocking me off balance again. I couldn't get my bearings. I couldn't see or feel a way out.

The wings around my heart fluttered.

I'd never been pulled into a mind like this before, unable to break free. I'd simply never run in to anyone with more juice than I had. The

Order didn't send operatives on no—win missions. I'd always thought I was the best at what I did. And *La Muerte* was older than time, the most powerful of the Horsemen. Together, we'd defeated the stronger being in the universe more than once. We'd taken control of our destiny.

We'd never been challenged by an archangel.

Sure, Michael had been an asshole and then a friend and then an asshole again, and so on. He'd given me orders I'd refused. But he'd never come after me at full throttle. If he had, which of us would have been left standing at the end?

Michael was my blood. Lucifer bore me no kindness or allegiance.

The Angel and I looked for something — anything — that would give us an advantage. A clue to Lucifer's hopes and fears. A clue as to what she really wanted. Her strategy. Her endgame.

The light beneath us broke into sections, some long, some short, whispering so that I could hear but not understand them. They stacked and angled and stretched themselves into walls on either side of me, not high enough to reach the ceiling, but too tall to see over. The whispers filled not just the space around me, but the whole room. Lucifer was building a labyrinth. Or a maze.

The Angel and I reached out, brushing our fingertips against the closest wall. It quivered against our skin, smooth and alive and vulnerable.

We shot forth frost from our hands. It should've frozen the wall, making it easy to crack, but it had no effect.

The air above us shimmered. I turned my palms up just as curved length of iron manifested, dropping into my grip like a bomb. It was a scythe. Death's scythe.

It had no handle. No hilt. Nothing to separate the sharp blade from my skin. If I closed my hand, it would slice me open to the bone.

I curled my fingers into a fist, screaming as the blade cleaved my palm. Blood gushed, running down the iron, dripping on to the foundation. I swung the scythe at the wall, spattering it with my blood, cutting through the quivering whispers and light like a hot knife through butter, opening a dark seam. A way out.

Hope flared in my chest — then the flame sputtered and spent as the edges of the seam closed.

I swung again. And again. Each time, the wounds I created healed.

The harsh sound of my breath and the thunder of my heartbeat drowned him out. This small corner of Lucifer's mind held us prisoner. It refused to bend or break in response to our magic. While we were trapped in here, our friends would be fighting to free us — or fighting for their lives.

If we couldn't break out, the best way to help them was to break in.

I stilled my body. For a moment, the harshness of my ragged breathing and the thunder of my heartbeat drowned out every other sound. I counted: breathe in, two, three, four. Breathe out, two, three, four, five, six. My nervous system calmed, my awareness dropping to my heart, the source and home of my magic. Thoughts raced through my mind. I paid them no heed, concentrating on the feelings that flowed through me.

The maze itself offered no clue, no direction. Wall after wall of whispers — walls of sound and fury — they were nothing but noise. I listened for lies, and heard them everywhere. I listened for truth, and heard a single, solitary drop of silence among the cacophany.

I turned toward the silence, moving with steady purpose, all my senses trained on it.

The maze faded, leaving *La Muerte* and I standing in silent darkness.

A voice bloomed in my mind. It was not the Angel's. It was Lucifer's.

Good.

She was testing us. Playing with us. Distracting us.

You're still bleeding, she said.

So I was. But I no longer felt the pain of the wound or noticed the red dripping from the blade or from my fingertips.

Why doesn't your angel heal you?

Good question. Healing had never been his primary purpose, but every time I shredded myself in battle, he sewed me together again. There was something about my blood, some meaning beyond the hurt. My thoughts circled back to the archangels. What they held in common. How they differed.

I won't let you go, Lucifer said.

The Angel answered for both of us. *All things die, including you. In the end, I will reap you, Lucifer.*

She laughed. The sound rang hollow.

The space around us began to shift, the darkness transforming to star—filled night once more. Lightning flashed so brightly, it blinded me. The ground underfoot tilted again. As I caught my balance, my sight returned.

I was no longer in Lucifer's mind. I had no idea how I knew that, only that it felt true. The stars in this night sky belonged to someone else. Each of them was an entire world filled with living beings, and every one of those beings had hopes and dreams and loves and value. Each life, and each world, obeyed a set of laws I could barely grasp. Laws that dictated the rotation of the earth on its axis, the patterns of planets, the cellular structures of mammals, reptiles, trees, mountains, and oceans.

Millions of lives.

I'd only experienced the human world, the In—Between, the realm of Faery. I'd touched the envelope of the angelic realm. I'd thought the number of worlds was finite. That there were only a few. I'd never imagined this vastness.

Words flowed across my mind's eye like an evening news chyron. I recognized the voice that spoke them.

What happens here—the choices you and the Angel make—affects them all. And that's just you. When you're working in concert with the other Horsemen, it's more critical. Amy must be able to control War. To keep him from igniting destruction across all the worlds. She must fight on the side of life. If she fails to do either, the universe as we know it faces destruction.

I took a deep breath and blew it out slowly. "I know all this. Why are you telling me?"

"Because Lucifer won't be the only one after her in the coming days, and you need to get your shit together, Night."

In front of me, a spark caught, spiraling into a six—foot high blaze.

The flames died as quick as they'd risen. In their wake stood a dark—haired man with fiery eyes. He wore black motorcycle boots, faded jeans, and a worn, black T—shirt emblazoned with *Ride the Lightning.* He slid his hands into his front pockets, casual as you please.

I looked at the manifestation of Michael in front of me, the human shape and metal T—shirt. We stood in a corner of his mind. The stars didn't represent worlds out there somewhere. They existed in here. Inside Michael.

I hadn't understood a fucking thing about who he was. What he did. The responsibility he carried on his fiery shoulders. If I'd known, would I have ignored his warnings? Would I have made the same choices?

Probably.

Definitely, he said.

I blinked at him. *You rescued me from Lucifer's mind.*

He nodded.

How?

Your blood. He glanced at my hand. At the scythe.

I followed his gaze, surprised to find that the bleeding had stopped. Not only that, but the blade was clean. I opened my hand. With an audible *pop,* the scythe disappeared. And a heavy weight settled in the bowl of my belly, as if the weapon had made a home inside me.

What about my blood? I asked.

I tasted it on the wind.

I've been hurt before. Bleeding. You didn't show.

You didn't need me.

I could argue the point. I could call him an asshole to his face. He'd deserve it and I'd feel better. But the Angel and I were still trapped, only inside a friendlier archangel. A friendlier prison.

The Angel's voice rang inside my heart. *When has the size of the adversary made a difference?*

Never.

I hadn't allowed fear to rule me since the night the Order assassinated my parents. I didn't fear death. I only feared not making a difference, not doing everything in my power to help. No one could make me do something I didn't want to do. No power in the universe was strong enough. I understood the big picture as much as any human could. What Michael didn't understand was that, along with that big picture, we were talking about a girl's life. She would have to decide on her own. Not because it wouldn't mean anything if he forced her hand, but because only her dignity, her agency, her essential self could accomplish what he wanted.

I held Michael's gaze. *I can't believe we're having this conversation again.*

Lucifer believes she knows best how to keep Amy safe because she understands what you don't. What's happening now is bigger than you. Bigger than humanity. Bigger than your world and all the worlds you know.

He thought I didn't know that. He thought I didn't understand. *This is about power. It's always about power and who holds it. It's about whether the End destroys everyone and everything, or whether we get to live.*

That's a start, he said. *If you want to help Amy, never forget it.*

Before I could think of a snappy reply, the bottom dropped out from under me once more — and, this time, there was no catching my balance. The Angel's and my magic — our consciousness — slammed back into my body with enough force to knock me off my feet and drive me into the floor. The impact stole my breath. For a hot second, I saw stars. Then they resolved into the lobby at Snake Bite Tattoo, the pristine white tile smeared with blood. I tasted copper at the back of my tongue and inhaled the twin stench of gunpowder and sulfur.

CHAPTER 10

MY VISION CLOUDED. I shook my head to clear it — a mistake. The room spun. Two quick breaths later, the spinning slowed. I rolled to my feet as quickly as I dared, reaching out with my magic, the Angel's power twined with mine, ready to strike with all the power we had left.

Lucifer had vanished. So had Michael.

The room looked like a hurricane had blown through it. Furniture overturned. Upholstery shredded. Blinds twisted and window glass cracked. Walls gouged. The air tasted burnt. My skin felt more than hot — it felt boiled. My ears rang, the sound piercing my nerves, pinning them down.

Time spun in circles, not moving forward, not moving at all. Dust motes floated past my face, bright dandelion shapes backlit by the light filtering through the window blinds. I knew this feeling.

Shock.

I didn't have time for it. The enemy had vanished from the room, but she could be behind me, in the back. After the defeat in the alley, another round of Order assassins were headed here right now. I turned my head toward the left, inspecting the shadows near the cash register and the spiderwebbed glass counter. No one there. I turned the other direction and froze.

Blood smeared the white tile to my right. Sunday lay still, red pooling around her head like an angel's halo. She was still bleeding — trickles of crimson rolling from the corners of her eyes. *Fuck.*

I scrambled to her, hands and boots slipping in the blood. She had the mother of all sunburns. In addition to the blood flowing from her eyes, shallow cuts lined her face, and deeper slashes across her chest and belly welled red, too. Her rose—gold halo, so fiery before, looked like ash. Gray, spent, ash.

A scream tore its way up my throat. I swallowed it hard and laid a hand over her heart, one on her forehead. The heat flowing off of her felt overwhelming.

I leaned in close. "Sunday."

She moaned, the sound so soft it was barely there. Her empty beside me grasped for something. I followed its trajectory. Saw the knife she'd held. The one she'd dropped, or that Lucifer had knocked from her grip. I set the handle in the center of her palm. She closed her fingers around it and exhaled a ragged breath.

"Look at me," I said. "I need to see how bad it is."

She did what I asked. Her eyes looked physically whole, thank all the powers. But magically?

"Night?"

"Your magic—"

"It's gone. I don't know how she did it."

I hadn't even known something like that could be done at all. The feeling of horror that flashed in the middle of my chest and wanted to creep out from there, take me over — it would have to wait.

A kaleidoscope of expressions crossed her face as she tucked away her emotions, putting herself back together. "Where is the enemy?"

"Not here yet."

"Can you stand?"

"Help me up."

Movement beside me had me reacting instinctively. I reached for the neck of the person who'd stepped too close, wrapping my fingers around their throat. Only then did I look at them.

Rude, Hawaiian shirt stained and torn, skin singed, stared at me with big black eyes. His hands glowed with spent power. "You shouldn't move her."

Sunday answered for both of them. "Get out of the way or fuck off, Davies."

"But you're hurt—"

"I can fight."

"You're blind," he said.

"No shit?"

He blinked at her.

"I can see fine in all the ways that matter."

Because that was how she'd been trained to use her magic. Our mentor inside the Order made sure her flock could fight, even when overpowered. She made sure we knew how our magic affected others, down to the smallest detail. She didn't need my help to stand. She just wanted to feel me here. To ground herself in my presence. That was what people did when they were off balance—when they had the luxury.

Rude blinked again. "I'll stay with Sunday. You get Shadow under control."

"The hell is wrong with him?"

"He's about to explode. Dude, I mean literally. I don't have the juice left to stop it. I can do something about Sunday's cuts with the power I've got left."

And if an Order operative walked through the door? What good would a spent Faery Seer be to Sunday then?

I heard his voice at the periphery of my mind. He projected at me, hoping I would hear.

I won't leave her.

Reassuring as that felt, and no matter how deadly Sunday could be, even with her magic taken, it wasn't enough. "I'm not leaving either of you. Follow me."

"Into the blast radius?"

That didn't deserve a response. I turned on my heel and marched into the back room, barreling into the overpowering stink of sulfur like walking into a wall.

The magical fortifications embedded in the walls, floor, and ceiling strobed like a disco alarm. An open portal to the In—Between glimmered to my left, where the full—length mirror should be, between the adjustable work bench and the bathroom. On my right, the long counter and sink looked as they always had, packed with supplies. The ever—present knife Malek used to add his blood to his inks trembled at the side of the sink, as if someone had knocked it. Or as if we were having an earthquake.

Shadow stood in the center of it all, blue fire licking at the edges of his halo. The same blue flames flashed in his eyes. His muscles screamed with barely contained tension. He wanted to move. He wanted to do something. But he couldn't.

I didn't see Amy with him.

"She went through the portal," I said.

He shook his head, his whole body trembling.

The shop provided nowhere to run and nowhere to hide. If she hadn't stepped into the In—Between, she'd been taken. Lucifer had taken her, like she'd taken Sunday's magic.

"Fuck," I said.

Wave after wave of rage flowed off him, striking me like punches to the gut, the jaw, the solar plexus. I shoved a magical shield in to place, blunting the blows. I took a step forward, then another. His halo expanded. He raised a hand.

The Angel and I lashed out with one strong wing and smacked it down.

Shadow voice lashed with power. "You were supposed to protect her."

He didn't wait for an answer. His face contorted with pain. He threw back his head, voice dripping with anguish.

This was going nowhere good, nowhere fast. The Angel and I slipped through the boundaries of mind.

The air in the room stirred to wind, blowing from zero to sixty in seconds, turning everything not nailed down into a missile. The bench and chairs skidded on the tile, metal feet squealing. The countertop along the right wall gave up its supplies, paper towels and bandages and a rainbow of ink bottles flew. Cabinet doors slammed open.

Shadow's mind and the fearful heart where his magic rooted — they were the eye of the storm, thick, rotating walls of electric magic. We could puncture them, but there was no reason there. No reaching through to talk him down. The Angel and I could put him down — knock him out and keep him there. But that would take everything we had right now, and we needed our reserves.

We pushed back agains the wind, turned our magic to forging a path through the force around him. He shoved the bench and chairs at us, trying to knock us off balance. He bombarded us with splattering ink, blunt objects, sharp instruments. We barreled through it all.

His magic anchored him to the floor and the foundation underneath, bracing.

I pressed my body to his, our ice and death to his fire. I wrapped my arms around him. He struggled against the hold. He was physically stronger than me. He'd break my grip any second. I didn't care. I only needed a second or two to contain him.

While he struggled against my human body, the Angel wrapped our wings around him.

Shadow shoved out of my hold, drawing his hands into fists. He threw a succession of quick, hard punches to my stomach. "Get the fuck off—"

He never finished the thought.

The tips of our wings met, forming a cage around us both. Instantly, the feathers hardened, turning to stone and plunging us into darkness.

He froze, shocked to stillness and silence. After a moment that felt like an eternity, he whispered. "What did you do?"

"Get your shit together, Shadow. We don't have time for this. The next round of Order operatives is on the way."

"Amy's gone."

"We're gonna find her. That's a promise. But we can't do that if we're fighting the Order. We have to go. Now."

He took hold of my shoulders, squeezing, but not hard enough to harm me. "We're going now."

"Yes."

The Angel spoke, loud and clear. *Now.*

Shadow sucked in a breath. "Okay."

The Angel and I released him, stone softening to feathers, opening wide as the door to the back room slammed. I spun on my heel in time to watch Rude lean Sunday against the wall. He stepped back, throwing silvery light from his fingertips into the seams around the door, like some kind of magical weld.

He shot words over his shoulder like bullets. "Right behind me. Three of them."

I shoved furniture out of the way to get to them. "Get her through the portal."

His eyebrows climbed to his hairline. "What are you doing?"

"Holding them off until you're gone. Shadow, go with them."

The nephilim finally moved. "You made a promise. Not letting you out of my sight."

The hell? Was he joking?

He stepped up beside me, taking the space Rude and Sunday vacated. So, apparently not.

I stared at him, marking the seconds, the flash of heat, the push of sulfur as Rude and Sunday entered the portal. I backpedaled, eyes on the door as it began to rattle inside the frame. Shadow kept pace with me. Kept himself within arm's reach.

Rude's silver magic seal melted, molten metal dripping down the frame, pooling on the tile. The hinges blew apart. The wood stayed in place for a split—second, as if it'd forgotten there was nothing to hold it up, before slamming to the floor, the imprint of a furious fist burned into the other side. A white woman with white—blond hair floated at the threshold, bottoms of her boots a good two inches off the floor. She zeroed on me with shining white eyes, no pupils.

I didn't know her. She'd come to the Order after my time or she was one of the mentors' secret projects.

Shadow's magic rose again, this time only half—wild. He aimed at her and let it fly.

She should've come apart at the seams, just like the door. Instead, she laughed and raised her hands. Lighting flashed at her fingertips. Before she could launch a blast, *La Muerte* spoke a word that shook me to the depths of my bones.

The woman's eyes widened. Her chest rose with a sudden drawn breath. Then, she dropped to the floor like a stone. One by one, the operatives behind her — the operatives I felt and knew were there, but couldn't see — followed. I didn't have to check them to understand they were dead. That the word the Angel uttered had killed them instantly.

My turn to freeze, for my mind and heart to try to catch reality. A rush of emotions crashed over me: the thrill of the kill. Joy at the destruction. Horror, too.

From the time I'd left the Order to this moment, I hadn't killed anyone who wasn't a direct, immediate threat to me and mine. I certainly had never enjoyed it. But this felt different. Dangerous.

Shadow wrapped his fingers around my wrist and tugged. "Night."

I turned to stare at him.

He cocked his head toward the portal. "We have to go."

We needed to stick together. The Order would know within minutes, if they didn't already, that their second team had been taken out. They would send a third. And a fourth. They wouldn't stop until they got what they wanted.

Amy.

Shadow pushed me through the portal first. Heat flashed, singing the ends of my hair, my eyelashes, the breath in my lungs. He dogged my heels as I stepped into sulfur—soaked air. My boots hit asphalt softened from the heat, the ground springy underfoot. The shadow of a great oak loomed to my right, the caw of a crow jolting my nervous system to even more exquisite attention.

I took a shallow breath through my mouth in defense against the rotten egg stench, surprised when the unexpected scent of saltwater coating my tongue. The sound of waves splintering on sand came from my left. I turned to look.

A short Latina woman, her long dark hair twisted into a loose bun on the top of her head, faced the incoming tide. The clouds overhead had gathered so thick, they blotted out the sun entirely, so that she cast no shadow on the sand. She was dressed all in powder blue from her denim shirt to her linen pants stood in the sand. White tendrils of foam grabbed at her bare ankles, threatening to drag her out to sea. She shook them off. A gust of wind tore at her updo until her locks streamed in the current, a godlike weathervane.

A storm was coming in. I could feel it in the way the fine hairs on my arms rose. I could taste faraway ozone.

Rude and Sunday were nowhere to be seen. I couldn't feel them, either. Same with Shadow, who should be right behind me. Something had dragged me off my intended path.

Something, or someone.

The woman turned slowly to meet my gaze, her brown eyes filled with moonlight and time. Her lips moved. I couldn't hear the sound she made, but I could read it. Worse, I could feel it, like a wound to the heart.

Nena.

The buffeting wind tore her name from my mouth, but from the way her lips curved, I know she heard it. Heard me.

Abuelita.

CHAPTER 11

MY BREATH CAUGHT in my throat. My *abuelita* walked toward me, leaving footprints in the sand like a mortal woman. She gathered her long, dark hair as she walked, twisting and tucking it into a bun that held against the wind. She closed the long distance between us in a handful of steps, bringing with her the perfume of salt and water and sand, concentrated so strongly they activated every childhood memory I had of her, playing my emotions like a movie soundtrack.

I saw the film in my mind's eye, too. *Abuelita* in front of the kitchen stove, cooking a mole sauce that made my mouth water even now. My view of the water from the sand when I was a child sitting in the V of *abuelita's* legs, her arms wrapped around me as she told me a story about the stars in the night sky and how I was like them. I felt longing. I felt as if I belonged to someone who understood me, who didn't fear me. And love—always love, but shattered and cruel at the edges.

She both was and wasn't my grandmother. She was an elder, older than time, one of the beings who created the worlds. Dream was her name and her title, her function. The raw power she carried had no equal, as far as I knew. Maybe she loved me. Maybe she didn't. In the end, that didn't matter. She had a job to do. A mission. And the mission mattered more than me.

I shook my head to clear it. I couldn't be here. Not with Amy in Lucifer's hands. Not with Shadow on the verge of blowing people I loved—and maybe the world—to smithereens. I launched my magic, searching this construct, this place on the astral or whatever it was, for weaknesses. For a way out.

No doors. No windows. Not even a goddamn crack to slip through.

I spoke through clenched teeth. "Let me go."

"Not until you hear me."

I stared at her.

"You're still pissed, *nena*. I don't blame you, but be mad later."

"I don't have time for this."

"There is no other time."

"We can fight our way out of here."

"You could." She shrugged. "But that would take longer than listening."

The last time I'd seen my *abuelita*, she'd deliberately exposed me to the contagion that cemented the Angel's and my transformation from two separate beings into one. She'd taken away my choice. Turned me into Death.

And if she hadn't, we wouldn't have been able to defeat the End. Everyone we knew and loved would probably have died. That didn't make it all right.

I hadn't given her much thought over the last few months of recovery but, seeing her now, I got that I hadn't put her out of my mind at all. I'd just swallowed the betrayal and uncertainty of what she'd done, and now it roiled in my gut.

I clenched my hands into fists. "I haven't forgiven you."

She nodded. "You're not going to like what I have to say now any more than you did then. I saw what you did at the serpent's shop. The way you killed your enemies."

"What about it?"

"You need to be careful, *nena*. The things you do now, at this sensitive juncture, will influence all of your actions to come. You're rewiring your mind and your nervous system. You're rewiring your heart, the seat of your magic."

"Rewiring them to do what?"

"To accommodate a weaving of souls that are no longer human into your human body."

Her words took me right back to the place where the End holed up, far underground on the west side of the Willamette where he'd opened a portal to the In—Between, setting a trap for the Angel and me.

The End wrapped his life force around our heart, a fist seeking to crush, to destroy. To make our home his own. His power against ours. He had total control. We could barely use what we had.

The snow beneath us clung to me, the End's ice seeping in with a cold so deep, it burned. My breath came shallow and quick. The sulfured air and the darkness seemed to close in, swallowing the space around us, hugging the edges of my body. Claustrophobia exploded under the surface of our skin, and fight or flight kicked in hard and fast—only our body still refused the order to move, so we could do neither.

The Angel's wings—those beside our heart—turned to smoke, from feathers we could feel to something more ephemeral, reshaping into something sharper. Talons that tore at the End, slicing through its black—hole being.

With every strike, every blow that ripped him apart, the End reconstituted himself, healing, covering, crafting better defenses.

Just before the transformation occurred. Before my human life ended. Before all my heart and blood connections burned out and I flatlined. Before I roared to life again as Death.

"Are you mad that I enjoyed killing them?"

"Are you mad that I sent you over the cliff or that I didn't tend your wounds after you climbed out of the pit?"

"Yes," I said.

"Which?"

"Both."

She sighed. "All creatures feel pleasure when they are able to express their true nature."

"And mine is death."

"Night—"

"She died."

"Night will always be a part of you. What would she think?"

Horror. Shame. But not guilt. The Angel and I did what needed to be done. I didn't say any of that aloud, but Dream seemed to hear it all the same.

"Don't take the path of least resistance, *nena*."

"What's that supposed to mean?"

"Don't become the villain you worked so hard not to be."

I held her gaze. "If you wanted a say in my choices, you should've treated me differently."

She held up both hands, but I wasn't stupid enough to interpret that as a sign of surrender. If she felt strongly enough to interfere in the first place, she'd find another way to try to get what she wanted.

"You never ask me what I want," I said.

"Because you always know. You've always been clear about what that is in every single moment."

My breath caught in my throat. "I do what has to be done to keep my people safe."

"And to keep the world spinning."

"The world is not my priority—the people I love are."

"It's a lot of people, Night. Your family. The children inside the Order. A girl chosen by an archangel to act as a vessel for a Horseman. A man in a coffee shop possessed by the End."

"So it might as well be the world."

She nodded.

"You miss my point."

"I don't think so, *nena*."

"My point is that what needs to be done and what I want aren't the same thing."

"No, your point is that you don't get to have a normal life, be a normal person. You didn't get to have an *abuelita* who bought you a dress for your *quincenera* or a *quincenera* at all. You don't get to settle down with your man and play house. You have great power—more power than any human should have. It could turn you into a monster."

She was right. I didn't get to have those things. Be those things. Do any of those things. But she was also wrong. "Power doesn't make monsters. The monster is always inside someone to begin with. They have to choose to wake it."

"And then what?"

"Deal with the consequences."

She frowned. "Are you sure you're ready for that?"

She thought I was a monster. "I don't need your warning. I don't want it."

"Then you're already lost."

I didn't have to listen to this. After everything she'd done, I didn't have to forgive, either. I wanted out. Now.

"Goodbye, *abuelita.*"

The Angel's and my magic rose at the prospect of freedom, frost kissing our skin. But there was no need for magic. Dream waved a hand and the clouds parted just enough to allow a ray of sun to burst through, turning a ribbon of sea into glittering diamonds so bright, they blinded. I blinked and Dream was gone, vanished without leaving so much as a footprint behind. The clouds faded to wisps, fluttering like feathers.

She'd left the door open and she'd left just like that. Just like before.

I took a deep breath and launched from the sand, wings catching a pocket of air, muscles straining against the buffeting wind one minute, then rocketing me forward in the next as the breeze died. The Angel and I knifed through the still air, magic at the ready, sliding through the rift and into the searing heat of the In—Between. I gulped the sulfur—stained air, fighting not to cough, and tumbled through a maze of interlocking portals, bouncing off the walls like a pinball.

When my feet hit the ground again, arms wrapped around me from behind, pinning the Angel's and my wings to my back. I whipped my magic, started to lash out. Then, the rich perfume of grass and earth overwhelmed my instinct.

Red.

He spun me around, fingers digging into my shoulders. "The hell have you been?"

Deep worry lines creased his forehead, a matching set framing the corners of his mouth. His hair looked as if he'd spent hours combing it with worried fingers. He sent a trickle of emotion through the heart link—a twin cocktail of fear and anger that hit me like a slap to the face. It didn't make any sense.

"Answer the question, Night." He tightened his grip.

"You know exactly where I went." Except that wasn't true. He knew I'd headed for Faery, but not anything that happened after that. "We got called into a fight."

"At Malek's place."

"I followed everyone through the portal and got hijacked."

He held my gaze, the sharpness in his eyes wicked enough to cut.

The conversation with *mi abuelita* couldn't have taken more than a few minutes. Unless— "How long have I been gone?"

"Two days."

Damn. Lucifer had a two—day head start hiding Amy. Two days to put her plans in motion. The world was fucking ending and people were in danger and maybe dying, and my grandmother had purposely kept me away.

I swallowed hard. "Sunday?"

"Sunday's fine. Well, fine as she can be."

"Her eyes?"

He shook his head.

I gritted my teeth. "Rude? Shadow?"

"Not here."

What did he mean, *not here*? "Where are they?"

He shook his head. "They never made it."

CHAPTER 12

R ED LET ME GO, leaving bruises on my shoulders. He didn't apologize, only looked at me, scanning every inch of my body while the room spun, swaying this way and that until it finally picked a side and dropped like a tossed coin. The skin on my arms pebbled into goosebumps. I curled my hands into fists, breathing in air dusted with bacon grease and coffee.

Slowly, my senses expanded to take in the white tile underfoot, the clock ticking above the stove, and the rain spattering against the back of the house.

"Night?"

I read my name on Red's lips, the sound a split—second behind. Something was wrong. Very wrong. I shuddered, forcing my gaze to rise so I could meet his. "Here."

"Sunday's in Addie's room."

That was the answer to the question I'd meant to ask before my senses had gone haywire. I spun on my heel, thanking the Powers when the room and my equilibrium held steady. Even so, the echo of our steps on the hardwood floor of the hall sounded too loud and the stair rail felt unreal against my palm as I climbed to the second floor, Red hot on my heels.

I knocked on Addie's door, not waiting for a response before I stepped inside. She leaned against the opposite wall, arms folded across her chest. Her dark brown skin glowed in the strange light that filtered through the window blinds. Usually, I could read her thoughts in her expression, but she'd boarded up all the holes and cracks. *Nothing to see here. Move along.*

Sunday sat on the bed, back flush against the headboard, a tall glass of water lifted halfway to her mouth. She didn't look at it, or at Red and me, although she'd clearly heard us come in.

"You stink, Sanchez. Sulfur and sand and brine. Either the In— Between has a beach or you've been with Dream."

"Yeah," I said.

"She come to help?"

"She delivered a message."

"What message?"

I hesitated. Telling them about Dream's warning would only make things worse. Things had been weird since the Angel and I became one. We were still learning how to be around each other. How to trust the new. But I'd also promised not to lie. Not to keep secrets from the people I loved.

"She told me to be careful so I don't go dark side."

"That's nerve after what she did." The anger on Sunday's face—in the blaze of her halo—matched the anger in Addie's and Red's eyes.

"She's an Elder," I said. "She does what she wants and the rest of us just have to live with it."

"Maybe not," Sunday said.

I could feel her mind working, thoughts turning this way and that as she worked the problem. She was an assassin. A temporarily wounded assassin. Eventually, we'd find Lucifer and kick her ass, and then Sunday would need a new target.

"No one deserves to have that kind of power over people," she said.

I couldn't disagree, but she was talking about offing *mi abuelita.* "Eyes on the prize."

"Really, Sanchez?"

My cheeks burned. "Sorry. Right now, we've got one mission."

Red shook his head. "Two."

Addie pushed away from the wall, hands dropping to her sides. "Lucifer says she's keeping Amy safe. She says she's giving her a choice. Say it's true."

I thought about my mentor and the Order. About Dream. About the Angel. "They all say they're giving you a choice. Then they carefully curate the options and manipulate you into choosing the lesser evil. What can you live with? What can't you live without?"

Red set a hand on my shoulder. "She's just like you used to be, Night. Confused. Pissed. Looking for a place to belong. She'll be easily fooled."

"Not for long," Sunday said. "When she realizes she's being played—"

My heart rate rose, and my magic with it. I took a deep breath. "All bets are off."

"What's that mean?" Red asked. "She simmers to a boil? She goes nuclear? What happens when a Horseman of the Apocalypse goes nuclear?"

"None of us know her well enough to say. Shadow does, but he's missing. Malek does."

"He's missing, too." Addie pressed her lips into a thin line. "Same time Sunday stepped out of the In—Between and into my kitchen, he vanished. One second, he was on the porch drinking the cup of coffee I made him, the next he was just gone."

"He walked away?" I asked.

"The porch chair he was rocking in was still moving. I found his mug on its side in the flowerpot beside the rocker, coffee soaking into the dirt. He was taken. Or he had an emergency so strong, he couldn't take the time to set down his drink before he magicked himself out of here."

An emergency. Like Lucifer kidnapping Amy. Malek cared that much about exactly two people in this world. "Where's Beth?"

"Here."

I glanced over my shoulder, meeting Beth's bleak gaze. The braids that snaked around her head were dull and frizzy, her skin still too pale. She leaned against the door jamb for support, but she didn't tremble as she had the other day. She looked like shit, but she felt stronger. She was healing.

Red took a step toward her. "You should be in bed."

Beth held up a hand. "Not a chance. You need me, and, besides, my family's gone *poof* and I will find them, with or without you and I don't care how long it takes or whether it kills me. Again. Understand?"

Red gave her a *do what I say, girl* look.

She rolled her eyes. "How do we find Amy and the others? How do we kick an archangel's ass, because that's what we're going to have to do, right? I mean, we can do one or the other because we're mighty, but both is kind of pushing it and Malek cannot be *gone*. He can't be. No one took him. No one is powerful enough and he'd kick their ass and make sure they died screaming. It's what he does and—"

She looked like she could hyperventilate any second. "Beth."

"—after we took care of the End, there's no one else. No one. He's the strongest and best and most ruthless and—"

She wasn't just pale anymore. Her face had taken on a bluish tint. "Beth."

"—he wouldn't have just left me like that."

No matter how pissed off at him she was for breaking trust with people she cared about, or how afraid she felt that he might kill her for disobedience. No, he wouldn't have just left her. Not without so much as a word.

"Take a breath." I modeled one for her, deep on the inhale, long on the exhale.

She followed my lead, the blue undertone fading from her skin. Her eyes shone, wet with a combustible mixture of rage and unshed tears and devastation. "He wouldn't."

"I know."

A tug on the heart link had me looking at Red from the corner of my eye. I tugged back, letting him know I felt him. He relaxed a hairsbreadth, but no further. Worry and agitation still had a hold on him, pushed down low, waiting to be sprung like a tripwire.

Addie removed her glasses and rubbed the bridge of her nose. "We need reinforcements. We have to call everyone."

Everyone meant sending a messenger for Kevin and Luna. Recalling Miguel from his quiet life and putting the kids to work, including and especially Faith. Dealing with my *abuelita* whether I wanted to or not.

After everything she'd said to me about duty and obligation—whether or not she'd used those words, that was what she'd meant—and after everything I'd said to her about how I only did what I did to protect the people I loved, I didn't want to look at her, much less work with her. That didn't matter. It couldn't. If I had to swallow my feelings, I'd shove them down even if I choked on them. I couldn't look at the anguish on Beth's face and do anything else.

Going up against an archangel also meant calling in another.

Sunday pushed up on her elbows and braced her back against the headboard. "What are you waiting for, Sanchez? Summon the asshole."

I looked at Addie. Her house, her rules, her choices.

She shrugged. "I could put up a ritual circle and be formal about it, but I don't think it works that way for you anymore, Night."

Now that I was a full—fledged Horseman of the Apocalypse. I nodded.

"You call Michael. Red, take Beth outside and call Kevin and Luna."

"What are you planning to do?" Red asked.

"Going to the kitchen. With this many magical beings gathering in one place, we're going to need some nourishment. And the house spirit's going to need to be fed." The corners of her mouth turned down. The stars in her night sky halo flickered.

She was hiding something, or at least not telling us everything. I should ask her what and why, but I hesitated. If she had something important to say, she'd share it. We trusted each other like that now. I watched her walk out, the expanse of her back a closed book. A moment later, the stairs creaked under her step.

Red offered Beth a shoulder to lean on. She took it, shooting me a determined glance as they followed Addie. Without them, the room felt to still. I could hear my own breathing, and Sunday's, and I could sense the kinetic energy of dust motes floating in the air.

"Well?" Sunday asked.

I closed my eyes, pushing my energy through the soles of my feet, feeling my center of gravity stable and strong. The Angel and I drew our magic from the edges of our skin into my heart. The magic built there, layer upon layer of darkness and cold, of strength and time, pulsing into my throat. I took one deep breath and blew it out slowly, then another. Each influx of energy fed the push of magic into the single word I spoke on the fourth exhale.

"Michael."

The space in front of the window began to shimmer like the air above asphalt on an August day, as if it was about to catch fire. A heartbeat later, it did. A single spark seared one of the floating motes, igniting the dust and oxygen all around it. The temperature shot through the roof—literally—scoring the paint on the ceiling and the wall, melting the edges of the window blinds. In the center of the heat and flames, a portal opened. A being stepped through it and into the room, too tall and too big for his own skin.

His hair streamed behind him, writhing flames of orange, yellow, red, and blue. He had three eyes, two in the usual places and a third in the center of his forehead. His armor glittered like diamonds. A sword with a golden hilt stood at attention in the sheath on his back.

Then the flames guttered and the archangel shrank down to something more man—sized. By the time the last of the smoke rose from his skin, he looked like any guy on the street. Black leather jacket. Black motorcycle boots on his feet. Black jeans and familiar black T—shirt emblazoned with faded white script—*Ride the Lightning*.

The bangs of his short black hair dusted his brow like feathers. He blinked at me, his three eyes resolving into two, but never making it to a human color. Fire burned inside. I wondered for a split second whether the flames ever went out, and what it must be like to burn like he did. To have the air itself bend in your presence because your power.

He opened his mouth, breaking my train of thought. "What?"

Sunday barked laughter. "For real? What? Don't you pay attention to what goes on down here? Wait—don't answer that. I know you do."

Michael didn't grace her with a single grace. He met my gaze and held it, waiting for an answer.

"Lucifer is here."

He didn't so much as raise a brow.

"But you knew that," I said. "Did you know she took Amy? That Shadow and Rude and Malek are missing? That she knocked the Angel and I down as if we were a house of cards in high wind? Of course you did. Just like you knew we'd be calling. So, what's the problem? And don't say it's that you're not allowed to interfere. We both know that's bullshit."

"The problem is that I had to break off tracking Lucifer to answer your call."

I blinked at him. "You're interfering."

"I had to choose a side. The powers or the world. I chose the world."

The sensation of his being too big for his own skin hit me again like an itch between my shoulder blades. He no longer felt comfortable or sure of his role. Of his place. "What's the price?"

"Nothing you need to worry about. I ask again: what do you want?"

"Your help against Lucifer."

He studied my face, gaze digging past the surface to excavate everything underneath. Thoughts, feelings—mine and the Angel's. As if he were trying to see not only what we'd done, but what we might do. Every path we could take from this moment forward, the consequences and repercussions, victories and defeats. Flashes of light and color and fleeting images of faces and places spiraled through my mind. I couldn't hold on to a single one.

I couldn't track what Michael saw. Neither could *La Muerte*.

Michael's face softened so briefly, I could've imagined it. "You should stay out of this, Death."

The impulse to squash that name came fast and hard. "Don't call me that."

"Because you don't like it."

I stared at him. "I'm not Death."

"You are," he said. "The longer and harder you fight that, the worse things will get."

"I get to choose."

He shook his head. "Fool."

I tried to set my hands on my hips, but they remained stubbornly at my sides, fingers curling into fists. I tried to hit him with words as hard as his own, but my mouth refused to move. Did I or did not not have control over my own body? Wasn't I in charge? Weren't the Angel and I a team?

Wait, the Angel whispered.

I didn't want to wait. I wanted the archangel in front of me, the one who never came when I called but only when he wanted, who told me he couldn't interfere and then found every way he could do so without getting caught, the one who claimed to trust me because my methods got results, even if they were different than what he wanted —the one whose blood ran in my veins—to answer my goddamn question.

"I don't want to fight with you. Will you help us?"

"You assume my choosing the world means I choose you," he said.

I shook my head. "I don't understand."

"You will."

"What does that mean?"

"It means no." He disappeared as quickly as he'd appeared, scorching dust and air in his wake and leaving a nasty burnt spot on Addie's bedroom carpet.

I stared at the empty space he'd left, unable to wrap my brain around what had just happened.

Sunday broke the silence. "I wish I could feel surprised. When has he ever done what we wanted?"

"Never," I said. "But that's not the problem."

"What is?"

I couldn't put my finger on it. "Something's different this time. Can you feel it?"

"Yeah," she said. "You are. You smell different. You move different. The things we all know about you, the ways we know you—everything's changed. Maybe that's Michael's point."

Maybe it wasn't. "You're reading his mind now?"

She rubbed her palms on the comforter. "Not touching that with a ten—foot pole. If Michael's out, then he's out. We can't wait for him to change his mind or depend on him for anything. Same shit, different day. Help me up."

I closed the distance to the bed. "Where to?"

"If we're meeting in the kitchen, then that's where we should all be."

She didn't have her sight or her magic, but even without those things she was formidable. Woe to anyone who underestimated her.

She grabbed the hem of my shirt and helped herself out of bed, taking up position behind me with her hands on my shoulders. "We're gonna need more than your standard battle plan, Night."

"I want to fight. Magic and guns and fists always get the job done —at least, they always have before."

"They will again."

I hoped she was right. She had to be.

Even thinking that felt like swimming against a rip current. Like being pulled out to sea and dragged under. I exhaled, pushing the feeling away, but it only tangled around me more tightly, like a net.

Like a trap.

CHAPTER 13

I LED SUNDAY slow and easy as much for my sake as hers. The silence upstairs and the feeling of *wrongness* wouldn't let me go. The brush of my boots against the carpet on the stairs, the echo of our footfalls on the hardwood in the hall, and the constriction of my wings to make room for Sunday behind me felt like razor wire on my nerves. I expected to hear Beth stack run—on sentences while Addie opened and shut drawers to retrieve silverware and cooking implements. I expected to taste coffee in the air, to sense Kev and Luna arrive by way of the basement portal. But I felt and tasted and heard none of those things.

Sunday stopped behind me, forcing me to do the same.

"Why is it so quiet?" she asked.

I took a step forward, tugging her along even when she tried to dig in, picking up the pace until we turned in to the kitchen. The rooster clock above the stove ticked away the seconds. The afternoon light filtered in through the window blinds. The wear on the white tile whispered memories of warmth and family, but that was all they were —memories. The room felt lonely.

The room was empty.

The back door was locked. Same with the windows. No signs of forced entry or exit. No pots or pans graced the stovetop. The refrigerator's motor hummed as if it were on its last legs. The air tasted stale. Dust everywhere, at least an inch thick and spiderwebs dangled in the corners of the ceiling.

I reached through the heart link for Red, but felt nothing. He wasn't there at all, not even a hint of his grass and earth.

I pressed a palm to my belly, sick to my stomach. "There's no one here."

"They're gone?"

I steered Sunday toward the closest chair and planted her in it. "Don't move."

"Screw you, Sanchez. I'm not helpless."

"I need to know exactly where you are if the shit hits the fan. And I need all your senses."

She didn't respond, just expanded her awareness like the pro she was. I knocked on the door of her mind and she let me in, inviting me to share her senses and reactions. This room was clear. No magical remnants. No sign of our family, or of anyone who might've taken them.

Sunday pulled a knife from its sheath at her side as I stepped out of the kitchen and into the living room with its facing sofas and photos on the mantle and black hole of a fireplace. The same layer of dust that had overtaken the kitchen made a home here, too. Not a single footprint or magical signature marred its surface. The deadbolt on the front door was engaged, the windows closed and locked.

I checked the basement next. The protective magic Addie maintained shimmered in the air, but weakly, as if it hadn't been reinforced in months, maybe years. The portal we'd built to travel from Addie's to the gym was simply gone. No trace of it remained, if it'd ever existed at all. The door that led out into the side yard was not only locked, but nailed and painted shut.

After that, I cleared each room of the house. Sunday saw everything I did, feeding me suggestions to look more closely at certain corners or in closets, to pull back curtains and look out the windows. I saw nothing out of the ordinary, except that everything continued to feel wrong. The more I tried to pin down the why, the more elusive it became.

The photos and art and fabrics—everything down to the rooster clock in the kitchen—belonged to Addie. They reflected her taste. I'd lived here, part— or full—time, for months. The place was home, but it felt unrecognizable all the same.

There was one thing I hadn't yet done, one being I hadn't felt or heard from in all of this—the spirit that protected the house. We'd called Michael and he'd come. People disappeared. All kinds of weirdness was going on. The house ought to consider any one of those things a threat. It should have contacted me. I should feel its hackles. I should feel it locking the place down. But I hadn't.

I reached out, searching for its solid presence, but found nothing at all.

I stalked into the kitchen again, knowing that Sunday still sat in the chair because I felt her there, real as the sun in the sky, but seeing her still opened a floodgate of relief.

She set the blade on the table beside her, her forehead creased with a deep V. "What happened here?"

"I'm not sure that's the right question."

"Something happened here. Something terrible."

"Maybe." I wrestled my uneasiness and jumbled thoughts into formation. "This is Addie's house. It looks like her house and feels in almost every way like her house, but it's not the place we know. It may not even belong to our Addie."

"Come again? Are you saying we're in an alternate dimension?"

"Or something like it."

She mulled that for a moment. "Are we really talking about that like it's normal? Like people slip into alternate spaces and other worlds without so much as a ripple and it's everyday news?"

I counted the evidence for normality on my fingers. "Faery. Demonic dimensions. The In—Between. The borderlands between this world and the angelic dimension where the Order made chameleons like Miguel and held *La Muerte* prisoner."

"Yeah, but I've never heard of anything like this before. This is actually weird."

I shot her side—eye, then remembered she couldn't see it. "The question we should be asking is what changed. Did the house change? Did we change?"

"How long have we been here? Does time run differently here?"

That was a rabbit hole waiting to suck us in because the questions were seemingly endless. "How do we get out, or at least find our people?"

"Who did this? Because somebody did this. This shit doesn't just happen."

The feathers around my heart fluttered.

"What was that?"

"A sign that you're on to something," I said. "This is a trap."

"A fucking elaborate trap. Lucifer?"

"She's our best bet." She wasn't the only being with enough power to pull off something like this. But I couldn't think of a reason why any of the others would try.

"What now?" Sunday asked. "Emergency blood link?"

Use the vestiges of the past spells that tied us all together to reach out. "It's worth a shot."

"You want to use the basement space?"

"It's a bad defensive position without the house spirit on guard duty. Here's fine."

She nodded. "What do you want me to do?"

"Let me in a little further. I need to tap whatever remains of the spell inside of you, and I might have to root around for it."

"Because Lucifer took my magic."

"Because Lucifer took your magic." I pulled the chair beside Sunday into position so that I could sit facing her, so that I could reach out and take her hands. "You trust me?"

"Always."

I needed to hear that. Even more, I needed to believe it.

"Let's not waste any more time. Do what you need to. I'll keep my senses pealed for both of us."

I closed my eyes and slowed my breathing, pushing my magic deeper into Sunday's mind. She opened up for me like a blooming rose, fragrant and familiar, all red velvet and dark shadows. I lit those dark places, chasing away ghosts, looking for her memories of the blood link we'd forged when we'd built the blood link before.

Prepping for battle in Addie's basement, with our witch Stacy casting the spell to bind us all together. Allowing us to share thoughts and feelings and skills. Allowing us to survive. To win.

Sunday's memory overtook mine like dye spreading through water.

I breathed in the scent of fabric softener and felt static electricity from the dryer. I felt the warmth of a hand in mine and felt pinned to the spot by Stacy's sharp blue stare. When the witch's spell passed over and through me in a crimson wave, a flood of emotion roared through. It was too much—so much, it stunned me. I held on to the anchor of my heartbeat, of my body— the weight of my feet on the floor and the tension of muscle over bone—to keep standing. To be ready. To fight.

I gathered that memory close, searching for traces of the magic, and found fragments floating free, unconnected to anything or anyone at all. When Lucifer had taken Sunday's magic, she'd taken the chain. She'd severed Sunday from the rest of us.

The connection had been broken along with Sunday's access to her magic, but the most important thing—the essential thing—remained.

We'd need the witch to reforge the link, but we had no time, and powers knew where Stacy was in this cracked up world or dimension. We'd have to make due with what we had right here and now, which meant *La Muerte* and me. The single being we'd become.

I didn't have to think about what to do. It came as naturally as breathing.

We reached for her heart—the seat of her magic, the part of her that made her who she was. It took only the slightest touch, the brush of a fingertip against muscle memory, magic memory. One touch, and her heart froze.

Time slowed and stopped, stretching and flattening until the blink of an eye lasted an eternity. Sunday's nervous system sent alarm after alarm, muddy and blurred and hopeless before the Angel's power. Without a heartbeat, it was only a matter of minutes before her brain would begin to die from lack of oxygen.

We didn't need minutes, only the seconds it took for the seed of the power she'd been born with, buried deep inside her heart, to burst forth from the ice. That seed of power was made of light so bright, nothing could hide from it, and even the power of Death was no match for a soul.

We couldn't regrow severed connections, but we could raise the dead with our power and the power of Sunday's soul.

"Stop."

The single word broke our magic, shocking us into releasing Sunday's heart from our cold, dead touch, throwing us out of her heart and her mind.

I slammed back into my body with so much force, I couldn't breathe. My vision blurred and grayed before I could focus again. I blinked hard and fast until I caught a glimpse of my daughter's face—light brown skin flushed with anger, fury in her brown eyes, dark hair like a lion's mane. Her silver—and—gold halo roared like flames. A second later, I felt her hands on me, fists gripping my shirt. She shoved me backwards, tipping my chair, smashing into the floor. My head cracked against the tile.

Faith spun on her heel, touching Sunday's face, searching for a carotid pulse, taking her by the shoulders and shaking her, sparks from her hands scorching Sunday's clothes and skin and hair. Faith laid a hand over Sunday's heart, whispering something that sounded like an incantation and a prayer rolled into one.

My skin began to crawl and my gut rolled over as the facts on the ground hit me like a punch. Sunday was dead. The Angel and I had killed her.

Sunday took a sharp, deep breath and coughed, eyes wide and unseeing as she clawed at Faith's back.

Faith drew her close, rocking her. "It's okay."

Sunday pulled away, but Faith refused to let her go. It took three tries before Sunday disengaged, pushing to her feet, breath ragged and fingers splayed at her sides. "Sanchez!"

I stood up, dizzy and slow and freaked the hell out. I hardly recognized the sound of my own voice. "Here."

"The hell did you do to me?"

I opened my mouth to reply, then snapped it shut again. In the moment, I'd felt so sure. I'd known exactly what I was doing—or *La Muerte* had. Now, I couldn't remember. The thought of that—so much less frightening than the reality—made me want to scream. But I had to say something. I couldn't just stand there silent and guilty and terrified.

"I don't know."

"I said it's okay." Faith put her body between us. In the moment, she didn't look much like my kid. She looked like the god she carried, the Awakened. God of magic itself.

"No," Sunday said.

"No," I agreed.

"You can fight or talk about it later, then. I found the others and we need you. Understand?"

"You found them where?" Sunday asked.

"Not important now. We need to go."

Fear wanted to eat my words. I forced them out into the open. "*All the others or some of them?*"

"Now, Mom." She reached out a hand to each of us.

I took the one offered to me. Sunday didn't hesitate to do the same. Her gaze never left mine—not when Faith opened a portal with the power of her will alone, filling the kitchen with heat and sulfur, or when we tumbled into the dark whirlpool of the time stream.

CHAPTER 14

A KALEIDOSCOPE OF white and steel and wood, of coffee and
frying eggs and bacon, of familiar voices assaulted me as I
stepped from the In—Between. Before my feet touched the ground, a
punch hit my right cheek. Pain raced like electricity from the point of
impact through my eye socket to the crown of my head and then
exploded. The blow knocked me sideways, left hip striking something
hard—edged—an oven handle. My magic flared as my senses fought
for a handhold and finally anchored me in time and space.

Another version of Addie's kitchen. Blinds drawn and back door
closed and locked, ticking from the rooster clock loud as ever. This
kitchen was full of people. Red and Faith and Addie. Kevin and Luna
and Beth. And Sunday, who'd hit me.

Her rose—gold halo glowed like a bomb about to go off, her hands
curled into fists as she moved with feline grace in front of me, heed-
less of Faith's shouted warning to back off and the shock on the
others' faces. She glared at me with malice and purpose.

She glared at me, taking in everything she saw.

"You can see," I said.

"You killed me."

"I did." There was no denying it. "You done?"

"You're kidding, right?" Magic licked her skin, flowing in clean lines toward her face. Toward her eyes.

She was preparing to use it on me. To take me down. The air around her began to come apart at the seams. Watcher's magic.

She froze. "Addie?"

"Settle down, Sunday."

"Sanchez is dangerous."

"She's always been dangerous, and you never cared about that before now."

Sunday tore her gaze away from me, turning it on Addie. "It's what we thought."

What they thought?

"How could it be when we didn't know what to think?"

Sunday furrowed her brow. "But—"

"Settle down, I said."

Sunday shook out her hands. "What are you going to do with her?"

Do with me?

"Not a damn thing—yet."

Sunday's mouth fell open.

"None of us is strong enough to bind her," Addie said.

"All of us—"

Red's drawl was pronounced. He was pissed. "There's no *all of us*. We're not in agreement on this. Night's your best fucking friend, so give her enough benefit of the doubt to talk to her."

I braced my hand on the oven top and straightened, holding on for more than physical balance. Every single person in the kitchen stopped talking and stared at me, half of them waiting for me to make a hostile move and the other half uncertain.

I knew how they felt. I couldn't stand here under the weight of it for another second.

"I'm going to sit in the living room. I need a minute, and so do you."

She let me walk away, though I felt her gaze on my back until I slipped out the door and around the corner, out of sight. The living room was pitch black, blinds drawn. I understood suddenly that it was dark outside, too.

My legs shook as I found my way to the sofas, choosing a seat facing the kitchen so I could see the others coming before my knees gave way. I dug my nails into the armrest. My heart beat too fast, my breath shallow. I couldn't seem to catch it. The raw pounding in my head threatened to take over, to become my whole world.

A touch at the nape of my neck stole my attention—the house spirit, checking in. It seemed to scan me from the crown of my head to the soles of my feet. What it was looking for, I couldn't say, but it seemed satisfied with what it found. I sent it a wave of gratitude.

I'd never realized how much I'd come to depend on it, not as much for protection as for a foundation of normalcy, security. That was the stuff dreams were made of, wasn't it? The knowledge that everything was all right at the root, that someone or something had our backs, that we weren't alone in the fight.

For great stretches of my life, I'd been without that, or I'd been that to someone else without any guarantees for myself. I'd shouldered the weight of the world because others depended on me to do it, and because I loved them. Strange how fast I'd gotten used to Addie and her house spirit taking that role for me. Even if it was an illusion—powers knew it was, because there were never any guarantees, not about anything—I wanted it.

A moment later, I caught a whiff of grass and earth, and Red's weight on the sofa beside me. He made no move to hold my hand or to touch me in any other way, but his presence comforted and calmed. My breathing evened and depend, and my skipping heart slowed to something like normal.

"Better?" he asked.

"Enough."

"You want to tell me what happened?"

"I don't know." I felt his regard as he studied my face, but couldn't turn to look at him. Not yet. "I mean, I know what I intended to do. I connected with Sunday, and we were about to reach out to see whether we could connect with all of you, and then it was like *La Muerte* took over. Like he knew what was needed."

"And you let him."

"I trust him."

He hesitated. "You have to. Trust him, that is. Because he's a part of you—more than a part. He's—"

"He is me, and I'm him."

"What'd he do?"

"I'm not sure of all the whys and wherefores."

"What, Night?"

"Stopped Sunday's heart."

"Jesus."

I nodded.

"And after that?"

I shrugged. "That's fuzzy, too."

"You gotta do better than that."

I looked at him then. "You don't think I know that?"

He reached for my face, sliding a fingertip along my cheekbone. "That's gonna bruise badly."

"That's changing the subject."

"It is. I was worried earlier about Amy going nuclear, but it never crossed my mind to worry that you would."

"You've been managing me since the change. Following me when I go out in the middle of the night, bringing me home. Making sure I don't stray too far off the beaten path."

"There is no beaten path for this, Night. Not even the Watchers have lore about what it means to be a Horseman of the Apocalypse. We only have you. Your experience. What you share with us. You keeping things to yourself you don't want us to know?"

"Not that I'm aware of. Besides, we've got the heart link."

"I know everything you're feeling. You can't hide that from me."

"I can't lie to you, and I don't want to."

"All right."

I took a deep breath and blew it out slow and steady. "Where'd you go? When Sunday and I got downstairs in the other house—wherever we were—you and Beth and Addie were gone. You were all gone. We thought maybe we were in another dimension."

Faith spoke up. "Timeline."

I searched and found her in the shadows near the corner bookcase. She seemed smaller, and her hair was no longer down. "You're quiet."

"I didn't want to interrupt."

"But you need to. Timeline?"

She nodded. "There are a handful of them right now—timelines where things are different. We're different. The world has ended in all of them except this one."

It took a second to process that. "How do you know this?"

"I've been to them, looking for you and Aunt Sunday. I knew they were there all of a sudden." She snapped her fingers. "Like that. Like, one minute it would never have occurred to me, and the next it just was. Super weird."

"No one told you," I said.

She shook her head.

"We've gotta figure this out." Red brushed the hair away from my forehead. "Sunday will forgive you, Night."

"Sunday hits like a girl."

"Who gave you a shiner."

"Wouldn't be the first time." But it was the first time she'd done it because I'd threatened her existence. "I feel out of control, Red. I don't want to feel that way."

"Let's see what we can do about it, then."

"Basement," Faith said.

The heart of magical operations. "The others?"

"Down there already, Mom."

It was one thing not to hear Faith padding into the living room while I freaked about what I'd done to Sunday, or while Red and I talked—for a normal human woman without my magic and training. I never missed an approach like Faith's.

She wasn't an enemy bent on catching me unaware. She was my kid. She loved me. She was trying to help.

I shouldn't have missed her, and no way would I have missed the crowd in the kitchen squeaking down hardwood floors, opening the basement door on its squealing hinges, pulling the chain on the overhead light, and clomping down the basement stairs.

"Why didn't I hear them?"

Red went still.

"Did you?" I asked.

"No," he whispered.

"I think we should go downstairs and talk about it," she said. "The timelines are—"

"Shifting?" That was the only explanation that made sense.

"Yes."

I held out a hand to Red, and he let me help him up. We held on to each other tightly as we descended the steps by the light of the bare, overhead bulb. The protections felt like the familiar weaving of Addie's and the house spirit's magic, of the additions the rest of us had made over the last several months.

When we stepped through the protective veil and into the basement proper, the sight of the bright rug and pillows in the center of the concrete floor and the rhythm of the dryer spinning a full load of sheets sent a shudder of relief along my spine. The far corner housed the portal to the gym, as it should. Everyone who'd been in the kitchen stood or paced, none of them comfortable enough to sit.

Addie fingered the hem of her flowing purple tunic. Her silver—rimmed glasses perched on the tip of her nose as she met my gaze with dark eyes. Her starry halo recognized mine, and mine hers.

Kevin, all in brown leather, brown eyes cautious and hyper—vigilant, looked past me, attention locked on me. Same with Luna. Her black mohawk stood tall and looked razor—sharp. Her green halo split itself into flames as I watched, the power of the Horseman she carried at the surface and at the ready. Beside her, Beth ran the fingers of both hands through wet, loose hair, her white tank informing me that *Driver picks the music. Shotgun shuts his cake hole.* Her jeans were threadbare at the knees, her feet shoved into her scuffed black Doc Martins, laces untied.

Sunday folded her arms across her chest, her rose—gold magic rising to the top of her head, shining like a crown. "So, we're all here. What do we do now?"

"We figure out how to stop the world from exploding," Faith said, sweeping past Red and me to meet the others. "Or imploding. Whatever it's doing."

I blinked, trying to clear my head and focus. "We know what's happening—or we can guess. But we don't know why."

"Sure we do," Kevin said.

Beth looked at him from the corner of her eye. "Enlighten us, Faery man."

He pointed at me. "It's her."

CHAPTER 15

"I'M NOT DOING ANYTHING." My voice echoed off the basement walls.

The concrete underfoot felt cold and hard and unyielding, like the floor of a tomb. The air stilled as it had before. Every bit of dust and lint floating in the air became visible as if backlit by some invisible force. I held my breath, waiting for the world or the timeline or whatever to shift, but nothing happened.

The stillness took on weight and strength, pressing down on me as I stared at Kevin, nut brown in the midst of the colorful rug and pillows. He stared right back at me, his white—feathered wings unfolding behind him, but not opening all the way. For a heartbeat, it seemed there was no one else in the basement except him and me.

All the power of Faery flowed into him and through him. Because of that, he could see through any magic or mask or denial I might throw down. He saw me clearly as a weaving of human and Horseman, just as he was a weaving of human and fae. Of all the people here, even more than Luna, he knew what it felt like to share consciousness and a soul with a being who had never been human and never would be, who had motivations and obligations of their own.

Not only did he have no reason to lie, he literally couldn't, although he could talk around and obfuscate like a champ.

If Kevin said I caused the timelines to move and combine, then it had to be true.

The others looked at him and then at me, eyes narrowed and teeth gritted and magical shields up. As they moved, the pressure of the stillness lifted. Their suspicion sliced at me like knives. The dryer buzzed, cutting a wedge through the silence.

"Maybe it's not you, Night. Your human parts," Kevin said. "Maybe it's the part of you that is the Angel."

I started to say it couldn't be, that *La Muerte* wouldn't do anything to put them in danger. The words hovered on my tongue, and they tasted of ashes. I still didn't have a handle on what had happened in the other timeline with Sunday. I had no business protesting or making guarantees.

I asked a silent question. *How is this possible?*

Images scrolled across my mind. The basement shifted from familiar and filled with my people to dusty and abandoned, as it had been in the other timeline. From abandoned to gore—splattered, bodies strewn along the floor. From bloody to empty and pristine with a single, glowing figure kneeling in the center, his diamond armor and fiery sword glittering with magic, the air bending around his body.

As if he sensed something wrong, something that shouldn't be there, Michael turned to look at me, the flames in his eyes roaring high at the sight of me, his mouth grimly set.

At that moment, I understood that the images weren't flowing through me. I flowed through the images—the spaces, the timelines.

"Death," Michael said.

Before I could respond, the timeline changed, depositing me where I'd started, in the basement with the Addie in the flowing purple tunic and the Beth who wore the tank celebrating her *Supernatural* fandom and the Kevin whose brown eyes widened as his gaze met mine once again.

Sunday stepped toward me. "What just happened?"

"I think I just took a timeline tour," I said.

"You didn't move. Not really. But you weren't here, either. Was she?"

Kevin shook his head.

Movement behind him caught my eye, energy flowing toward a single point and coalescing into something solid and man—shaped. Someone with glittering armor and a sword who didn't bother to disguise his angelic nature with a T—shirt and jeans.

Michael shoved past Kevin and Sunday, knocking them aside, gathering speed as he barreled toward me. His eyes shot flames. Sparks flew from his fingertips. He reached for the sword at his back, drawing it with a crystal shriek that drove Addie and Beth to their knees and reverberated inside my bones.

I felt the air around Red displace before he inhaled, before the heart link between us lit up. Before he shoved forward to defend me. I moved back, blocking him, pushing him toward Faith and hoping she would know to shelter him from the impending firestorm.

Michael brought the sword down with all the might of the powers behind it.

The Angel's and my magic streamed to meet it—ice and doom and deliverance. The sword sliced through our magic as if it were smoke.

We shot out a hand, the intention clear as the noonday sun in a summer sky. The human in me screamed. The Horseman in me laughed.

We blocked the blade with the palm of our hand, wrapping our fingers around the flaming steel.

The blade should've taken off half my hand. My arm. It should've buried itself in my shoulder. Found its way to my heart. Instead, its forward motion halted with the force of a speeding car striking another head—on, the collision a cacophony of screeching metal and shattering glass. The impact shuddered through us. It didn't move us, not a sliver of an inch.

Michael's eyes narrowed. He tried to force the blade through our hand. When that didn't work, he tried to pull it back. *La Muerte* and I refused to let go.

Behind us, footfalls sounded on the stairs. I felt Faith turn to protect against the intruder, and I felt her backpedal before searing heat flashed at my back.

The man that strode past her and Red—past *La Muerte* and me—carried a sword of his own, pommel up. He ran at Michael, transferring all the energy and power he carried into his arm as he swung. He slammed the pommel into the side of Michael's head.

The archangel went down in a shiny diamond heap, his hand slipping from the hilt of his own blade, leaving us holding the thing as he hit the concrete, the flames in his eyes fading, lashes finally fluttering closed.

The Angel and I looked at the intruder who'd taken down Michael with that single blow, shock rippling through us as we took in the black hair and fiery eyes, the jeans and motorcycle boots, the T—shirt with its faded *Ride the Lightning* script.

This was our Michael. The one from our timeline. The corners of his mouth turned down as he surveyed the lot of us. "This is bad."

"Understatement of the year." This was worse than bad. This was off the charts." "How is this happening?"

He turned to the Angel and me, his brow furrowed. "The same way the timelines are combining and shifting—because of you."

"I'm not doing anything." Saying it again, this time to Michael, didn't change a thing. If Kevin and Michael were convinced I was making this happen, then they were probably right. I didn't have to consciously act in order to influence the people around me. No one did. Just by being who I was, my body language, other subtle cues, I could change the course of a conversation or other interaction. It stood to reason that I could do more than that.

Because I wasn't just me. I was *La Muerte*, too. The Angel lived and breathed in all the worlds. In all the timelines.

Fuck.

I swallowed hard. "I thought you were staying out of this."

"I thought you had better sense."

I raised a brow. "You've never thought that."

Addie brought her hands together, the sound a clap of thunder.

I looked at her, while Michael kept his gaze focused on me.

"What in heaven's name is going on here?" she demanded.

"Night's altered our reality," he said.

Addie glanced at the archangel laid out at my feet. "Not just ours."

Michael sheathed his sword, then squatted to retrieve the one on the floor. From his low vantage, he surveyed the damage to the other Michael's head. "He'll be out for a while."

What did he mean by "a while?" "Then what? He picks up where he left off?"

"Trying to kill you?" Michael looked up at me. "Yeah, probably. I'll talk to him."

"You expect that to do any good?" Addie asked. "By the time people get to the killing stage, they're usually past talking to."

"It worked for you and Night," he said.

Addie flashed a rueful grin. "You planning to tie him up?"

Michael shook his head. "Restraints don't work on us. Besides, you've had enough people tied up in this basement. Don't you think?"

Luna cleared her throat. The green light of her halo flickered. "Co —signed."

I couldn't argue with her, seeing as she'd been one of those people.

"Can't you take him somewhere else?" Addie asked.

Michael and I responded in unison. "No."

I cocked my head, curious about his answer.

"If we move him, it will make it harder to send him back where he belongs."

We couldn't take that chance. "I want him here. I have questions for him about why he wants me dead, what his world is like, and whether he traveled here on purpose or by accident. We need information."

Michael rose. "Get comfortable."

Addie sighed. "I'll go upstairs and bring down some food and drink."

Sounded great in theory, but what if she walked upstairs and into a different timeline? "Take someone with you."

"I don't think that's going to be good enough," she said.

"To keep you in this timeline? You're right. But if you end up somewhere else, at least you won't be alone."

She granted me the point. "Beth?"

"I get the best bacon." She followed Addie toward the edge of the protective veil, pausing before she passed through. "Don't fuck anything else up until I get back."

Red looked at her with wonder as she disappeared from view. "She wants a front row seat."

"She'll get one," Michael said. "You want to help me with him?"

"I thought you said to leave him where he is."

"Maybe he'll be less murderous if we make sure he's comfortable?"

Michael nodded.

Michael, Red, and I dragged him on to the rug, and placed a pillow under his head. As an afterthought, Luna pulled a warm sheet from the dryer and covered him with it. That was all the comfort we had to offer.

Michael insisted that the others stay back while he crouched in the line of fire. Luna huddled with Kevin checked on Beth.

Red closed the distance between us, drawing me in and speaking low in my ear. "What was that?"

He tugged on the heart link. I felt the hurt and simmering anger that flowed through it.

"An archangel attacked me with a sword."

"You stepped in front of me."

"You wanted to protect me."

He nodded.

He was in no position to go up against a being with that kind of power. He knew it. I knew it. So, what was he trying to prove? "I didn't want you to get hurt."

"I'm not helpless, Night. I have power. We're supposed to be in this together."

"We are."

He raised a brow. "You sure about that? Because I'm not. Every fight changes you. The last one changed you so much, I'm still trying to get used to who you are now, what you've become. One more fight might be too much."

I met his gaze and held it. "You're asking me not to fight?"

"No." He took a deep breath. Blew it out. "Yes." Another breath. "I don't know."

"Yes, you do." I could see it in his halo, the way the green deepened and the brown grew richer. I could not only smell the grass and earth on him, I could taste it.

He set his hands on his hips. "I don't want you to take it all on by yourself."

I still didn't understand where this was coming from. "We'd never have got this far if we weren't a team."

"The team backs you up. You take the biggest risks."

That was just how it worked because I had the Angel, and now I was the Angel and the Angel was me. That made it more important than ever that we take point. Take the risk. Take the brunt of the blows.

Red worried he wouldn't recognize me. I got that. I really did. He worried he'd lose me, but we'd been over that ground more than once. Was this wounded male pride? Maybe. But there was something else going on here.

"I do that to protect the people I love," I said.

"You need to trust us. Trust me."

I didn't look at any of them—at him—as if he was a stranger. They looked at me like that. They treated me like a bomb about to explode, something they had to handle with kid gloves. "I'm not the one with the trust problem here."

"That's not fair."

Of course it wasn't. Not for any of us. "I know you love me, Red. I also know you're managing me. Following me in the middle of the night to see where I go, to make sure I don't reveal myself, that I'm not accidentally seen. That I don't hurt anyone."

He flinched. "You never said anything."

"Because I understand. Doesn't mean I'm okay with it."

He dropped his arms to his sides. "I'm not sorry."

"I know." If I were in his shoes, I'd have done the same damn thing.

He nodded once and walked away, leaving me with a belly full of acid and a weight on my heart.

Sunday caught my eye with a cant of her head. She angled it toward the corner of the room that housed the portal. I followed her her lead, watching the changes in her halo as she moved. I didn't expect her to turn around and punch me as she had in the kitchen, but I wanted to be ready, just in case.

Finally, she stopped and turned, pitching her voice so low, only I could hear her. "You want to tell me what you just did?"

"Which part?"

"The part where you turned into the full—glory Angel of Death and blocked an archangel's sword with your bare hand by grabbing hold of the blade."

"I don't know," I said, immediately feeling like an ass. I'd just bitten into Red for saying those words.

"You're the same person I've always known, and then you're really, really not. How are you not freaking out?"

"Who says I'm not?"

She looked at me as if I'd lost my mind. "You don't even look a little bit bothered. You're not even fucking bleeding."

I looked at my hand, my palm whole and unmarked. "It felt normal."

Her eyebrows climbed to her hairline. "You literally have no idea."

"About what?"

"How you look to the rest of us when this kind of shit happens."

I shook my head. "How do I look?"

"Like a Horseman of the Apocalypse."

Not like Night. Not like me.

"There's another problem here: How can we strategize? How can we fight if we don't know your capabilities?"

Now we were getting closer to the heart of the matter. "*That's* what this conversation's about?"

"You expected to rehash trying to kill me?"

One—hundred percent. "We're not done with that."

"Even if I forgive you, you're never living it down. Here's the thing: if you don't know what's going on, the Angel must. Why isn't he telling you anything?"

When had *La Muerte* ever told me much? He'd given me clues I needed to fight—what, where, who. He'd healed my physical wounds, putting me back together after I'd given it all to save my people, time and time again. We were on the same side of the battle.

The months since he'd first appeared had flown by. First, I'd fought for survival. Later, just to get my bearings. Everything had moved so fast, and it was all new. I'd been too busy just trying to be.

"I should've asked more questions," I said. "If I'd known more going in—"

Sunday held up a hand. "Not what I was getting at. Not interested in would've, could've, should've. I'm saying that either the Angel has an agenda he's not willing to share, or he's sharing but you're not hearing him. And I also think you never really had a choice, Night."

I narrowed my eyes. "What?"

"Choice. You didn't get one. Not unless you would ever consider not saving your kid or not saving all the other magical children the Order held prisoner. Would you ever not go up against the End? Would you have held on to your humanity and let him take the world because the price was too high?"

"Those questions don't deserve answers."

"I know—stupid, right?"

That I didn't have a choice with the Angel. That I could not have done anything differently because of who I was. "If you're not forgiving me, why are you saying that?"

"Because it's true, and you need to hear it."

Sunday always told me the truth. I loved her for it. I wished I could give her something in return. A glimmer of information from the Angel. A way to strategize, above and beyond what we could do now.

Michael's voice carried to us. "Night?"

I turned to look at him.

He kept his expression well—schooled, but his eyes told a different story. He'd heard every word of our conversation. "He's waking up."

CHAPTER 16

MICHAEL INSISTED on acting as a barrier between his twin and me. He kept his body between us, shifting as I paced the rug. I wanted to appreciate that, but his protectiveness felt wrong and weird. And, as much as I didn't want to think about going full—on Angel of Death and stopping the sword's lethal blow by grabbing the blade—or any of the other things I'd done today that marked me as different or dangerous—I had no choice.

No choice.

I wanted to clock the shit out of something—anything. I hated feeling out of control. I hated everything about what was happening.

I didn't like the way the others watched me. They were wary. I didn't want to blame them, but couldn't help myself. Still, they fanned out between us and the exit. No idea what most of them could do against an archangel if one wanted to punch his way through them, but they wouldn't let him loose in our world without a fight.

The twin's eyes fluttered open, pupils black and rimmed with orange like glowing coals. He took in my Michael's face and form, as well as the energy behind them. His brow beetled, a deep V framing his third eye. He started to say something, but couldn't spit it out.

Michael spoke to me without splitting his focus. "Water."

Thirst was such a human thing. "Archangels need that?"

"Something's wrong with this one."

The protective veil parted, footfalls echoing on the concrete—Addie and Beth returning. Beth took one look at the situation and took the breakfast platters to the laundry area, setting them down on top of the dryer. Addie held an enormous thermos and a stack of mugs.

"Coffee?" she asked.

"It's not perfect, but yes." Michael stuck out a hand behind him, still unwilling to tear his gaze from the other one.

Addie handed him the thermos. He unscrewed the cap and offered the whole thing to his twin.

After a long swallow, the twin sighed with palpable, physical relief before setting the thermos down beside him. "Thank you, brother."

"For the drink, or for knocking you out?"

The twin glanced past him, gaze locking on me. He tried to rise, his intent as clear as it had been before. Michael pushed him down twice before he got the message.

The glowing coals in the twin's eyes ignited, flames flaring in their depths. "You're protecting her? She destroyed the world!"

"She's never been to your world."

The twin froze. "Mine?"

Michael raised a brow. "This world—this timeline—is still very much alive. You're in the wrong place, brother."

"That's not possible."

"I'm sorry, but it's true."

The twin peered at me more closely, the fire in his eyes burning so hot, the flames turned blue. He didn't try to make a move again, however. "It's her. She's doing this."

"We think so."

"Then why are you protecting her?"

"Because she's our kin. She's a protector of this and all the worlds. And she doesn't understand what's going on."

"She's a Horseman."

Michael cocked his thumb, unerringly pointing at Luna. "So is she."

His twin blinked. "You're harboring two? Where are the others?"

"One has joined forces with the End. The other has not yet been possessed by her Horseman. She's been stolen from us."

"By Lucifer," the twin said. "In my world, Lucifer has taken the fourth."

"Here, as well. By Lucifer."

The twin's eyes widened. "These two—"

"Are on our side."

"They can't be trusted."

"They can. And I do."

The twin held his gaze for a long moment. "That will be your downfall."

"Maybe." Michael stood, holding out a hand to his twin.

The twin let Michael help him up. He stepped around Michael, and this time Michael allowed it. He made his way toward me, steps slow and steady.

He felt like Michael—the same fire and strength, but the air didn't bend around his body the way it did his brother's. His fiery halo was faded, like denim left out in the sun and weather so long, it barely had a color.

As closely as I studied him, he studied me as well. "You're not the same as the one in my timeline."

"How am I different?"

"You're a mother."

"You can tell that by looking at me?"

He canted his head toward Faith, who'd taken up position directly behind him. "I can tell that by how she's looking at you."

"Is that all?"

"Do you refer to your Michael as 'asshole?'"

"Not to his face," I said.

The corner of his mouth quirked.

I didn't for a moment take that as a friendly overture, but maybe it meant he wouldn't try to kill me again right away. Maybe he'd answer questions if we asked nicely. "Can you tell us exactly what's happening in your timeline? You said the world had been destroyed."

"I said you destroyed it."

"Why?"

He considered his words carefully. "The fourth Horseman. You were so bent on finding her, on taking her back from Lucifer. When you couldn't get what you wanted, you burned it all down. You refused to protect the world against the End. After everything you'd sacrificed to defeat him before, you surrendered. You made it impossible to reimagine, to rebuild. There's nothing left—a few of us, hidden in the shadows."

I couldn't wrap my mind around any of that. Just hearing it, imagining the blood and suffering, made me want to throw up. "I don't believe you."

"I don't require your belief."

"What's wrong with you?"

"Why am I so weak?"

I nodded.

"This is what the End does when he finally wins. He eats souls piece by piece, savoring their disintegration, their digestion. Parts of you disappear as if they'd never existed. Eventually, you're left with scattered memories, smaller and smaller fractions of what you were, and then you fade altogether. Most of the world is gone. Those of us that remain are like this. In a week, a month, there will be nothing left."

My legs wanted to give out. A wave of feeling poured from my heart, the texture like shattered glass and the taste like grief.

"I don't require your belief," he said again, and this time each word was a slap in the face "I require your death. But since I'm not strong enough to kill you, and since I can't bear to watch what's already happened in my timeline happen in this one, you will send me back. Now."

He didn't want to be here, and everything he said—everything about him—made me want to crawl into a hole and die. "You can leave any time."

"Send. Me. Back."

"I didn't bring you here."

He glanced at Michael. "Does she really know nothing?"

Michael shook his head.

"It doesn't matter whether you're different from the Night in my timeline. It doesn't matter because you are Death. Death is not confined to one human body, or one dimension, one world. Death is not confined to one timeline. Death is everywhere, all the time. As soon as we are born, we are dying. It's just that most of your species does not realize that until they've grown so old, their bodies begin to remind them. You are Death. You are everywhere. You can be everywhere at once. So it doesn't matter whether you are the same Night as the one in my timeline. You might be here in this timeline, and she might be there in that timeline, but part of you – the part that is Death – is one and the same. So, you see, you are the one who destroyed my world. When I saw you, all I could think of was vengeance. The sight of you makes my blood boil. Even if my brother allowed me to strike you down–"

"He does not allow anything here. This is my house," Addie said.

He did not pause or even look at her, just steamrolled over her words. Every syllable was a hammer strike on a nail, driving me down, bending me, breaking me.

"Even if he allowed me to strike you down, it would make no difference. I would be killing your human self. But Death lives on. If you know what's good for you—for the people you love—you'll let Michael lock you away. Maybe then, all of the damage you've wrought can be atoned for. Maybe then, the rest of us will have a goddamn chance. If you're not that smart, well, powers help us all. You think the End is the worst enemy we'll ever face? You are. Now send. Me. Back."

What could I possibly say to that? I couldn't even breathe.

"Pity," he said.

That one cold word wanted to drive me to my knees.

The fire in his eyes clawed for purchase before it went out like a match in unrelenting wind. His halo faded utterly, and a heartbeat later, he vanished like so much smoke.

Sunday took a hesitant step. "What?"

I stared at the spot where Michael's twin had stood. There was no evidence he had ever been there. Not an impression in the rug, not a scent. He might never have been there at all, but his pain and rage echoed inside me.

I'd destroyed his world, but he'd never told me exactly what I'd done—just that it had happened because of who I was. Death. *La Muerte.* That was enough.

I turned to my Michael, my asshole. "The fuck—"

Michael held up a hand.

"Don't do that. What just happened to him?"

"I think you drew him here, into our timeline."

"How did I accomplish this magical feat? I wasn't thinking about him. I was thinking about you. How in the hell did I open the door to another timeline and bring your doppelgänger into ours?"

"I don't know," he said.

"Bullshit." Sunday closed the distance between us. "You people keep using that phrase. *I don't know. I don't know.*"

Michael cocked his head, looked at her. "This has never happened before."

"No shit. There's only one Apocalypse."

Michael looked at her as if she'd grown three heads. "There have been many. If we're fortunate, there will be many more."

Her head snapped back. "You know that book, the Bible—that sort of true, sort of not true book that all of your people insist on shoving down our throats? According to that book, there is just one. The end of the world."

Michael shook his head. "You haven't read it closely enough. The world was destroyed by water."

"The flood. Noah. The ark."

"Yes, that. And next time it will be destroyed by fire."

"God's wrath."

"No." Michael pointed at me. "Hers."

CHAPTER 17

SUNDAY STARED. "You've gotta be kidding. Night would never do that."

No, Night would not. But I wasn't only Night anymore, was I? I had wings and black eyes without pupils and crumbling inhibitions and I was a full—fledged Horseman of the fucking Apocalypse. Standing in Addie's basement among splashes of color and concrete with the people who'd become my chosen family, who'd fought beside me and risked their lives for me to save a world that my ancestor, the archangel Michael, now said I was destined to destroy.

I refused to believe it.

Michael glanced at me from the corner of his eye as if he'd heard my thoughts. "You think you have a choice here?"

"There's always a choice." Always, even if the options were awful and worse. My choices made me who I was, from the little girl who'd killed the assassins sent to murder my parents and me, to the assassin who thought rivers of blood would quench my rage, to the moment I'd changed my and Faith's destinies forever, when I'd saved both our lives.

"That's naive."

I hadn't been innocent enough to be called naive since the age of three. I looked around the room. At Sunday, thrown out of her home to defend herself on the street. At Red, who championed kids who needed someone in their corner. At Faith, who'd lived on the run with me for years. At Addie, who'd cut ties with the teachers and mentors who'd raised her in order to do what was right. Beth had given up her mortal life, apprenticed to Malek. And Luna and Kevin—none of us was naive.

I shook my head.

The air that bent around Michael's body contracted, as if he gathered patience along with breath. The letters on his black T—shirt squeezed together like an accordion. "It's a cycle that repeats itself, over and over, through centuries, through millennia. The flood and the coming fire are the ones that have been foretold by the prophets in that book. You know that book isn't meant to be taken literally because it was written by humans. But even if a god had written it themselves, without the aid of humans, it would still be fallible. There are too many choices influencing the present and the future in too many interconnected worlds to say for sure what will happen and when."

Addie's starry halo flashed brightly. "You're talking about free will."

"Precisely."

She looked him up and down. "Do you miss it?"

"How can I miss what I've never had?" he asked.

"You sure about that?"

He narrowed his eyes. "Are you mocking me?"

She shook her head. "I used to buy in to what the Watchers taught me. Free will is only for humans. God has a plan for us all. Everything happens for a reason. But the older I've gotten and the more experience I've gained working with this lot, the blurrier the lines have become. You know what I mean?"

His lips curved. "Less black and white. More gray."

She inclined her head. "That's the truth. The rules exist to be bent."

"Not broken."

Beth cleared her throat and twirled a braid around her finger. "This is great and all, but can we get back to the time thing because it's breaking my brain. Interconnected worlds means interconnected and interdependent lives and choices. It means we're creating the present and the future together all the time, every day."

Sunday held up a hand. "Not sure how you got from A to B."

"The future isn't set. Maybe there's a blueprint and maybe it's just a super violent, patriarchal, misogynist bedtime story about a capricious angry god more interested in punishing people who hurt his feelings than in making things right. Either way, we have input. We can choose to make the world a better place."

"Said every newbie motherfucker ever."

"I used to be a newbie at all this," Beth said. "Working for Malek yanks that out of you, throws it on the ground, and stomps it to death."

Listening to them go round and round, all I felt was a fist inside my chest, wrapping itself around my heart, squeezing until I wanted to explode. "The other Michael doesn't know."

"No."

"It really is up to us."

The corners of his mouth curved into a wry grin.

Beth sighed. "I just said all that."

Red set a hand on her shoulder, ignoring the anger that flashed across her face. "What did you mean when you said that it was Night's wrath that causes the world to end?"

"It's always Death," Michael said. "The situation gets out of hand. The forces that fight kill until the streets run red with blood, until there's no hope. The only thing that can be done is to wipe the slate clean and start over. It's not wrath. It's…necessary."

"You talking about this like it's a good thing," Red said.

Addie turned to him. "Michael's opening a window into a world we never get a chance to see. Giving us a glimpse of forces we can't hope to understand because their experience is so far outside of our own, it's in comprehensible. We think, because we have no real idea, that Michael and the others like him know what they're doing."

"You're saying he's as scared and clueless as we are?"

"Yes," I said.

I had more to say, but I couldn't form the words. The thoughts tumbled around inside my brain, devolving into images and colors, sounds and silences. I tried to make sense of them—no luck. Thinking wouldn't solve the puzzle. What made the difference here was magic. Magic came from the heart.

My heart told me that every word Michael spoke was true. It told me more than that.

"He's saying is that we're all in this together. He's saying that he does not know how to fix what's happening anymore than any of us. He's not omnipotent. He's not all powerful. He's just older, with more experience, and he's got more power than most of us. He can exert all his influence on the course of events, and one of us–any one of us– could screw it up."

"Or create a miracle," Beth said.

Exactly. "It's not just about choice or free will, or whatever we want to call it. It's about responsibility. If we can prevent something terrible from happening, stop suffering, keep life as we know it from being wiped out, we have a responsibility to do that."

I believed every word I'd uttered, but I couldn't shake the feeling that I'd missed something important. I glanced at Michael, but read nothing in his eyes.

"And we're just supposed to trust you?" Beth asked.

"Trust me or don't."

"It's not that simple," she said.

"No, it's not. But I'm not gonna walk on eggshells or beg. I'm not gonna hide or wait or second guess."

Sunday nodded. "That's not what we do. We act."

"Damn right."

"What if you fuck it all up?" Beth asked. "What if you bring on the fiery apocalypse even though you didn't mean to?"

It was possible. Given what Michael said, probable, even. My heart hurt with the weight of it. All this time I'd been working to prevent the Apocalypse. Was it all for nothing? After everything was said and done, would I wipe the slate clean? Would all the people I love die because of me?

I felt Addie's eyes on me, measuring me and finding me wanting. I read that in her halo, in the way the stars in her night sky seemed to judge me. She would be thinking of how to stop me. She would be thinking on how to do that permanently, if necessary.

"If we take Night off the board, won't that change things?" she asked.

"It will buy you time," Michael said. "But no more than that. If something were to happen to Night, Death will find another host. Perhaps not one as strong, but he will find one. And when he does, the danger will front—and—center."

Luna spoke for the first time, her voice low and commanding. "Whoever his new host is, we won't know them. They won't know us. We won't trust them. They could be like me, or they could be like Famine. I'll take my chances with Night."

I didn't want to listen to the people I loved talk about whether they trusted me, whether they should kill me, whether that might be necessary in the end. Some of them would be in my corner automatically, like Luna. Some of them, the jury was still out.

Sunday gazed at me the same way she always had: ride or die, she had my six. "*What ifs* like that are useless. All we have is the moment. We take into account everything we know and everything we feel, and then we do something."

She was right.

There was only one thing to do. "We find our friends. We bring them home."

CHAPTER 18

W*E FIND OUR FRIENDS.*
My gut told me that we needed them for the battle to come. Each confrontation, every step of the way, felt like the final fight, as if the world would end if we fell. No lie there. But every time the stakes grew, and now with the end of the world barreling toward us, we stood at the edge of a cliff. Either we stopped the other side before we went over, or the world as we knew it would change irrevocably. Maybe something of the old would survive. Maybe it would be gone forever.

Suddenly, the weight of my body felt like too much. The wings at my back felt alien, as did the Angel's consciousness, enmeshed with mine. I looked at my people, one by one, all their eyes on me. Doubt and uncertainty, expectation, fear—everything I saw in them threatened to beat me down until my legs buckled and took me to the concrete underfoot. The rhythmic spin of the clothes dryer and the scent of fabric softener seemed so out of place, so *normal,* I laughed.

The sound scared me. It felt out of control. *I* felt out of control.

I met Beth's gaze and saw my own reflection in the lenses of her glasses. I looked like a monster. Like the Angel of Death.

A heartbeat later, she turned to Michael. "If we're going to find them, we need your help."

"Which means finding Lucifer," Beth said, hope lighting her face. "Michael, you're our dude, right? You can get a bead on your sister for us and take us to her and have our back with that because you're our friend now, right? No more straddling the fence. You took sides. You took our side. We need you on this one and you're going to come through."

He took his time answering—so long, Beth's expression faltered. "No. I can't—"

"Do not say you can't interfere. We're done with that, aren't we?"

"I've done much more than I should've already."

"So you're drawing your arbitrary line here?"

"It's not arbitrary."

"What does that even mean?" she asked.

"I am what I am."

"You're not God."

"No," he said matter—of—factly.

"You really are an asshole, you know that?"

"I know." He met my gaze.

I understood that this was it. If I called him again, he wouldn't answer, and it wasn't because he'd done too much to help us already. That was an excuse. Window dressing. Or I interpreted his words the way I'd wanted to hear them.

Michael, like the Angel and me, played a role. He maintained a part of the world's—the universe's—order. His aid had never been about friendship or trust. All of his help from the moment he'd appeared to us to this one was predicated on that one irrevocable truth.

The proper order, as unbelievable as it seemed, had been restored. The world as we knew it was on track to go down in flames at the Angel's and my hands. That was how it should be. Michael could step back now and watch it all unfold.

"Will you even shed a tear for the poor souls you're leaving behind?"

He pressed his lips into a thin line. He didn't want to answer. He wanted to turn away. I could feel it.

After a moment, he took a deep breath. "Yes."

Beth looked from Michael to me and back again. "Bullshit."

But he wasn't lying. He had no reason to. I shook my head.

"What we need is your power. What good will it do for you to cry?" Beth demanded.

None at all, but that wasn't the point.

He held my gaze. "Thank you."

Beth spat a comment so hard and sharp, it might as well have been a bullet.

He paid it no mind, all of his focus trained on me.

Standing under the lens of his attention felt like a fly under a magnifying glass on a summer day. "What did I do?"

"You surprised me."

"How?"

He glanced away for a fraction of a second, searching for words. When he looked at me again, amusement shone in his eyes. "You never gave up. Not on them."

My family.

"Not on me."

My breath caught in my throat. I complained about him. I couldn't depend on him. His blood ran in my veins, but that didn't make me special to him.

"Thank you for allowing me to help."

He'd told me over and over again that he couldn't intervene, but I called him anyway. I changed circumstances if I had to. I opened the door and he'd walked through it when we needed him.

When I needed him. "Thanks for helping."

He nodded. "You won't see me again."

"I know."

For a moment, I thought he'd vanish like his twin had. Instead, he simply walked out of the circle the way he'd entered, disappearing as he stepped through the protections.

Beth stamped her foot, the smack against the concrete a hard shock. "The fuck, Night? You made googly eyes at him when you should've kicked his ass."

"Googly eyes?" I wasn't in love or lust with Michael. He was my ancestor, for crying out loud.

"You know what I meant. The hell was all that?"

Wasn't it obvious? "Goodbye."

She poured on the sarcasm. "Well thanks so much. We're totally screwed beyond all belief."

"You can't make him do anything, Beth."

"You could."

I shook my head. "I'm not all powerful."

"He said you are. He said you're going to end the world, for chrissakes. Act like it."

I stared at her. "I can't believe you just said that."

She scowled. The anger drained for her words as they flowed, shading toward despair. "How are we supposed to find Lucifer and Rude and Shadow without him?"

How, indeed.

I closed my eyes, *La Muerte*'s presence rising around and within me. He should know how to find Lucifer, shouldn't he? I listened deeply, waiting for his answer.

Images and feelings flashed in my mind's eye and across my skin:

The cold beauty of Lucifer's face, her electric eyes, the curve of her lips.

The overpowering energy of her magic as she tore at me. The metallic taste of my own fear.

I caught fragments of memories that didn't belong to me. The Angel's memories. The sinuous movement of Lucifer's arms as she danced. The flash of white as she smiled. Her whisper in his ear and the way it made the fine hairs on his arms rise and lust quicken in his groin. Yes, *La Muerte* knew her. Had known her, when he'd walked the earth before.

Where is she now?

No answer.

If everything Michael said was true and I could be in any timeline I wanted, and if Death knew her, shouldn't I be able to find her and go to her?

The Angel's voice echoed in my heart and mind. *That's not what we are for.*

I was "for" helping my family. For helping, period. If I couldn't do that, why be here at all?

We are the Law.

What on earth did that mean — *the Law?*

Natural Law. It kept the planet spinning on its axis, and the gravity that anchored us to its surface. It was the food chain — predators and prey, life feeding on life, truth and consequences. And it was bigger than us. Bigger than the small world on which we lived and depended.

It ruled all beings in all the worlds. *Ruled* being the operative word. The rules we lived by, whether or not we understood them consciously, derived from it. Just like Michael, we were constrained by who and what we were.

The Angel's and my purpose was to enforce the rules of Death. No, more than that — *La Muerte* had been created not only to deal with the dying and the souls of the dead, but to kill the world and everyone in it once a certain set of events had been triggered. All but one of those events had already happened over the course of centuries. It didn't matter what they were or whether anyone could've stopped them. It was far too late for that.

The world would die and be reborn, but he didn't care about that any more than he cared about the creatures who would die, how they would perish, or why any of it needed to occur.

Amy was the final event — or, the coming of the fourth Horseman, at any rate. If she accepted her fate, all the pieces would fall into place and the Apocalypse would rain down on us.

My desire to help Amy, to protect her, to make sure she understood what was happening to her — it meant nothing to the Angel. She didn't matter — not as a human being.

That's not acceptable.

The Angel didn't respond, not with even so much as a feeling.

With the other powers, I'd mostly found a way to get what I wanted in the end. The Angel had never told me no. He'd never stopped me from acting or speaking. But, in everything we'd done together, we'd been traveling the same path. Working toward the same goals — or so I'd thought.

What now? I asked.

We go.

To Lucifer. To find Amy and bring her home. *Not yet.*

Pressure built in my chest, filling me up with the need to move. My breath caught in my throat. I met Red's gaze. "The Angel wants to go now."

Red shook his head. "We're not ready."

Sunday picked up where he left off. "Damn right, we're not. We've got no recon, and no reason to go in blind. You could be walking straight into a trap. After what Lucifer did to you last time you faced off, you really want to risk that?"

"No, but—"

"We go the old—fashioned way, Sanchez. Divination. Farseeing. Getting the lay of the land."

I looked at her, the Angel seeing through my eyes.

Her eyebrows climbed to her hairline. "Fuck. Me."

The feathers around my heart fluttered again and again, demanding my attention. No – demanding that I do what the Angel wanted. And what he wanted was to find Amy and bring her back here now, without delay. Rude and Shadow were unimportant. My family's opinions and concerns didn't matter.

Sunday wrapped her fingers around my wrists. "Night, what's happening in there?"

La Muerte was trying to convince me to bend to his will. If I refused, what then?

I tried to tell her, but the words that came out were, "I need a minute."

She tightened her grip. "I'm not letting you go anywhere alone."

The fluttering and the pressure mounted. I swallowed hard and my gorge rose. It was all I could do not to throw up.

The Angel pushed. My body swayed, but I anchored my feet to the concrete.

"Please." I didn't know whether I was asking Sunday or the Angel. I only knew I needed a minute to think. A minute to feel emotions that belonged to me, and me alone.

Red laid a hand on Sunday's shoulder. "I've got her."

"Don't let her go, Red."

"I won't."

Sunday opened her mouth to say more, then snapped it shut. She didn't need to tell him she'd kill him if he screwed up. It was written all over her face.

He held her gaze.

Finally, she broke eye contact. But I felt the rose gold of her magic follow us through the protections to the stair landing. We had ten, maybe fifteen minutes at the outside before she came looking for us.

I needed space alone with Red to tell him what was happening inside of me.

The Angel coiled within, biding his time. But not for long.

CHAPTER 19

WITH EVERY STEP upon the stairs, the Angel's presence grew heavier, until I could barely put one foot in front of the other, much less climb to the top. Opening the door into the hallway, I might as well have been pushing on steel instead of wood. I made it halfway to my room before my legs gave out. My shins smacked the hardwood as I went down. I reached for the wall, nails scraping paint as I struggled for purchase.

Red scooped me up, carrying me the rest of the way and setting me down gently on the unmade bed in the dark. The afternoon light that forced its way in through the slats of the blinds formed a pattern on the floor and across the blanket that reminded me of prison bars.

The thought didn't feel like mine. It felt like *La Muerte*'s.

I drew a shallow, shuddering breath that tasted of sleep and sex. The backlit dust floating in the air seemed too thick. For a moment, I couldn't get enough oxygen.

Then, Red knelt in front of me. "You're gonna have to tell me what's wrong, Night."

I reached for him through the heart link, sending him a shot of fear.

"Whoa." He set his hands on my shoulders. "Calm down."

I felt a swell of anger. Had anyone in the history of the world every calmed down because someone told them to?

I forced myself to breathe deeper, to feel my lungs expand all the way down, so that my belly rose with each inhalation. I gave the anger to the outbreath, letting the motion carry it up and out. I didn't want to be pissed at Red.

It took a long minute to organize my thoughts, to remind myself how to speak. My words came out as a croak. "The Angel wants to go after Amy. Right now. I'm fighting him."

"I thought you were one being, one entity. If your consciousness and his are woven together, if there's no difference between you, how can you fight him? How can he fight you?"

I wished I understood better what had happened to me. I wish there was a roadmap, so that I knew which step followed which in this process of merging. All I could do was react. It was fucking exhausting. "I can only tell you what I think, because I don't know anything for sure. I think that the parts of us that have merged together are all energy. Souls. But mind and will? I don't think we have those two things down just yet. I think there is his mind and my mind, his will and my will."

"Who the hell is in charge, then?"

I let out a shaky laugh. "Whoever's stronger."

"That's a recipe for disaster."

"Agreed."

He studied my face. "What do you need?"

The short answer? "For you to trust me."

"Always."

"You sure about that? Because I feel as if you've been wrangling me for the past few months."

"That's called 'keeping you safe.'"

I could take care of myself. And what I couldn't handle, the Angel could. "Keeping me under wraps."

He shot me some side—eye. "You're pissed about that?"

I started to tell him yes, but let the words fade on my tongue. What really bothered me wasn't that he didn't want me to be seen by the general public or the cops. "I'm afraid one of these days you're gonna look at me the way most of the others do."

"Like a stranger."

I nodded.

He leaned forward, brushing his lips against mine. "I'm always gonna know you, Night."

I believed him. No hope or faith necessary. If he said it, it was true.

He looked me in the eye. "I'm always gonna do what's right."

I trusted that, too. It lifted a weight from my shoulders.

"So, what are we gonna do about the Angel?" he asked.

"I really don't know."

"You gotta do better than that."

"You're right. But, right now, it feels like all I can do is fight the impulse to give in."

He rubbed my forearms, intending to sooth, but his fingertips felt like sandpaper on my skin. "There might be something I can do. Strength I can lend."

He had that in spades. Strength and compassion. It ran in his veins and lived in his heart and his magic. "That'd be good."

"It could be better if I can get some help from Beth. Get her to tattoo a sigil for you. Something to set the magic in your body."

"You think she has the juice for that right now?"

Beth was still recovering. Even if she could manage a magical tattoo, I didn't want it to drain her, or cause more harm. If she heard what I was thinking, she'd smack me on the back of the head. She'd do what needed to be done, damn the torpedoes.

"I'll go downstairs and ask."

"Thanks."

He rose and slipped out of the room, leaving me to cascading thoughts and fears that curled my toes inside my shoes and closed my hands into fists. Just a few more minutes until he returned with Beth, and a little breathing room for me.

A muscle at the nape of my neck contracted into a hard knot in the space of seconds. I bent and stretched and kneaded it with my knuckles, but no amount of effort released it. I stood, shaking off waves of tension, but that didn't help either. Something was *wrong*—something bigger and worse than I imagined.

"Get it together, Night." The sound of my own voice grated my every raw nerve.

I needed to get it together. Now. We had work to do. Friends to save. My family depended on me. I couldn't let them down.

I took a deep breath, on the exhale sending my energy and attention through my belly and legs, down through the soles of my feet, through the floorboards and the foundation of the house and into the earth below. On a second deep breath, I sent my attention and energy through my shoulders and neck, through my head, and up and out of the crown, connecting with the air above me. I shot it the second story of the house and the roof, all the way to the sky. Ruthlessly, I routed out all the tendrils of worry, fear of what had happened and what might happen, fear of who I once had been and who I might become. I breathed them out, willing the air to take them.

All of that rooted and grounded and cemented my place in the here and now. Everything would be all right. How could I possibly know that? I had no objective evidence. The powers involved felt incomprehensibly huge to me, even if I carried one of them within me. But I knew it with such certainty. In my bones. In my heart.

I no longer wanted to wait here for Red and Beth. Going to them would help me feel better, more in control of the sensations I felt. And they would know I stood with them, no doubts or questions asked.

Let's go, I said to the Angel.

He didn't answer, but when I breathed in, I felt him inhale. When I breathed out, I felt him exhale. The beating of my heart didn't belong to me alone. It was his heartbeat, too.

I took a single step toward the door, and then the world imploded.

Air rushed toward me from all directions, buffeting my hair and clothes and lifting me off the floor. My heartbeat, steady a second ago, stuttered, then stilled. I couldn't breathe. I couldn't move. The feathers surrounding my heart fluttered. The Angel expanded inside me—not just his magic and consciousness. This was physical. *La Muerte* was a solid thing inside my body, alive and thriving in my flesh and blood and bones. He pushed against my edges. Took up all the space within me, shoving my thoughts and feelings out of the way. Disintegrating my boundaries. Overtaking my will.

I fought back. Marshaled all my magic. I threw it at him, expecting him to back off. He waved it away, as if it were a mosquito buzzing in his ear. I sent the power again, shaping it into knives mean to cut through any shields, to slip inside his defenses the way I'd slipped inside the defenses of every target I'd ever taken down. The blades struck an invisible wall with one thud after another, falling, clattering to an invisible floor.

I screamed, the magic in the sound loud and strong enough to shatter. It had no effect at all.

I couldn't wrap my mind around what was happening. After the Angel and I had merged, I hadn't been able to tell the difference between us for weeks. There'd been no I, only we. This was something else. This was a violation. An obliteration.

He overran me, a wave of Death. There was no more us. Only him.

I hung on by a thread. My senses felt far away. I saw through my eyes, but colors and shapes seemed alien, as if I were gazing through his eyes. The creak of wood floors underfoot, squeal of hinges, thump of closing doors sounded muffled, as if blurred and softened by distance or fog. The weight of my body, suspended above the floor, was the only thing that felt real and true. Then, the Angel stole that from me, too.

He focused all of this magic on a single point. An image bloomed in his mind: fair skin, eyes the deep blue color of twilight, power so great that, as with Michael, the air bent around her body.

Lucifer. *La Muerte* was thinking of Lucifer.

Time stopped for the space of a heartbeat. As quickly as it had expanded, the Angel's magic tightened, racing from large to impossibly small. Compressing my body into something microscopic. We slipped into the space between the human world and a world I recognized from the split second it'd taken Faith to draw Sunday and me home from the other timeline.

The heat and sulfur of the In—Between grabbed at my clothes and seared my skin. Darkness swallowed my vision and an invisible force spun me until I couldn't tell up from down or inside from out. Nausea tightened its fist around me, squeezing from the bottom up, determined to pop me like a piñata. Any second now, I would die.

Except I couldn't. The Angel wouldn't let me. And we were in the goddamn time stream.

The sick disorientation ended with a sudden break, like a spine snapping with the twist of a neck. We dropped out of the stream on to the concrete floor of a converted warehouse. I blinked as my vision refocused on a long, narrow room with unpainted red brick walls, new blond wood and steel structural beams, and electrical wires snaking across the exposed ceiling. The lights were off, but afternoon light spilled in through high, rectangular windows punched into the brick. Closed glass doors on either side of the room gave way to darker spaces. At first blush, we were alone. But first impressions didn't always pan out.

The Angel scanned the space, taking in every detail the human eye could gather. He fanned my magic out like radar, seeking the hidden, searching for magical signatures, for halos, for the presence of minds we expected. Lucifer's. Amy's. For a long moment, nothing responded. Then the tiniest blip made itself known in the otherwise empty room.

A point of light so dim hung suspended near one of the windows across from us, blending with the sun's rays, its shade subtly darker, the difference so slight I wouldn't have noticed no matter how hard I searched. The Angel caught it because of the way it tasted, like royalty and guile.

The light swooped down to eye—level, keeping its distance.

The Angel cleared my throat. Spoke with my voice. His words echoed inside my head. "Why hide, sister? If you believe in what you're doing, stand in your truth for all to see."

The light stretched into a line that flowed to the concrete. Only then did I understand what we saw—a tear in reality. A rip in the fabric of the human realm.

Lucifer stepped from the break, as beautiful and shining as I remembered from Malek's shop. Amber hair that flowed in waves to her waist. Doe eyes. Ruby red lips. Gold loops at her ears. Flames licked at her body, fading to reveal a black leather vest and pants that hugged her considerable curves. Her feet were bare.

Either she wasn't expecting company so soon or the Angel didn't scare her.

"If you're here to fight, get on with it," she said.

A rumble shook me from bones to breath. The sound of her voice? No. Not an earthquake, either. The unmistakable wail of a train horn and the shear of wheels on rails helped me name the sensation.

The Angel took a step toward her.

She neither matched it nor stepped back, but held her ground. "You could learn a thing or two from Night."

The Angel cocked my head, playing confused. "I am Night."

"You've shoved her into a corner so you can take control. You don't have enough patience. You never have. It's always about now. Because you can't wait, you make a lousy strategist."

The Angel slid my hands into my pockets. "Death comes for everyone. It cannot be denied."

She raised a brow. "You think so?"

He gathered the magic he'd sent out, using his will alone, not giving her any sign. He didn't so much as twitch. Tendrils of power, thin and faint, began to circulate near her feet, but not close enough to be noticed by someone as powerful as she.

"What have you done with Amy?" he asked.

"I promised to give her the space to make up her own mind, and I meant it."

"As long as she decides to go your way."

"What do you think my way is?" Lucifer asked.

Either she stood on the side of life, or she'd thrown in her lot with the destruction. "There is no in between, only life or destruction."

"There are more than two choices."

He shook his head. "No great power can remain neutral in this."

"I'm not neutral," she said. "I want the lot of you to fuck off, go home, and leave the rest of us in peace. The worlds don't need your family feud. Your death and disintegration."

"Events have been set in motion. Millenia—long cycles have come to fruition."

"Screw your events and your cycles."

What Lucifer wanted was to keep the Angel from realizing his purpose. He would not tolerate that. He'd destroy her first.

The magic he'd seen into motion constricted around her, pinning her to the spot, leaving her at his mercy.

"I haven't acted against you," she said.

"Your intention is an act of war."

"If war is what you want."

That was a tease. She mocked him. "Stop meddling. Fall in line."

"I can't."

"You won't."

She didn't deny it. Instead, she flashed a Cheshire grin. "You want Amy's opinion, you should ask her. She's standing right behind you."

CHAPTER 20

THE ANGEL TURNED his head, catching a glimpse of Amy from the corner of his eye. Her blue—black hair dazzled in the filtered sunlight. Grime and purple paint streaked her plain white T—shirt and faded jeans. She'd stuffed her feet into motorcycle boots without taking the time to zip them, but she'd managed a few seconds to grab her sword. It rested in the sheath on her back. Wearing it, she looked like a knight of old. But she was much more than that. Much more important.

"You here to rescue me?" Her tone was neutral.

Given that she'd been kidnapped and should want to be anywhere but here, neutrality was an elephant—sized red flag.

The Angel met her gaze. "If what Lucifer says is true, you're free to choose where you want to be and what you want to do."

"So, why haven't I already left her? That's what you're asking your-self, isn't it?"

He nodded.

Amy took a step forward, then cocked her head. "You're not Night."

"I am always Night," he said. "We are one."

"Whatever this is, it's not that. You took over."

"I did what was necessary."

"What about her?"

"She's healthy and well."

And trapped underneath *La Muerte*'s boot. Listening to them talk about me as if I weren't here made me want to scream. Hearing the Angel describe pushing me aside and stealing control of my body tapped a fountain of rage.

I struggled against the Angel's consciousness, against his will. Every movement seemed to drag me deeper, like quicksand.

Lucifer laughed, the sound a seduction. "You see? You can't trust him."

Amy squared her shoulders. "I haven't had a lot of good experience with trusting other people. They always let you down."

"So you trust no one?" Lucifer asked.

"Didn't say that." Amy searched the Angel's eyes.

He didn't understand what she was looking for. Neither did I. I only wanted her to see me.

"I trust people to have their own best interests at heart. To do what they need to do to survive." Amy looked at Lucifer. "You've told me the truth. You laid it all out for me so I could make the only sensible choice—to do what you think I should."

"I'm glad to hear that," Lucifer said.

Amy drew War from its sheath. The blade chimed as she did. Beneath the ringing, a cacophony of voices whispered. There were too many to make out the words, but the emotion in them hit the Angel like a punch in the gut. Anguish. Betrayal.

The feelings didn't belong to Amy. They belonged to the dead, the ghosts whose memories lived within the blade, chronicling the wars of the fae. The Angel understood them well enough. The energy he drew from them was like oxygen. They slithered over me in my cocoon, slashing with poisoned fangs. Could they set me free if they found a way in?

Lucifer nodded. "They call out for blood."

Amy stepped back. Away from a fight.

Lucifer's shoulders tensed. "Use the sword. That's what it's for."

Using the blade against the Angel meant using it against me. He couldn't be killed. While I hosted him, neither could I. But being sliced and diced would hurt like hell. Enough damage, the Angel would be forced to get us out of here. He couldn't fight Lucifer and Amy with a broken body.

Lucifer's voice became a command, her words a compulsion. "Strike down this abomination who's come to bend you to his will."

Amy stilled, face wiped blank. A single corner of her mouth moved, frowning with effort.

Through the Angel's presence, I felt the sway in Lucifer's words. The way they poured into Amy with just enough spin to make the girl believe the idea to take down the Angel was her own. She had no choice. No—there *was* no choice. Only the order given by an archangel with all her will behind it.

Amy moved the hand that held the blade, ever so slightly. Not to raise it, but to lower it.

Lucifer pushed, seizing the connection she'd made with Amy. Tightening. Twisting.

The Angel glanced from the archangel to Amy and back again. How could a girl fight Lucifer?

But she wasn't just fighting. She was winning. I could see it. I felt it.

The Angel disagreed. Her defeat was inevitable. He had to act now. He committed, his decision flowing through my limbs, launching us toward Amy. She was the mission. Get her out of here. Bring her back with us. Plug her in to the Apocalypse and let her play in blood and destruction. Once she understood she had no choice, she'd do what she'd been born for.

The second he turned his back on Lucifer, she struck.

A wave of magic shoved him off his feet. He stretched out his arms, pushing against the power. He righted himself, landing on the balls of his feet like a cat. He ducked low and spun into the force of Lucifer's magic, drew a breath, and blew a wind of power.

A bolt of frost raced across the floor, fast as lightning. The space between them crackled. Fine droplets of moisture ripped from the air and fell like tears of ice, shattered on the ground. Lucifer stilled, breath frozen in her lungs. Her arms trembled as she tried to raise them. She managed a flick of her fingertips.

The frost melted. Water ran in rivulets on the concrete, pressing their way toward the Angel. Lucifer's spell never materialized. The magic couldn't reach the Angel without crystallizing. Without triggering a backlash. Lucifer's legs trembled. She fell to her knees.

The Angel rose to full height, wings snapping wide. He coiled, ready to launch himself at her. To do to her what she wanted to do to him. He had the upper hand. He'd never get another chance. Not like this.

A blade's edge stung the back of his neck. He stilled, his power a live wire ready to snap. He started to speak.

"Not interested in anything you have to say. I want to talk to Night."

"She can't do this. Only I can."

Amy increased the pressure, drawing the blood Lucifer claimed the sword thirsted for.

He hissed. "You can't kill me."

"Then why not just take me out? Why argue with me at all?"

Because he could see the way that would play out, with Amy's serious injury or death. With his own injury at precisely the wrong time. The magic he'd used to bind Lucifer would fail, leaving him—and me—vulnerable and at her mercy.

If Amy or I died, others would be chosen to carry our Horsemen. But that would take time, maybe a lot of time. The Angel wouldn't wait.

The hell was his hurry?

He allowed my consciousness to rise and connect with my body, enough that the muffling of my senses cleared. I could see Lucifer trapped in a cocoon of ice through the lattice of my frozen lashes. The scoring where hers and the Angel's magic had bitten the concrete. My skin was more than a forest of gooseflesh. Frost slicked every bare surface, numbing me to the bone. The sword remained pinned against my neck, one deft gesture away from severing my spinal column.

I tried my voice. A little rusty. "Amy."

She sounded as relieved as I felt. "Night, what's going on here?"

"What's it look like?"

"The Angel took over."

"Yeah."

"Is that supposed to happen?" she asked.

"Never has before. We can talk later. Right now, we have to move."

"I'm not going anywhere with him."

"Even if he's the only choice you've got?" The Angel hadn't let me go. He had no intention of doing so until he accomplished the mission.

"He can do what I say or he can go screw himself."

He mulled the odds. Judged the angles. Looked for a way through.

Not going to find one, I said silently. *She's not bluffing.*

He held on a heartbeat longer before he acknowledged the futility of it. My will began to bleed through his like warm air rising through his cold, blooming against the edges of my mind, my heart, my skin. The numbness cleared, giving me freedom to move. With the sword still at my neck, I didn't dare try too much. Fingers, closing them into fists, releasing them again.

"Night?"

"Let's go."

She removed the blade, lowering it but not sheathing it. I didn't have to lay eyes on her halo to know she expected a trick. When I didn't turn on her, she relaxed just enough to reason with.

"Take my hand."

She twined her fingers with mine. "Were are we going?"

"Home." To the only people I had.

People who loved me, but didn't trust me. I'd blamed them for it because I hadn't understood how they could believe I'd changed so much, it was no longer a given. And I needed them more than I'd ever needed anyone in my life.

How could I ask them to trust me when I couldn't trust myself?

CHAPTER 21

THE WAREHOUSE VANISHED as the Angel propelled us across time and space to Addie's house. The searing heat of the In—Between burned away the unclean feeling of full possession and imprisonment from my body, but it couldn't touch the seed of fear rooting inside. Crossing the magical boundaries of Addie's land filled my mouth with the tastes of rosemary and lavender. I heard the thump of her tuxedo cat's feet as it jumped from its seat on the porch rail to land on creaking wood. The house spirit's recognition felt like a benediction, but it didn't open the way as it usually did. It encircled me in magical chains and dragged me into the timeline, forcing me to land not in the kitchen, but in the basement. Inside the circle designed to contain magic. To protect the rest of the house and everyone in it from what it held.

I blinked, focusing on the warmth of Amy's hand in mine. On the weight of my body, the contact of my shoes with red rug underfoot. I inhaled the scent of fabric softener and, fainter, the perfume of coffee wafting from upstairs.

Amy let go of my hand, taking a look around. There wasn't much to see because the basement was empty of everyone except one person. Not one I expected to see—not Addie or Red or Faith or Sunday, but Beth.

She'd gathered her braids into a knot at the crown of her head, held in place with a cobalt blue ceramic chopstick from the kitchen drawer. She wore a long—sleeved flannel shirt of the same color over a black T—shirt emblazoned with faded white words proclaiming *I TOLD YOU SO.* Her bony knees poked out of the holes in her black jeans, and she'd stuffed her feet into thick hiking socks.

She waved like a princess—elbow, elbow, wrist, wrist. "Glad you could make it, Night."

Not what I'd expected to hear. "Not *where the fuck have you been?*"

"Or *am I talking to Night or the Angel of Death?*"

Even after Amy had forced the Angel to retreat, I wasn't stupid enough to believe he'd done more than back off. If he could take over so easily, so completely, then I couldn't answer Beth the way I wanted. "Good question."

"Right?"

"You don't seem to be taking this seriously."

"Oh, I'm deadly serious. Homicidally serious. It's just that I've been expecting this to happen for months and how could I be surprised that, when it finally happens, it's when we need you most."

I stared at her. "I didn't expect it at all."

"Because you're you. You're so freakin' competent. No—exceptional. And it's all worked out just how you wanted it to all this time."

"I didn't want any of this."

"You didn't say no."

Why was I indulging this argument? I'd had this conversation with myself a hundred times, and it always turned out the same. "If I'd said no, we'd all be dead."

"Not me. I have a get out of dead free membership card."

Because she belonged to Malek.

"You think you can save everybody, Night. That's a problem, because it's a lie. You're not gonna be able to save the whole world. It's not possible. Not because you won't try hard enough or give enough or martyr yourself if the Angel will let you. Because it's literally impossible. Get that through your thick skull before the others come down here."

I'd proved time and again that she was wrong. The proof was my family, living and breathing and thriving as best they could under the circumstances.

"You've got that look on your face again," she said. "Vertical line cutting through the middle of your forehead and your lips all pressed together like you're grinding your teeth behind them. You don't have to believe me, but you're not dumb, so think about what I'd said. I know what I'm talking about."

"How can you?" She'd never been in my shoes.

She smiled softly, and spoke with a gentleness I'd never seen in her. "I know what it's like to be saved the way you want to save the people you love. I've had it done to me over and over, and each time, I die a little inside."

Comparing what I'd gone through to save my family to Malek's bringing her back from the dead was just wrong. "It's not the same."

She didn't try to hide the disappointment in her voice. "That's what I thought you'd say."

Amy sighed. "You done, drama queen?"

"Fuck you, too." Beth plucked her phone from her back pocket and texted. "The others should be down in a minute. Everyone who's left, anyway."

Amy sheathed her blade. Its whispering voices dimmed, but didn't fade entirely. I could still hear a faint buzz, like seeing something I wasn't quite sure was there from the corner of my eye. "What do you mean?"

"They're scared. They left."

"And went where?"

"N.O.Y.B."

"What are you, like, five?" Amy asked.

Beth tucked her phone away. "I'm, like, over it. The whole shebang. Angels and Horsemen and apocalypses."

"Lions and tigers and bears!"

Beth ignored her. "I'm tired of worrying that people I love are turning into the enemy."

"You need to chill. No one here is planning to kill you, although I'd watch out for smacks to the head."

Beth rolled her eyes. "Missed you, sis."

Amy grinned. "You, too."

A squeal of hinges signaled the basement door opening. I counted three people's footfalls on the stairs. A moment later, Addie, Sunday, and Red stepped through the protections.

The first thing I felt, before I could even register expressions or take a measure of magical intent, was a mixture of love and anxiety flowing through the heart link between Red and me. I matched it with my own and felt him accept the emotion and the goodwill behind it. My nerves quieted a notch. It wasn't much, but at the same time it was everything. It made the distance I saw in his eyes a little easier to bear. His grass—and—earth halo looked muddy, like a forest floor after a hard rain.

He combed his hair back with shaky fingertips, threading them together on top of his head. "Were you followed?"

Not *what happened?* Or *you promised you wouldn't leave.* Or *I was worried sick.* Just a simple question about whether Lucifer dogged our heels.

I didn't believe she'd followed. I hadn't picked up on it at any rate, and my instincts about that kind of thing were still on point. I asked the question of the Angel anyway, because he'd been the one with a hold on her. They'd been connected before we escaped.

"No," I said. "She didn't come after us."

Addie wrinkled her nose. The overhead light struck the lenses of her glasses just the right way, making it impossible to see her eyes. "But she might."

"She definitely will."

Amy folded her arms across her chest. "She didn't get what she wanted from me. We can expect to see her."

"What did she say she wants?" Addie asked.

"For me to refuse the call to join the Horseman society. For the

Angel and all the other Horsemen to go fuck themselves. She wants the world to stay exactly the way it is. No end and no new beginning."

Sunday whistled, her rose—gold halo flashing red. "She couldn't have put in her order earlier? Saved us all this trouble?"

"Right?" Beth slid her thumbs into her front pockets. "Lucifer always has a reason for showing up. It's probably not what she told you. Or it's more than that."

"You want to tell us what that is?" Sunday asked.

"Sure, Sunday. As soon as I call the boss man."

"You need to warn him?"

"I need his permission."

Beth didn't ask permission. She asked forgiveness. That was what always got her in trouble. She hadn't suddenly turned over a new leaf. Whatever she needed to say about Lucifer was personal to Malek. She'd sworn an oath. I understood. I'd sworn an oath to him myself, one I'd just broken by bringing Amy home and into the fold.

"What are we supposed to do with you in the meantime?" Addie asked.

"That's a rhetorical question." Addie's power as a Watcher to weave and unmake reality was a threat, but her magic didn't stack up high enough against *La Muerte*'s. Not enough for her to hold me here in this protective circle, and certainly not enough for her to bind me or hurt me beyond the Angel's power to free or heal.

She set her hands on her hips. "We're supposed to be past this, you and me."

"I thought we were."

She swallowed hard. "I was raised to worship your Angel, to pray that one day I would act in his service. That he counted my people as special, that he would welcome us into his purpose and we would be his hands and voices here in the human world. I wanted you dead before I met you."

Because I was the magical wild card who'd entered her territory. Before that, because she and hers considered me too dangerous to live as a child. "Before I was even grown."

"I always thought I'd been righteous in that desire. Protecting the world, the natural order of things. But you made me realize that I'd been *self*—righteous. How dangerous thinking I'm above ego and petty considerations could be. So, I stood outside it all, watching you take on powers you had no chance of defeating. Watching you kick their asses to Hell and back, how you did it with the Angel's help. How you handled having him inside your head without breaking down, taking greater and greater chances with your life in service of ours. Now that you and the Angel are one and the same, I wonder whether you're like I was, thinking you know better than anyone else. Can't you see you're in over your head, Night?"

That was some speech. The Addie I'd known all these months would never have said all of that to me in private, much less in front of other people. I felt the truth in her experience. She meant every word. She had every reason to tell me all this now that the Angel had shown he could take over in spite of my ancestry, my power, my skill.

She grimaced. "I'm not too proud to admit I'm envious."

Not too proud, but it hurt her to say it. "Of me losing control?"

"Yes. Didn't you hear me when I said I'd always wanted what you have? You know what it's like to be this wrong?"

She knew who'd raised me, indoctrinated me, stamped and starved any seed of decency or sense of ethics I held on to. "You know I do."

"So, where are we supposed to go from here?"

She didn't want to harm me. I didn't want to harm her, either. I loved her. I loved all of them. They'd funneled Amy and me into the basement, within the protections, not because they meant to hold us here. We could break out if given no other choice. The house spirit was strong, but we were stronger.

The protections served as a boundary between this space and the rest of the house — and the outside world. The others who hadn't come with Addie, Sunday, and Red were out there. Doing something they didn't want me to know about.

I stretched my magic, brushing against the protections' barrier, searching for a chink in the armor, a place to slip through. The barrier was impenetrable. No way was I catching a glimpse outside its circumference without blasting through.

"Why are you stalling for time?" I asked.

She pursed her lips. "Obviously, we can't handle the Angel if he re —emerges."

So they were bringing in someone who presumably could. "Who?"

"Your grandmother."

"You called Dream?"

Before Addie could answer, movement at the edge of the circle caught my attention.

Faith stepped through the barrier, her silver and gold halo so bright, it hurt my eyes. "I did."

CHAPTER 22

I MET FAITH'S GAZE, noting concern in the cant of her brows and the downturn of her mouth. Her long, dark hair fell in waves below her shoulders, the ends frizzed with the electric energy of her magic. The god inside her shone through, burnishing her light brown skin to gold. She was so young, so new, and she read me as if I were a neon sign on a pitch—black night. She wasn't the one in trouble. I was. And she'd rescue me even if it cost her everything. So, she'd brought the one being who could push every one of my buttons the same way I could push hers. The one with a hope in Hell of handling the Angel.

I wanted to be angry. Faith knew how I felt about Dream. But I couldn't make the anger rise high or hard enough.

La Muerte could, however. He did *not* want my grandmother anywhere near me.

"This is your kid?" Amy asked.

I glanced at her from the corner of my eye. "She is."

"Damn."

A heartbeat later, Dream stepped into the circle, pushing her way past Red, Sunday, and Addie. She set her hands on her hips. A strand of dark hair fell from her perfectly gathered hair into her eyes. The rolled hems of her jeans were wet and smelled of brine. Wet sand clung to her forearms, dried salt streaking the rolled sleeves of her denim shirt. Magic streamed from her halo, battering the space and everyone in it over and over, waves breaking on our shore, splattering us with salt and foam.

Amy's mouth fell open.

Dream bent at the waist, focusing all her intensity on me. "What did I tell you, *nena?*"

"That's an Elder," Amy said.

Mi abuelita looked at her sideways. "Hmmph."

"What's that mean?"

Neither of us answered her. I trained my gaze on my grandmother. "To be careful."

"To watch out. Not to give in to him. And what did you do?"

"Got run over by an Angel—sized truck."

She shook her head. "I shouldn't have let you go."

"But you did."

"I didn't want to fight you, Night. I still don't."

"I haven't done anything wrong," I said. "I have less control than I thought I would, but I'm not the bad guy here."

She held my gaze. "You need to stop thinking in terms of good and bad, *nena*. The worlds are more complicated that that."

I shook my head. "You want them to be, because that would mean you're not the bad guy, you're just complicated. We both know better."

Dream reached for me, took me by the shoulders, and shook me hard. The touch startled me, making me freeze up, giving her room to hook in to my halo. She narrowed her eyes. Clearly, she didn't like what she saw or felt.

Amy reached for the blade at her back.

Dream brushed her off. "Don't be stupid."

To Amy's credit, she didn't back down, wrapping her hand around the hilt and raising the sword an inch from its sheath. "Let her go."

"Not until she understands."

I understood perfectly well. "Not until I forgive you."

Dream flinched. "We're can go round and and round with this, but we don't have the time. Don't make me put you down."

The Angel's power surged, threading from my halo into Dream's hands, turning them cold as ice. Pushing. Demanding. Fighting to gain ground.

Dream sighed.

The taste of brine filled my mouth. Salt scraped my skin. One moment, I stood in the protective circle in Addie's basement beside Amy. In the next, I lost every anchor. Connection to my body, to flesh and blood and bone and the weight of my feet on the concrete? Washed away. Control over my magic, over my skill and craft? Ripped from its mooring. The flutter of the Angel's wings around my heart? Shredded by a hurricane wind. The heart link to Red? Shattered under the pressure of the ocean depths.

My consciousness swam, grabbing on to anything and anyone in the vicinity like a drowning woman, climbing for the surface. Dragged toward the bottom.

I tried to breathe, but couldn't draw air — only magic. It shoved me into darkness. Into dream.

I lay in bed, skin chilled and pimpled with goosebumps, sheet pulled over my head. Muffled voices broke the darkness and silence. My father and another man arguing in the living room.

A car drove by on the street out front, engine groaning and belts squealing like a wounded pig. I prayed for the driver to stop. To help. I prayed they would keep on driving, because if they stopped to help, they would die, too.

There was nothing but death in the house tonight. It hadn't announced itself, given its name. But I tasted it all the same, like chocolate—coated poison.

The soft conversation grew more heated. I started to catch words and phrases. Order of the Blood Moon. Here to assist. To heal. To make the problem go away.

I was the problem. Where would I go? Would my parents come with me?

The doorknob turned, my mother slipping into my bedroom. So quiet. Her fear was a solid thing, a sticky, sickly green that tinged her normal human halo and reached out to caress my skin. To punch through my chest and curl its fist around my heart.

Rosa, *she whispered.* We have to go. We have to go now.

I blinked. In that fraction of a second, her shape warped and shifted until the woman I saw no longer looked like my mother. She was so much younger, her brown skin bleached white, the cuticles of her coarse hair smoothed and shining blue—black, like crow's wings. She wore a harness that reminded me of one I'd seen on cop shows, only this one didn't have a holster for a gun, but a long sheath that ran along her spine. Silver glinted from the sheath. A sword.

Amy.

She frowned, the corners of her mouth trembling. She hurried toward me. As she drew closer, I could see that her whole body shook as if she were vibrating with electricity. Not power, but fear.

Amy was just as terrified as my mother had been.

Night, the monster is coming. We have to get out of here.

That wasn't right at all. The assassin who'd entered my parents' home stood in the living room with my father, about to follow his orders to take me out and leave no witnesses behind.

No, *Amy said.* He's already dead. You killed him.

I shoved off my covers, swinging my feet toward the floor and hopping down from the bed. You don't make any sense.

Nothing did. The room around me, the sounds of conversation coming from the other room, the fact that I was so small and so young, that Amy stood in my childhood room, scared to death.

This was what happened to the people I turned my magic on. This kind of mind—warp. I sought out their deepest fears and activated them. Trapped them. Until they died.

The bedroom door burst open, slamming so hard against the wall, the knob buried itself in the sheetrock. Amy stepped in front of me as my mother had, arms raised to shield me from the magic the assassin would aim me. Any second now, the flames would come. Everyone and everything inside the house would catch, and I'd walk out the back door, into the night, drenched in soot and gore and grief.

Someone stepped through the door. Not the assassin. Not a man, even. A woman who looked like Amy.

The woman balled her hands into fists. Her breath came hard and fast. She opened her mouth, but no identifiable words rolled out, only a sharp whine, like a dog in pain.

Amy backpedaled, looming over my small body. She blocked most of my view, but what I couldn't see, I could smell and taste and feel. The stench of shit. The copper penny taste of blood. The rabid infection of the woman's halo, pulsing like a bomb about to go off.

Amy sucked in a shaky breath. Mom?

Amy's mom was dead, just like mine. None of this was real. This was a dream. Abuelita *in action. If she'd trapped my consciousness in this twilight zone of a lie, what were she and the others doing to my body? My magic?*

As if my realization reflected my reality, Amy's mother vanished. And Amy began to shape—shift, growing taller and broader. Her blue—black hair became feathers, falling out and see—sawing as they floated to the floor. Her skin turned so pale, I could see the faint color of her blood vessels. Her eyes faded too gray. The smell of old parchment filled the air as her denim and cotton transformed to leather and menace. As Amy became Malek.

He raised his hands to sign. Why are you here?

The question hit me like a splash of cold water. This was a dream. I got why my mother appeared. Why Amy showed up. I even understood why I'd seen Amy's mother.

But Malek?

The edges of the bedroom stretched and reshaped themselves. The bed shattered into a thousand sharp shards of glass.

For a moment, I felt something else break. No, not something—someone.

I searched for an energy signature. A color, a scent. A halo. Anything to tell me what had just happened. Who we'd hurt.

I caught a whiff of cold winter's night and a taste of saltwater and sand. Of snakeskin and fire. Of metal and magic. Dream and Addie. Beth and Faith. All of them, straining to hold the Angel and me inside the dream construct.

But no grass and earth. No Red.

The Angel wiped my worry and fear as if they were software. One second there, gone the next. He didn't care about any of them. He only wanted to escape. His need overran mine. Filled every empty place, leaving no stone unturned. Nothing for my humanity to hold on to.

We looked at Malek.

The tile underfoot became solid, clean enough to eat off of. The darkness outside faded, replaced by light and heat that slipped through the window blinds. Humidity battled arctic air conditioning. I backpedaled, running into a black vinyl sofa hard enough to lose my balance, land on the seat.

Malek advanced, taking a knee in front of me, hands moving again. Why, Night?

Was he as real as he seemed, or just another manifestation of Dream's magic?

I took a deep breath, sending power down my spine, through my legs, out of the soles of my feet on the exhale. On a second breath, I sent power up through the crown of my head. On the third breath, I slowed my exhale, forcing myself to breath out longer than I breathed in. Calming my nervous system. Giving myself a chance to see what was real. To feel. To know.

My grandmother had trapped me, but I didn't have to remain stuck. If the Angel and I tried to fight her directly, maybe we'd lose or maybe we'd win, but the fallout would be a disaster. My family would be caught in the crossfire.

If we sidestepped the fight, we could get free.

The feathers around my heart fluttered at the thought.

I didn't care whose magic did the trick, the Angel's or mine. We wanted out.

Move back, *I said.*

Malek narrowed his eyes. For a long moment, I didn't think he'd do it. But he braced his forearm on his thigh and pushed to his feet, stepping away. Making room for me to do the same.

Standing felt like fighting my way from watery depths to the surface, lungs screaming for air, fingers clawing for purchase on something — anything — to pull me out. I felt a thud and heard a crash. I didn't dare look to see what caused them. I pushed and shoved and battled my way through the water until I could breathe again. Until the concrete underfoot and the vinyl sofa pressing against my calves and the shape and scent of Malek himself felt real and solid and right here and now.

My stomach executed a slow, forward roll, nausea blooming bright and hard. I gritted my teeth, willing the feeling away. Concentrating on the information my senses took in. Breathing in the scents of cleaner and aged paper, ink and fire. Underneath it all, traces of old blood in the air.

A hand on my shoulder captured my attention. I stared at it, skin so pale I could almost see through it, and followed the arm it was attached to all the way to Malek's face. Worry lines at the corners of his gray eyes crinkled.

He drew back his hand and signed. *You all right?*

It took a moment to make my voice work the way it should. "I'm okay. I'm not gonna fall over or disappear. I'm here."

Good.

Good? "You brought me here. Why?"

Because I need you to be free to act, and things were getting dicey at Addie's.

"You were spying."

Not me.

For the love of all the powers. "Beth?"

He nodded.

"You two are on the outs."

I asked her to keep a weather eye, and she did.

"You've been trying not to kill her for betraying you, and she just said, sure, I'll do whatever you want? She trusts you not to punish her?"

There's trust, and there's trust. Personal feelings can't keep us from doing what we know is right.

Personal feelings—that felt like a gross understatement. But Malek was spot—on. "My grandmother believes I'm too dangerous to walk around free."

Are you?

"Faith thinks so. Dream thinks so. The rest of my people didn't make a move to stop all of this. So, probably."

He furrowed his brow. *What makes you think I won't do the same thing? Cage you? Keep you from using your magic?*

The truth was, he might try to do exactly that. The only thing he feared, as far as I knew, were the Four Horsemen. I was one of them. The most powerful of them. "If you take me out of the equation, you're safe."

He nodded. *But if I do that, I have no allies. No one to trust.*

There was that word again. "What if what I think is right turns out to be the opposite of what you want?"

The answer arrived out loud, in a voice that dripped with richness and promise.

"Then we have a problem."

I turned toward the doorway to Malek's work room, and the archangel who filled the frame.

Lucifer.

CHAPTER 23

I BACKPEDALED FAST, shoving the black vinyl sofa behind me so hard, it dented the Sheetrock. My skin pimpled with gooseflesh, cold and clammy. My heart pounded, the rush of my own blood filling my ears. It took an act of will to access my training. To slow my pulse.

Lucifer wore a human disguise, waves of amber hair drawn into a French braid that ended midway down her back. Black jeans replaced leather pants. A crisp, white button—down shirt with sleeves rolled to the elbows showed off fire tattoos at her wrists. that flowed in waves to her waist. Pristine, white leather sneakers completed the package. As with Michael, the air bent around her body.

The Angel curled our hands into fists.

She held up a hand in truce. "No need for that."

"You're joking."

She'd kicked the Angel's and my ass all over Snake Bite last night. Amy and I had barely escaped from her just hours ago. And now here she was again, looking right at home, and Malek hadn't flinched at the sound of her voice. He'd known she was here. He'd invited her in.

I met his steady, gray gaze, keeping a weather eye on Lucifer in my periphery.

Listen first, he signed. *Fight later.*

The Angel calmed. Because we were outmatched? Because we might learn something useful? It didn't matter.

I nodded. "We'll listen. For now."

"Now is good enough." Lucifer motioned toward the sofa. She wanted me to sit down. To have a civilized conversation.

"Fine." I settled on the arm of the couch closest to the shop door.

She grinned, amusement dancing in her eyes. One moment, they were brown. The next, they filled with starlight.

She settled across from me. "I made a mistake.

I blinked.

"Don't look so surprised. It happens all the time, even if my brothers are loath to admit it. We're not infallible, Night." She exchanged a pointed glance with Malek. "I shouldn't have taken Amy. I thought if I separated her from you and Luna, if I kept her safe from Famine, that I could turn the tide of this war before it became too late to make a difference."

"You couldn't keep me from Amy."

"More than that, I doubt I could've kept Amy from you if she wanted to leave. Each of you is powerful. You may be the strongest, but Amy's not far behind you, and she hasn't yet been possessed by her Horseman."

"I want to help her with that." I didn't want her to go through what Luna had endured. I refused to allow her to end up like Famine.

"And I don't want her to become possessed at all. Even if you're able to stop the destruction of the world by fire, Night, what remains will never be the same."

"Maybe that's a good thing." There was so much wrong with the world. So much violence. Hatred, bigotry, greed.

"I know what you're thinking. It's commendable, wanting to change the world for the better. It's also impossible, unless you're planning to do away with human beings altogether."

The wings surrounding my heart fluttered, then stilled. "You don't believe that people can change? That, if given a second chance, they'd do better?"

"You've been given a second chance. Have you done any better?"

I stared at her. "I'm not an assassin. I don't work for the Order. I don't kill people because I'm ordered to. I take care of my family. I protect them. I've saved the goddamn world more than once."

"You want to stop the Apocalypse, but every action you've taken has only drawn it closer."

"The Angel doesn't want the world to end."

She shook her head. "The Angel won't give the world to the End."

The End wanted the destruction of all things. All beings. All worlds. The Angel wanted to remake the world. To create something new.

"I can see it in your eyes," she said. "You understand what I mean."

"There's a difference."

"It's a fine line."

I didn't see it that way. "You're afraid."

"You should be, too, Night. The fact that you're not is a problem. That's why Dream wants you caged—until she can figure out how to stop you."

If only my grandmother—my family—trusted me. If the people who knew me best couldn't do that, how could Malek and Lucifer?

"Why are you talking to me like this?"

Lucifer glanced at Malek.

He signed. *It all comes down to you, Night. What you choose.*

Everyone wanted me to choose. And everyone wanted me to choose them.

I took a deep breath and blew it out slowly. "So, what now? You expect me to try to stop the Angel?"

We can help you.

"How?"

Blood. Ink.

A tattoo, spelled with Malek's poisonous, powerful blood. "To do what, exactly?"

Malek didn't answer right away. I listened carefully, my magic rising to determine the finest shift in his expression. His body language. To tell truth from lies.

La Muerte listened, too. He saw and felt with his senses and mine. His magic and mine.

The space between us and them tightened, a high wire they would have to walk without slipping. Without falling.

You should never have merged with the Angel.

Not an answer to my question. Not a deflection, either.

You did it to win the battle.

"Because it had to be done," I said. "If I hadn't—"

You would've died. Your daughter would've died. And the End would've won.

Lucifer stood, shrugging away tension. "Instead, the End was so soundly defeated, it will take generations for him to rise with enough power to try again."

"That's a good thing."

She nodded. "We owe you debt of gratitude we can never repay. I don't just mean Malek and myself. I mean all of us. The Elders. The Powers. Humans. Fae. All of us."

"I didn't do it for gratitude or to collect a debt."

"No. You did it because you're you, Night. It's who you are. It's not who the Angel is."

"Really? Without him, none of us would be here."

Her halo glimmered at the edges. She began to pace, a handful of steps back and forth between the sofa and the display counter, her light illuminating the jewelry behind the glass and the silver back of the cash register. Every movement carried such stunning grace, it mesmerized.

Malek snapped his fingers. I tore my gaze away from Lucifer as he signed.

The Angel helps you because it serves his ends, not yours. You should know that by now, after he took you to Amy against your will. That will continue to happen, and it will get worse. He will do what he wants, and you will be a prisoner inside your own body. Trapped. Helpless. You want that?

Of course I didn't. I opened my mouth to tell him so, but couldn't form words.

The Angel's power roared inside me, exploding through my skin, my eyes, my mouth. The Angel aimed the cold and dark at Malek, but the magic slammed into a barrier a foot from my body. The impact shook me to the bone.

My legs gave out. I hit the floor on my hands and knees. Pushed up immediately, but couldn't rise beyond a crouch.

Malek hadn't moved an inch. The magic that held me didn't feel like his. It felt bright. Fiery. Graceful.

Lucifer.

She'd caged us. Just like my grandmother.

The Angel and I pushed our power against the edges of the prison, searching for a fault in the magic. A crack in the facade. We found none.

I didn't bother to look over my shoulder. To look at her. I met Malek's gaze.

He signed. *I can't take the chance that you'll lose yourself.*

He could've waited for me to hear them out. To think. To decide.

The Angel's voice echoed inside my head. The finality in them stole my breath.

You made the decision when you died. When you and I became one. There's no going back from that. No way to separate us. You're mine until I let you go.

I knew in my heart—in the seat of my magic—that he spoke the truth. That I'd never had a hope in hell of figuring out how to co—exist with him.

He was more powerful than I could ever be. He allowed me to help my family, to fight the End, because it was convenient for him. Now, my wants and needs—my life—no longer mattered. *La Muerte* had control. I had nothing.

I understood now. *Mi abuelita.* Lucifer. Malek. Why they thought I had to be stopped.

If I had any agency left—any will of my own—I needed to marshal it now.

Unless *La Muerte* found a way out of this trap in the next few moments, Lucifer and Malek would take whatever action they had planned to keep the Angel from destroying us all. And I would have no voice. No choice at all.

I held Malek's gaze. I needed him to see. To see me.

The wings around my heart fluttered.

I ignored them.

The Angel spoke, his voice rising inside my head until it became loud enough to drown out every conscious. Until instinct lifted my hands to cover my ears in a futile attempt to drown his words.

He'd found a way out. He could break the bars of the cage enough to transport us to another timeline. We could be free.

He short—circuited my nervous system. Flooded me with emotion.

With desire that flashed low in my belly and spread like wildfire.

With hope that we could craft a better, brighter tomorrow. That no one else would ever have to crawl on their hands and knees to belong, to survive, to live.

With love for me. My true self. The child who'd been born without any understanding or hint of magic and on whom it had been bestowed, a dark gift. The girl who'd been saved by the Order, found a place to belong, learned how to defend herself and how to kill—because life fed on life, and those who could not curse could not heal. The woman who chose the path of the heart in the end, who tried every single day to protect the people she loved.

If I bent my will to his, we could give this gift to all beings in all the worlds. We could break the chains that held them down. We could all be free.

Free.

That word—that feeling—was everything. Nothing and no one was more important. It was all I'd wanted, all my life. To break my bonds. To be all of who I was inside. To let that shine through.

If I let him, the Angel would not only show me how, he would take me to that place. This was a vow he would not break. A promise I couldn't deny.

Except that was all a lie. Not because it wasn't true, but because it wasn't about me at all.

The Angel wanted those things. He needed them the way a drowning person needed oxygen.

He'd been born at the beginning of time. All those millenia, and only once had he been loosed upon the world and allowed to create it in his own image. The freedom he craved lasted only long enough for the rain to fall and the floods to rise. Once the waters receded and the sun shone, the Powers chained him again.

He'd waited long enough. The Powers owed him this. The worlds owed him. And so did I. I knew what it meant to be trapped by my own nature. To be imprisoned by beings more powerful than I could ever hope to be. To bend my will to theirs because I had no choice, if I wanted to live.

I understood him.

I breathed deep, tasting power in the air. Tasting life.

That was at stake here. My life. Malek's and Lucifer's. Faith's and Red's and Sunday's. Kevin's and Amy's. Addie's and the kids'.

Rude's and Shadow's.

They stood behind Malek now. Behind the sofa. Between us and the door to the work room, as if I'd summoned them with my thoughts. Hope flared in my heart. I'd lost them, but they'd found me. They were safe.

Rude's face looked deadly serious, his cheeks flushed the same color as his buzzed orange hair, his eyes stormy. He'd changed into fresh clothes since the last time I'd seen him. Khaki shorts. Key lime Hawaiian shirt. Not a single scuff on his white hightop sneaks. His magic pulsed, ready to leap.

Shadow met my gaze with steely eyes. His mouth turned down at the corners, tight with loss. The stars seemed to have fled his halo, leaving it coal black. He wore clean clothing as well. And a blade shoved into a brown leather sheath at his front right pocket. It had been spelled, the power it carried visible even through the leather.

It felt dangerous, but not to everyone. Only to me.

Instinct demanded I step back, but I couldn't move. The feeling grew stronger with every passing second.

Shadow reached for me with his magic. With the Angel focused on breaking Lucifer's cage, Shadow slipped into my mind and froze for a single heartbeat. In that small space and time, I shared his feelings. His thoughts. His horror at what he saw happening inside me.

The moment passed. He anchored his feet to the floor and shook out his arms. He braced his magic, and spoke for me alone to hear.

Amy?

I'd left her with Addie and the others in the basement. But she'd appeared in the dream spell *mi abuelita* had woven. I'd broken free from the spell. I'd broken Amy.

The thought smacked me hard. I shook my head to clear it, but it didn't work. Something was wrong. I'd done something bad. But what?

She's with Addie? Shadow asked.

Yes. Of that much, I was sure. *You're with Malek and Lucifer. You and Rude.*

Yes.

Just the one word, enough for all the puzzle pieces to fall into place. *You brought them together.*

Brokered a peace between them, he said. *This is more important than old hurts or differences of opinion.*

I agreed. And I also knew that Shadow and Rude would join their magic with the serpent's and the archangel's if they needed to. If the Angel and I threatened to break free.

Shadow would use the blade.

He'd killed me once and he wouldn't hesitate to do it again. Last time, the Angel brought me back, as he always did. I was *La Muerte's* embodied form in the world. I could act where and when he could not. I was his home. And together we were strong, but were we strong enough to defeat the four powers in this room?

Shadow held my gaze. His voice rang in my mind.

Decide.

CHAPTER 24

S HADOW'S QUESTION ECHOED in my psyche and in my heart. He waited for my answer, maintaining the connection between us so he would hear not only my words, but my intention. His hand strayed to the sheath at his side. He unsnapped the strip of leather that braced the spelled blade and wrapped his fingers around the hilt.

The thud of my heartbeat felt strong enough to break my ribs. The overhead lights seemed hot enough to burn. The silence in the room was so heavy, it threatened to flatten me against the cold, white tile. Then, Rude broke it, splaying his fingers before contracting them again, knuckles cracking.

Behind me, Lucifer shifted her weight. The soft brush of her pants legs against one another raised every hair on the back of my neck.

Malek leaned forward, the vinyl sofa creaking beneath him. He, too, had a knife to hand. But this one wasn't a magical mystery. He used it to draw his own blood before mixing that blood into his inks.

I understood the choice they were asking me to make. One knife or the other. One kind of death, or another.

The wings near my heart fluttered. This time, I read desperation in their touch.

I felt the Angel move deep inside of me—in my bones and in my blood. I couldn't tell what he was up to, though. Not without going just as deep as he was. To do that, I'd have to tear my attention away from Rude and Shadow. From Malek and Lucifer. And I could not do that.

It went against every ounce of training I'd undergone and every survival instinct.

The Angel wanted his freedom. He wanted to act. I got why. I didn't even disagree with him. He was part of me, and I wanted to give him everything he asked for. I felt that in every cell, so strongly I vibrated with the emotion.

Separating myself from the Angel proved impossible. Everywhere I turned, there he was.

But we hadn't been one long enough for me to forget who and what I'd been before the night we joined. I remembered the need that drove me before. To be good. To do what was right. To belong to people who cared about me, not for the destruction I could wreak, but for the healing I could bring. To love and be loved.

Those things burned in my heart. More than that, they burned in my soul.

Because the soul I'd been born with had shattered under the weight of the lives I'd taken and been rebuilt from the souls of my victims. They'd given me that gift for a reason. Redemption.

I'd earned my family. Their respect. Their love. The Angel had already led me into shaky territory with them, breaking trust. If I followed him, the rest would unravel. It was inevitable.

I refused to destroy myself—my soul—in service to him.

Before I completed the thought, my vision blurred. My hands fell to my sides, out of my control. The Angel, taking over. He'd done it before. He could do it again—and he would.

I inhaled, tasting the power in the air. Tasting life. I used that life force to find the magic in my heart that belonged to me. The old me, before the Angel's power joined with mine. The new me, magic augmented by the ancient power the Angel carried. Every ounce of power I could get my hands on.

I used it to stop the takeover. To put up a walls and doors. To bar and lock them. Once, I'd had enough strength to imprison the Angel in my mind. Now, I had no idea how long I could hold him off.

Minutes, maybe seconds. I hoped it was enough.

I tried for words, but making a sound—any sound—would break the spell I wove.

But Shadow was still inside my head, his presence faded from a shout to a whisper. He could feel the battle of wills. He could hear me. Speak for me.

He pulled back, leaving a hole with his sudden absence. "Whatever you're going to do, do it now."

Lucifer tightened her grip. The world turned gray. Colors washed out. Borders between people and things, between thoughts and feelings, vanished.

I felt Malek *move*. I couldn't see him clearly, only the magic he wielded.

He pricked the fat pad of his thumb with his blade. Bright red beaded on his pale skin. He didn't need that, though—the thin film of blood on the blade would be enough. He sliced my forearm—not deep. Just enough to infect me with his poison.

All the stories I'd heard about his blood—how the touch of it meant agony—I knew they were true. But not for me. Because of *La Muerte*.

I was Death. I could not be killed. Not even by Malek's blood.

But it could slow me. It could shadow my consciousness. Render me powerless for moments longer. That was all Malek needed.

The buzz of his instrument washed over me like a thousand angry bees. The vibration. The slip and flutter of wings. The stab of stingers. With every prick of the needles, he wove a spell of his own. One that augmented mine.

He made the walls I'd built too high to climb and too strong to break through. The doors so thick, no magic could penetrate. The locks so complex, they carried bindings within bindings—more than I could see and name.

With every layer of power he crafted, my senses cleared, until I could finally make out the shape of his fingers and taste the copper in the air. Until I could smell the ancient paper scent of him and feel the implacable edges of his magic—and the unexpected kindness inside of them.

Finally, he pulled his arm away. No more stabbing. No more vibration. Just the sight and smell of my blood mingled with his. He met my gaze, searching my eyes for the Angel.

"Do you see him?" Lucifer asked.

Malek shook his head.

La Muerte was still inside me. Malek's working hadn't expelled him —but then, I didn't think anyone or anything could do that. Malek had built a fortress around him, though. One much stronger than any I'd ever crafted. One that ought to hold the Angel indefinitely.

Words tumbled from my lips, hoarse and barely there. "He's fighting it."

Shadow nodded. "Is he beating it?"

"No." Just the one word, but it was a word full of hope.

Lucifer relaxed her grip slowly, allowing me a full, deep breath. Allowing oxygen to reach my brain and suffuse my magic. My racing heart dialed back just as slowly. I stopped trying to hold myself up, letting myself collapse into a heap of flesh and bone. The tile beneath me felt cool and comforting. I'd fallen, but it wouldn't let me fall any further.

"Dude, you okay?"

I looked up at Rude. "You're joking."

He grinned. "It'll get better. Malek's whammy is kind of overwhelming."

Rude would know. The tattoo of the city on his back tied him to the land, the bayous, the people who lived here. That kind of magic was more than overwhelming. It was life changing.

I pulled my legs under me one at a time, arranging my body from the bottom up until I sat cross—legged, forearms resting against my knees. Malek reached out a hand for me to take. When I did, he squeezed. More kindness from a god, one from whom I expected nothing of the sort.

"I need you to explain what you did," I said. "I think I understand most of it, but not all."

He let go to sign. *It's better if you don't know everything.*

I filled in the words he didn't say. "Because if I know it all, the chance increases that the Angel finds a way out."

He nodded again.

Lucifer stepped back, releasing me. "It's good you understand that."

"Don't poke the bear," I said.

Power flared around Rude. He gathered it and shaped it into a portal to his right. I recognized the place it opened to on the opposite end. The concrete floor. The red rug in the center with its circle of brightly colored pillows. The rhythmic tumble of the dryer and the scent of fabric softener came through so clearly, I could've been in Addie's basement.

Three people stepped through the portal into the lobby of Snake Bite Tattoo before the portal closed behind them.

Sunday, outfitted in solid black with every weapon she could conceal on her person in place. She'd tied off her long, blond curls at the nape of her neck with a strip of black ribbon. Her rose gold halo flared, ready to take on any threat.

Faith came behind her in a shimmer of silver and gold that blurred her cobalt blue sweater and black jeans, her eyes ringed with the same silver and gold. The Awakened lay just underneath the surface of her skin. She took up position behind Rude. Rear guard.

At the end of the line, Red. The muscles in his shoulders tensed, pulling at the fabric of his navy T—shirt. His faded blue jeans frayed at the knees, his feet stuffed into worn, brown hikers he hadn't taken a moment to tie.

I met his green gaze, wondering what I'd see there—caution, distrust, anger. They were guarded, the emotions behind the shield like roiling waves in a stormy sea. The heart link between us remained, a solid anchor. His magic flooded through it, the compassion of the sacred heart, searching the state of my power and finding me. Finding the trap that imprisoned the Angel. He sighed, his relief flowing through the link.

I'd never been more glad to see anyone in my life than I was to see the three of them.

Sunday surveyed the scene, eyes narrowing as her gaze swept Shadow, Lucifer, and Malek, finally locking on mine. "Davies, you're in deep shit. You should've told me what you were planning."

"Would you have cooperated if I'd told you?"

She snorted, then raised her chin at me. "You all right?"

"Not even close." I was about as far from all right as I'd ever been, with the saving grace that I didn't have to fight the Angel as well as my own turbulent feelings.

Faith relaxed a hairsbreadth. "We tried to tell you. We tried to help you."

"This isn't her fault," Sunday said.

Malek signed. *Could Night have made different decisions? Probably. Would we all still be standing here, alive and well, if she had? Probably not. Fault does not matter. Responsibility does.*

I didn't know whether I agreed with him. With the Angel beaten back, the thoughts and feelings he'd wiped from my mind surged forward. I remembered fighting to free myself from the dream construct my grandmother had built. I remembered turning all my will and all of my magic—and the Angel's magic—against it. Someone had broken.

I pushed to my feet on shaky legs, bracing myself as best I could. "Who did I hurt?"

Faith shook her head. "It wasn't you."

"Who?"

"Amy."

Shadow took Faith by the shoulders and shook her. "Is she all right?"

Faith opened her mouth to answer, then snapped it shut again.

Worry and fear gnawed at the pit of my belly. I'd been trying to save Amy. To keep her out of Lucifer's hands. To help her with her Horseman.

Red cleared his throat. "Amy pushed Addie and Beth out of the way. Got in front of them. She took the brunt of it. And, no, she's not okay."

Shadow's fingers dug in to Faith's shoulders. She held his gaze without flinching. After a long moment, he let go and turned his anguished, furious gaze on me.

I needed something to hold on to before I fell again. Malek stood. Offered his arm.

I stared at him.

He pressed the arm into my grasp. Holding on to him was like holding on to iron.

Red held my gaze. "She's not dead."

I closed my eyes tight enough to see stars. "How bad is she?"

"Not going anywhere, anytime soon. Addie and Beth and the kids are working to put her back together. Malek will have to heal what they can't."

Beside me, Malek nodded.

I looked at Red again, asking without speaking.

"Most of the bones in her body are fractured or broken."

I couldn't escape the harsh sound of those words as they rolled from his mouth. Nor could I escape the emotions that powered them or the images that flashed behind his eyes and through the heart link.

Amy on the concrete floor of Addie's basement, blood in her black hair. Lip split. The catch of bubbles in her throat as she tried to suck in oxygen. Red kneeling at her side, laying on hands, allowing his magic to flow in to her as Addie did the same.

Amy's voice, a whisper and a croak. "Don't. Let. Me. Die."

Red cut off the flow of images and feelings. He'd shown me what I needed to see.

A sound escaped my mouth, somewhere between a moan and a keen. Red's face softened a little. I didn't want his softness.

I wanted to die.

He looked at Malek. "We need to take Night home."

Malek placed his hand over mine and left it there.

Lucifer spoke for both of them. "You can't handle her."

Red narrowed his eyes. "The Angel is trapped. She's herself again."

"That doesn't suddenly make her safe as houses," Lucifer said. "She's a ticking bomb."

"She's our ticking bomb."

He'd said "our," but meant "my." I felt a sharp edge through the heart link. He wouldn't back down, and he didn't care what he had to do to enforce his will.

Lucifer met Sunday's gaze. "He can't see reason, but maybe you can. You know what she's capable of, even on her own."

Lucifer was talking about my power. My training. The Order hadn't been able to hold me, nor had they been able to lay a hand on me after I ran. Not until I put down roots and made a stand had any operative even come close.

If I wanted to run again, I could, and my family wouldn't be able to stop me. If I had to fight any of them to get away, chances were I'd come out on top. And, once I'd disappeared, none of them would find me unless I wanted them to.

Meanwhile, the Angel would do everything he could to break Malek's blood spell. To break free.

Sunday folded her arms across her chest. "What's the plan?"

"She stays here. We keep an eye on her. And we figure out a solution to our problem."

Red bristled. "Night's not anybody's problem."

Lucifer rolled her eyes. It was such a human gesture on such an inhuman being that for a second it confused my magical sight. I blinked at her.

She caught my confusion from the corner of her eye and raised a brow before she returned all of her attention to Sunday. "We'll need all the Horsemen."

"In one place," Sunday said.

Lucifer nodded.

"Three, we've got—or two—and—a—half, anyway. Amy's not fully possessed and she doesn't want to be."

"I didn't want her to take that step, either. It was better for her—for all of us—if she rejected War."

"The Apocalypse would never come. That's what you wanted, you and Malek. You can still have that. Amy stays Amy. The world spins on."

"We thought so, too," Lucifer said. "What we wouldn't give for that to be enough. But it won't be, because now Amy is weakened, which gives War a stronger hold on her. And we—I—underestimated the Angel of Death."

I took a deep breath and blew it out slowly. "He'll get free. It's only a matter of time."

Lucifer turned to me. "And then it's all over."

Sunday scoffed, but her heart wasn't in the sound. "There has to be a way to work this that doesn't involve Famine."

"We need all four Horsemen. Their magic together. That is how bindings of this magnitude are created."

"Bindings?"

"Yes, we're binding the Angel of Death."

Sunday turned that over in her mind, considering all the angles. I watched the conclusions flash across her face one by one, until she came to the end of the line. "Wait."

Lucifer held up a hand. "For how long?"

Sunday opened her mouth to reply, then snapped it shut again.

Faith sought my gaze. The silver—and—gold shine of her halo faded. She no longer looked like the Awakened. She looked like a girl. My little girl who carried the god of magic, who knew that binding the Angel of Death meant binding her mother. Because the Angel and I were one—magic, body, and soul.

There was no line between him and me. No demarcation as to what belonged to him and what was mine. At best, I would become a normal. Only human, no magic to speak of. At worst, what Lucifer and Malek proposed would trap my consciousness, my soul, in whatever prison they built for the Angel.

Faith narrowed her eyes. Her expression hardened. "No."

CHAPTER 25

TIME SLOWED. The smallest details grew large: The angle of the sun seeping through the blinds. The long puddles of light on the white tile. The air tasted of fear. Anger. Adrenaline.

It bombarded my senses—not just mine. Malek loosened his grip on me. Lucifer widened her stance, driving the bottom of her halo through the floor as she tried to ground her perception.

Sunday flanked Rude and Shadow, surging past them before they could react. Her halo flashed rose—gold fire as she skirted the end of the sofa. I caught a flash of silver in her hand—a blade. Malek and Lucifer saw it, too. Trained their attention on it just as Sunday unleashed a blinding bolt of power, all the strength of it focused on Lucifer.

The archangel caught the blast in a single hand, as if it were a ball. She closed that hand, crushing the life from the magic she held.

In the split—second it took her to destroy it, Sunday launched herself into the air. She struck Lucifer head—first in the gut. Tackled her to the floor. Silver flashed. And red. I breathed in the perfume of blood.

Sunday's blood.

She was outmatched and Lucifer would fucking kill her over my own goddamn dead body.

I ripped my arm from Malek's grasp. Dove toward the fight.

I never made it.

The air itself stopped my momentum. Held me in place, froze above the fray. No, not the air—Malek. Because he'd cut me. Because he'd spelled me with his blood, he controlled me. All I could do was watch as Lucifer threw Sunday off of her. As Sunday rolled across the tile into the base of the glass counter, boneless as a rag doll.

A scream clawed its way up my throat.

Across the room, Rude and Shadow recovered their senses. Red faced off with the Faery seer. Faith, with Shadow. The scent of grass and earth exploded, not around Red, but around me, a shield against magical attack. Faith's silver and gold halo glittered, the shine transforming to a glow, pulsing to a light so bright, it turned everyone and everything photonegative.

The scream filled my mouth. Raked it raw inside.

Shadow's starry halo flashed. The floor beneath his feet disintegrated—not just to dust, to molecules. To the matter of creation.

The wall behind Rude opened like a giant's mouth, all fae shadows and teeth.

They were going to blow everyone and everything to smithereens, including themselves.

The scream punched through my lips.

"Stop!"

The sound reverberated off the walls. It shook the whole damn building like an earthquake, knocking over jewelry inside the counter case, loosing ceiling tiles, cracking windows. It echoed through flesh and blood and bone. And, finally, faded into silence.

Malek let me go. I fell to the floor in a heap.

I inhaled a shuddering breath as I scraped myself up and pushed to my knees. "Stop this."

The hush that followed was all tension and nerves, but no one moved so much as a muscle, thank all the Powers.

Faith's voice claimed the silence. "You can't do this to her. We won't let you."

"I won't let you destroy yourselves trying to save me," I said.

"You underestimate us, Mom."

I shook my head. "I know exactly how powerful you are, Faith. How powerful all of you are. That's the problem. You're willing to pay any price because you haven't learned that sometimes the price is too high."

She took a step toward me. Rude and Shadow allowed her to pass. Sparks fell from her fingertips, leaving a tail of ash behind her.

I pointed to Sunday. "Check her."

Faith did as I asked, squatting beside Sunday and laying two fingers at the pulse point of Sunday's throat. "Her heartbeat's fine. She's breathing all right. She's just knocked out—a combination of the impact with the floor and Lucifer's magic."

Faith narrowed her eyes at Lucifer.

The archangel shrugged. "She came at me. I wanted her out of the way."

But not dead. I closed my eyes for a moment and gave thanks. I could hear Faith's footfalls as she closed the distance between us. I could hear the sizzle of the sparks and smell the burning tile as they fell. I didn't want to look at her, but she knelt in front of me and set her hands on my shoulders. They were so warm, her hands. She shook me until I met her gaze.

"You've always done whatever it takes," she said. "How can you ask us to give up?"

Was that how she saw it? I'd never give up. Never. "Is it so wrong to want you to live?"

She searched my face. I didn't know what answer she hoped to find.

"Is it so wrong to want that for you, too?" she asked.

"I won't die."

"How can you be sure?"

"Because the Angel and I are one, and he can't be killed. Any binding they craft won't hold forever. The Angel is a force of nature too big and too strong to hold for eternity. But if he can be held long enough, that might give all the worlds a chance to find a different path forward—one that doesn't involve destroying the worlds to save them."

And, in the meantime, everyone I loved and everything I cared about would move on without me. If the binding held long enough, they'd all be gone before the Angel broke free, or before Lucifer and Malek found that better way.

The heart link between Red and me surged with love, fear, and doubt—but, most of all, pain. I tore my gaze from Faith's and looked at him. His grass and earth scent grew so strong, it overwhelmed every other smell in the room.

"Hell, no," he said.

His words hit my like a punch to the gut. How else could they possibly feel? Red was my home, and I understood all the way to my marrow that I was his, too.

The question I had to ask hurt even worse. "If it's the only way?"

"Then, fuck the world. Fuck you, Malek. And you, too, Lucifer. Fuck all of you. This isn't an intellectual exercise. It's life and death and heartbreak. You can't ask us to make this sacrifice, and you sure as hell can't demand it."

"But we can," Lucifer said. "Don't you see?"

Because they were ancient and more powerful and they could call on allies with the kind of magic we couldn't possibly dream of. They'd wipe the floor with my family and then do what they wanted to anyway.

"I don't care," Red said. "If you take Night, I'm going with her."

Malek snapped his fingers, drawing everyone's attention. *No hasty decisions.*

"Hasty, my ass."

We need you in order to find the solution to this problem.

"What makes you think I care?"

It's who you are. What you are.

Red glared at Malek. "I decide that. Not you. And don't give me any bullshit about my magic taking over and doing whatever you think is right. I'm in control, not it. It answers to my will."

Malek pressed his lips into a thin line. He could use his power to spell Red the way he had the Angel. It wouldn't take much—enough juice to overpower Red and one or two drops of blood. Malek didn't have to say that to bring it home to Red. It was written all over the serpent's pale face.

"Don't even try. I'll fight like hell every step of the way. I'll do all the damage I can. No matter what you do to me, I'll find a way to take you down with my dying breath. I learned how to do that from the best." Red nodded at me.

Malek looked at Red—and through him—in a way that made every hair on my arms stand straight up. I held my breath for a long moment, until Malek broke off eye contact.

The serpent set a hand on Faith's shoulder. She stood tall.

He raised his hands to sign. *What do you say?*

"I'm with Red. I think I can speak for Sunday, too. What you're trying to do here is wrong. It doesn't matter that it's for the right reasons." She turned to me. "You're wrong, too, Mom. I learned in just about every way possible that some prices are too high to pay. I learned it from you."

Damn.

I thought I'd done the right thing—the only thing to keep us all alive and together. To save Faith, first from the Order's assassin, and then from the Angel. To stop the Watchers from taking control of the Angel. To save magical children and destroy the Order. To save Luna's soul. To stop the End from turning all the worlds into so much dust and darkness.

I refused to second—guess every thought, every action and reaction. Down to brass tacks, all of us had done the best we could with what we had. We would do that now, too, because we had no other choice.

Backs against the wall. Hell on the way. And my man and my kid, showing two of the oldest, most powerful beings in all the worlds—showing *me*—how it was done.

Lucifer stepped slowly into the middle of the room, placing herself at the center of our rough circle. "So, that's it? We're back to where we started?"

"No." I pushed to my feet and met her gaze. "We still have a job to do."

"Save the world."

Yes. "How were you two planning to get a hold of Famine? Or do you already have her?"

"She's hard to lure into the open," Lucifer said. "I tried."

"With promises and temptations." Neither of which would capture Famine's attention. Not for a hot minute.

I raised a brow at Malek. He had a vested interest in keeping the four Horsemen apart. He'd made me promise to help him do just that, and here he was doing the opposite.

Some things are bigger than me, he said.

Had I misread his hands? Because it sounded to me as if he'd admitted that he wasn't the end—all, be—all of everything. He'd spent millennia maintaining his position in the hierarchy of gods and keeping himself safe from the likes of me.

"What changed?" I asked.

Beth. She disobeyed me, more than once. I should care. I should take it out of her hide. He shook his head. *I can't do it. I don't care what it costs me.*

If I were him and we were talking about Faith instead...I understood.

He addressed the group. *There's something I need to tell you all.*

I held his flank as he signed the story of his first and only meeting with the four Horsemen. How the End had ordered us to take his speech. We'd removed the one thing that made him who he was and changed him forever.

We were the only real danger to him in all the worlds. We were also, right now, his only hope.

As he went on, the energy of the room shifted from surprise to fearfulness, then finally to something approaching community. There were no more secrets. We were all in this together.

"So, if promises and temptation aren't enough for Famine," Lucifer asked, "what is?"

I turned to Malek. "You're her boss."

He flashed a wry smile. *Sometimes, I think it's the other way around.*

"She has a tendency to get what she wants."

She may not want this.

"A chance to beat Famine?"

To be asked to do it by either of us.

Red interrupted. "She understands more than you give her credit for—who you are, the rules you're bound by, why you do what you do."

Malek mulled that over. *We'll find out.*

<h1 style="text-align:center">CHAPTER 26</h1>

BETH WAITED FOR US in Addie's kitchen, sitting cross—legged on a chair dragged from the table and planted in the middle of the floor. She cradled a cup of coffee in both hands. Her brown hair was loose, kinked from her usual braids, and still wet at the ends. She wore faded jeans with holes at the knees and a black T—shirt that said YOU'RE GOING TO NEED A BIGGER BOAT. Her feet were bare and her orange and black halo brighter than I'd seen it in a long time.

The air tasted of magic—the violence I'd committed, grave—chilled and midnight dark. The burning, alchemical fusion of Addie's power. Shed serpent's skin and fire—that was Beth. And something new that I recognized because the Angel recognized it: molten metal.

The scent of a Horseman's power. War's power.

She looked us over: Malek in black leather, his bald head gleaming under the overhead light. Lucifer in white and Sunday, with her arm braced across Lucifer's shoulders to help her stand. Rude in his Hawaiian shirt. Shadow, a ball of barely contained nerves and anger. Faith, whose fingertips still sparked. Red, who stood at my flank and refused to allow more than two feet of air between us. And, finally, me.

Her eyes narrowed. "Which one are you?"

"Night," I said.

"The Angel?"

"On a leash."

"Well, thank God for small favors."

The house spirit seemed to agree. I felt it all around me, pushed up against the edges of my skin, testing my magic. After a moment, it backed off, but not by much. I got its point. It would be watching me. One false move and it would show me the exit. No second chances.

It could back up that threat as well. In the short time I'd been gone, it had been augmented. I caught wind of Addie's magical signature, along with those of the kids. The house spirit carried some of Ben's ability to shield, Jess's Watcher powers, and Corey's ability to summon and speak with the dead.

I didn't want to hurt the house spirit. My intention didn't matter, only the Angel trapped inside me.

A touch of sadness squeezed my heart. Addie and I had worked hard to get along, to be good allies, even friends. All of that undone in the space of seconds by *la Muerte*. But it was also true that I didn't matter here—not how I felt or what I wanted. Only the mission counted. The outcome. The safety of my family and all other beings.

I swallowed hard. "You knew we were coming?"

"I hoped." She unfolded from the chair, standing slowly. "And I hoped it would be all of you—in one piece."

Malek showed her a ghost of a grin.

She cocked her head. "Does that mean I'm forgiven?"

He lifted his hands to sign. *Nothing to forgive.*

She sighed, her relief a palpable thing. "So, we're working together again. What are we doing?"

"Going to get Famine," I said.

Beth blinked. "Whose terrible idea was this?"

Malek raised his hand.

"Wonders never fucking cease."

I agreed. "We need to get downstairs, Beth. Talk with Addie and the kids. And we need Amy."

"Jess, Ben, and Corey are upstairs. Amy's not conscious yet and Addie will probably beat your ass before she talks to you."

"I'd deserve it."

"You know, it's hard to stay mad at you when you talk like that." Beth chugged the last of her coffee and smacked the mug down on the counter.

"I'm sure you'll manage." There was one more question I needed to ask.

Beth answered before I could get the first word out. "Dream is with the kids. She's making friends."

"Friends?"

"You know, priming the next generation. If they trust her, she can get them to do what she wants. Isn't that how all you Elders are?" Beth looked pointedly at Malek.

He stared back.

She winked. "C'mon."

She led us down the hall, the hardwood floor creaking under our steps. Between the house spirit and Red, I felt surrounded. As we drew closer to the basement door, my belly filled with butterflies. The single bulb inside the door was broken, the glass etched with a hundred jagged lines. It hadn't yet shattered, but it could any moment.

That made for a dark trip down the stairs, hands on the railing to the left, fingertips skimming the wall to the right. The protective circle opened for us. There were only two people inside, one unconscious and helpless, the other standing—or sitting—guard.

Blood smeared on the concrete floor. White towels stained red formed a breadcrumb trail from the edge of the protective circle to the center of the room, where Amy lay on the red rug, head propped up on a pillow that had been bright yellow, now also streaked with crimson. Her chest rose and fell. Her skin was too pale, but there were spots of color in her cheeks. The fae sword War was laid out lengthwise along the midline of her body, her hands wrapped loosely around its hilt.

"She wouldn't let go of it," Beth said.

Because it was part of her. Because she was part of it. If her will remained that strong, she stood an excellent chance of healing completely. I exhaled the breath I hadn't realized I'd been holding.

Addie knelt between us and Amy, eyes closed, palms flat against her thighs. She wore a sky—blue terry bathrobe over a pair of black leggings, her top discarded and balled up behind Amy. Addie glanced up as we approached, meeting Malek's gaze first, then Lucifer's. She marked Red and Sunday, Rude and Shadow. And then me.

"You here to fix this, Night? Because if you're not, you can get out now."

I took the verbal punch to the gut, feeling the sting and then letting it flow over me. "There's no time to fix this the way I want to. To finish healing Amy as best we can with magic. To give her the days or weeks she'd need afterward for her bones to finish knitting together and her mind and spirit to mend."

"Whose fault is that?"

"Mine," I said.

"You're not blaming the Angel?"

"I blame him plenty, but I'm the one who trusted him enough to let this happen. I didn't ask the right questions, and maybe he wouldn't have answered them anyway. I assumed he was on my side because he helped me—helped us. I didn't think he could overpower me. I was wrong."

"Yes, you were." She pursed her lips. "You brought the cavalry. At least there's that. No more warring amongst ourselves."

She might think differently in a minute. "How's Amy healing?"

"Like a champ. That spell Malek tattooed on her ankle—the one that turned her fae—it saved her life. If she'd been human, you'd have killed her, Night. There wouldn't have been anything I could do."

I hadn't taken the life of an innocent since leaving the Order. If I'd killed Amy, I wouldn't have been able to forgive myself.

Something shifted near my heart. For a bleak second, I thought the Angel had already found a way to break free. But then I realized the feeling had nothing to do with those signal feathers fluttering. It went deeper than that.

Addie stared at me. "Night?"

I held up a hand to stall. I remembered this heart—shift as if it were something from a long lost dream. It was important, very important. I needed to dig. To find the memory.

Red reached for me through the heart link, flooding me with grass and earth. I lost my grip on the feeling. It fled.

He laid a hand on my shoulder. "You all right?"

I glanced back at him, ready to vent my frustration. But the care in his eyes washed that away, too.

"Good," I said. "The Angel is still in his cage."

Addie rose, dusting off her pants. "So you're going to tell me what you're planning?"

"We need all of the Horsemen in one place."

"What the hell for?"

Lucifer answered. "We wanted to use their power to bind the Angel of Death."

Addie's brows climbed to her hairline. "No."

"That's what Night's people said as well."

"To be clear, I'm also Night's people," Addie said.

I blinked at her.

She waved her hand. "Don't look so surprised. I may not always like you, and I might want to kick your ass half the time, but we've been through so much together—all of us. I don't trust the Angel worth a flip, but I do trust you, Night."

Sunday grinned. "Ride or die."

Addie nodded. "So, if we're not binding the Angel, and Night along with him, why do we need all the Horsemen in one place?"

Because if the four Horsemen together were powerful enough to harm Malek—the only force powerful enough to kill him—then we might be strong enough to do something equally impossible. We might, in fact, be the only ones who could.

"If we can use our magic to bring on the Apocalypse, we should be able to use our magic to stop it. Not just for today, but permanently."

"Nothing in this world is permanent, Night," Addie said.

Malek raised his hands to sign. *Without extraordinary interference,*

I'm immortal. So is Lucifer. And Michael and Gabriel. What Night proposes is no different.

Addie folded her arms across her chest and bowed her head, thoughts rising to the surface of her face and falling again. Finally, she met Malek's gaze. "Forever, at least as far as we can imagine it."

He nodded.

"That's a long time," she said. "I hope to all the Powers it will be good enough."

I did, too. "That's not up to us."

Faith twined her fingers together and rested them on the crown of her head. "If we augment the Horseman's magic with all of ours, maybe we can do better than good enough."

Sunday pulled away from Red, standing tentatively on her own. He reached to steady her, but she shook her head. "I'm okay."

"You have a concussion."

"It's not my first."

Which made this worse, not better. He gave her some serious side—eye.

She ignored him. "Sanchez here has always been our captain, but we've saved the worlds—and each other—together. We're better together. We're a team. We're a family. That's how it's been, and that's how it's got to be now. No one goes off on their own. We connect psychically and physically the way we've done before and we stay that way until this is done, no matter what happens. Agreed?"

She looked at me, challenge in her eyes. She expected me to object.

I wanted to.

She was one—hundred percent right. I couldn't argue with any of it. But the facts on the ground might make what she proposed very dangerous for her and the rest of our family.

"If the Angel breaks free and takes me over again, then he would be connected psychically and physically to our family. He could use your power or prevent you from using it. Worse, he could threaten to harm or kill you and make good on those threats from the inside. You have to understand that."

"I do," she said.

I felt no lie in her words, and love was the only thing I read on her face. She'd gladly throw herself into a fight, but she wasn't stupid. She knew the risks and she'd take them for my sake. She didn't back down from threats. She dealt with them. And the Angel could go fuck himself.

A glimmer of hope sparked in my heart. It felt fragile and precious and I clung to it, but there was hope and then there was foolishness. One, we couldn't win without. The other, we couldn't have at all.

I swept my gaze over every face in the room as I spoke. "This is a decision everyone needs to make for themselves. No one should take this risk out of sentimentality or because they're worried about what the rest of us might think. We're playing for keeps, and, if we lose, we lose everything."

As the sound of my voice fell away, silence took its place. I listened to the quality of that silence, measuring the push and pull of my family's thoughts and feelings, of truth and wishful thinking, of refusal and acceptance. It was a magic all its own.

Lucifer broke that spell, at first pacing in an arc between the group and the circle's edge, then with a waterfall of words.

"I'm not your family. I don't know most of you. I don't know whether what you're suggesting is the bravest thing I've witnessed in my extraordinarily long life, or whether I'm looking at a herd of beasts about to hurl themselves, knowingly and willingly, over a cliff. If this is what you all meant by finding another way—if this is what you've been doing all along—I have no idea how you've survived thus far."

Behind her, the protections opened. I expected to see Ben or Jess or Corey—but none of them had ever appeared in a huge ball of fire that scorched the concrete and the air around them.

My magic rose, ready for a fight. But even as it did, I realized I knew this particular mass of writhing flame with his three eyes, two in the usual places and a third in the center of his forehead. With his armor that glittered like diamonds. With his golden sword in the sheath on his back, air bending around his body in deference to his power.

Then, the flames guttered, revealing Michael, all in black. Short hair, leather jacket, jeans, motorcycle boots. T—shirt emblazoned with the same faded white script—Ride the Lightning. The only thing about him that still burned were his eyes.

"Lucifer may not be part of your family, but I am."

I sucked in a breath. "What?"

"If you'll have me, that is."

He said I wouldn't see him again. He wasn't supposed to be here. He was, as always supposed to stay out of it. But hadn't he bent the rules, over and over again, to find a way to help?

Michael was my blood, and I was his. That was what had gotten me into this mess in the first place—the ability to hold the Angel of Death without burning up from the inside out. If I looked at it that way, Michael's offering to join this fight was the least he could do.

I opened my mouth to tell him so, to continue our long battle of words, then swallowed every syllable before it could roll off my tongue. He might be still be an asshole, but he was our asshole.

"Thank you," I said.

The fire in his eyes banked to glowing coals. He seemed more solid. More present.

Lucifer looked from me to Michael and back again. "You're serious, both of you?"

We nodded.

She set her hands on her hips. "Damn."

Michael laid a hand on her shoulder. "Decide, sister."

I'd have to re—evaluate everything I'd ever heard about Michael and Lucifer. They didn't seem like enemies. Or perhaps, when it came down to brass tacks, they both wanted the same things. For the world to spin on. For life to go on.

"I'll regret this, won't I?" she asked.

"Only if we lose."

A wisp of a smile touched her lips. "When you put it that way, how can I refuse?"

Sunday whistled. "Some team we've got here. We're still missing a couple of players."

Yes, we were. Our witch and our Faery King. "Rude, can you get a hold of Stacy and Kevin?"

"On it." He turned and stepped out of the circle.

"Faith, will you get the others?" I asked.

She nodded and followed the faery seer.

Sunday met my gaze, her eyes flashing to meet the challenge. "So, what now, Sanchez?"

"We heal Amy. We bring Famine here. Then, we play for all the marbles, and we play for keeps." I turned to Beth. She didn't yet have all her strength back. That worried me more than a little. "You ready?"

"I was born for this," she said.

We all were. For right here. Right now. This moment.

I hoped to all the Powers we survived it.

CHAPTER 27

MY CHOSEN FAMILY stood in a circle around the red rug in the center of the basement. We were as different from each other as we could be.

Red stood to my right, Sunday to my left. I couldn't ask for more than they'd already given, but they offered it anyway. Beside Sunday, Faith glowed silver and gold. Then Michael in denim and black and Lucifer all in white. Luna, all the gel and spray washed out of her black Mohawk, her brown skin shining under the basement lights. Addie and Shadow and Jess, halos full of stars. Rude in his Hawaiian shirt and his best friend, Kevin, the Faery King, in linen and brown leather. Malek and Beth, twinned serpents. Ben, his halo gray and stony. Corey, surrounded by the spirits of her ancestors. Then, the witch Stacy, fresh out of the portal from Houston, her blond curls a riot around her freckled face. She thrummed with power, drawing up the magic to connect us all as she'd done before.

Last, but far from least, Dream. She met my gaze, love in the depths of her dark eyes.

How was I supposed to respond to that? I loved her, too, and I understood why she'd tried to pin the Angel and me down. I even felt glad she'd done it. But I didn't know how to trust her.

No—that wasn't true, not exactly. I could trust her to be herself, to act in her own best interests, and, as a distant third, to act in what she perceived as mine.

"Abuelita," I said.

She inclined her head. "Nena."

I felt for the energetic edges of my body and soul—the beat of my heart, the weight of my feet on the floor. The cool air that flowed into me as I inhaled, the rise of my chest and belly, the warmth I breathed out. I slowed my exhales, calming my nerves, making myself present right here and right now.

We were Watchers and seers and kings. Elders. Witches and those who spoke with the dead. Shields and assassins. The girl who carried the god of magic and the two women who carried Horsemen of the Apocalypse. Two archangels. Black, brown, and white. From families of blood, broken and whole. All of us, bent towards a single purpose. Together, we could save each other and save all the worlds.

I had to believe that.

Amy still lay unconscious in the center of the room, her face a testimony to the pain of knitting bones and healing bruises. Her halo sparked and flared, all her energy directed inward, her grip tighter on the hilt of her faery sword. Its blade shone softly, like twilight.

The presence of the Horseman she was meant to carry hovered around her. I couldn't see it with my magical sight, but I felt it in the prickling at the back of my neck and the chill that settled along my spine. Luna met my gaze, her pupils rimmed with same glowing green as her halo. The fine dark hairs on her forearms raised like antennae. She felt it, too.

Amy wouldn't have a chance to make a conscious decision as to whether she would carry War. We didn't have the time to wait for her to wake and sort out the pros and cons. We needed War to help us capture Famine. We needed War to help us turn back the Apocalypse.

Amy could still reject the Horseman. Even unconscious, her will still held sway. If she refused to let War in, refused to allow him to take root in her body, mind, and soul, then everything we did from that moment forward might be for nothing.

No pressure.

Luna took a big breath and blew a stray lock of hair from her forehead. She opened herself to my magic, and I slipped into her mind.

Her voice brimmed with raw emotion. *You know, I remember when you did this to me. How you and Red talked me into taking on Pestilence.*

You're putting a kind face on it.

It's better to say you used all your magic and all your will to bend mine?

I shook my head.

She set her hands on her hips. After a moment, she let them fall to her sides. *I'm not sorry. You gave me another chance to live. To make a difference. If it's not the life I had in mind, so what? It's better than having my soul destroyed and being turned into nothing at all. Maybe it's even better than the life I thought I wanted.*

That was the kind of thing people said when they tried to talk themselves into accepting the unacceptable, but from Luna it felt true. I had no idea how she arrived at that kind of forgiveness. I didn't think I could, if I were in her shoes.

She answered my thought with firm words that closed the door on that part of our conversation. *I'm not forgiving you and Red because there's nothing to forgive. I would've made the same choice you did.*

That surprised me. How could anyone feel that way? But I heard no lie in her words.

You're okay with carrying Pestilence.

I believed you when you told me my humanity could change him. That I was necessary.

Even after everything you've seen with la Muerte *and me, you still feel that way?*

Yeah. But I can tell you have doubts. I can feel them like tree roots growing through cracks in a sidewalk.

If left to their own devices, tree roots broke and displaced concrete. They took over.

Is that what you want them to do? she asked.

It's what I fear.

Take care that fear doesn't become your reality, Night.

I blinked at her, and her lips curved into a small smile.

I'd never thought of Luna as my kid—not the way I did with Faith —but I did think of her as someone I mentored. Here she was, teaching me. *Thanks.*

She took the conversation public. "So, how do we do this?"

A minute ago, I'd have taken that "we" as rhetorical. If I used too much of my magic and opened an accidental way out for the Angel, or if I did something to break the prison Malek had built for the Angel, this whole operation and everything that came after it would become a disaster. Every word of that was true, but those words, thoughts, and feelings had been born of fear.

Who was in charge here? Fear, or me?

"We ground and center, and then we go in. You ride my magic, Luna. We'll both be inside Amy's mind."

"Got it."

"Red, can you stay with me through the heart link? Can you sweep up behind us, fill in the gaps, soothe Amy if she needs it?"

He raised a hand and pressed his palm to my back, between my shoulder blades. His magic pulsed in and through my heart. "Do what you need to. I've got you."

"I know." He wouldn't let me down. I looked around the circle. "We'll need the rest of you to back us up. Hold a container so that nothing gets in or out."

Nods all around.

"Ready?" I asked Luna.

As I'll ever be, she replied.

Her thoughts and feelings, her heart and mind, twined with mine. I turned toward Amy and dove in.

Agony slammed into me at highway speed. It stole my breath before it shattered like glass, slicing my magic to tattered ribbons. I screamed.

I felt hands on my body—Red's, Sunday's. A flow of power opened up behind my heart, feeding me strength. Feeding me healing. It tasted of ozone, like fire harnessed by a god. Not fire—lightning. Not a god—an archangel—one who felt like family. Michael.

My magic knitted together as quickly as it shredded.The lightning bent the air around me, creating a perimeter the pain couldn't punch through. My heart raced. I sucked air, every muscle tensed and ready for a fight. With every breath, I willed my heartbeat to slow and the tension to drain. I needed a clear head. I needed to think and to see Amy as she was without pain and fear—hers and mine—overwhelming my senses.

A sense of calm settled in my skin, in the bowl of my belly. My thoughts schooled themselves. I looked at Amy's pain. I felt it in my bones. In my heart.

Some of it was because of me. Because of *la Muerte*. We'd broken her body, and Addie's ministrations, along with Amy's fae nature, were healing it rapidly. Healing was no joy ride. It hurt like hell, and maybe in the end you came out stronger and wiser, but never the same.

Underneath the physical processes, the Horseman she was meant to carry had found a way in. I felt him coursing through her bloodstream, in the molecules of oxygen she breathed in and the carbon dioxide she exhaled. But he couldn't enter her heart, the seat of her magic, without her consent. So, his power built and built within her, displacing her own, pushing against organs and shoving against the inside of her skin, scrambling her thoughts and feelings. That hurt as bad or worse as reweaving bone.

Luna?

Here.

You all right?

Okay. Pestilence took the brunt of that blast.

As the Angel would've done for me, if he weren't trapped inside the cage Malek built. *You see what I'm seeing?*

How are we supposed to get through all that? How do we speak to Amy? How can she hear us?

We'd have to go where War could not.

Even before I sent the question into his mind and the need through the heart link, Red sent his consciousness right where we needed him. With us.

The grass and earth of his magic wove with ours, and the power of the Sacred Heart that only he could wield flowed strong. Every small, lonely place inside my heart, every fear that hid around corners I refused to explore, every dark and shadowed place suddenly lit with the gentle light of dawn. Before they could feel naked and exposed, Red's compassion covered them. I steadied myself in the river of his power. I felt held by him in ways I never had before. Because he saw me—and what was imprisoned inside me—and did not judge.

Jesus, Luna said.

Not off the mark—at least as far as the magic was concerned.

My lips curved into a wry grin. *Follow me.*

I dove into Amy's heart, Luna and Red right behind me. Not a single shield stood in my way. Amy had deployed them all against War. I should've understood that as a warning rather than an opportunity.

If Amy's pain had felt like agony before, what greeted me inside her heart was a Mt. Everest of trauma. The dream my grandmother had shoved me into had given me a glimpse inside Amy's past, but I'd only seen the edges, the beginnings and endings.

Her heart held everything in between, a roaring waterfall of time and memory, hate and love, trust and betrayal.

Her parents' raised voices and raging tempers. The way her mother pulled her in, tethering her in a net of feeling Amy could never escape from—and making love and care conditional on that emotional enmeshment. I witnessed the moment she met Kevin, tumbled into a swimming pool at a party in Rude's backyard. She dared to trust him, to open up to him and let him in to places she never welcomed anyone else, but then he'd fallen in love with someone else she couldn't hope to compete with. Her ability to trust crumbled completely—not only other people, but worst of all, herself.

When a friend and classmate summoned a demon, the spell that fell over Houston and its residents transformed her parents into monsters. They either died or vanished in the cataclysm, leaving Amy alone, an orphan.

She needed to help stop the demon. Unlike her friends, she had no magic. What she had was determination and desperation that took her to Malek. He'd given her one of his magical tattoos, changing her nature in the space of hours from human to fae.

I felt the smooth roll and weight of water on my skin the way she'd felt it, living for months as a mermaid in Houston's Buffalo Bayou, refusing to talk to the people who'd been her friends. Only surfacing to talk with Malek—the only one who didn't act as if he was sorry for her.

The night Kevin's mate—the Faery Queen—drafted Amy for help in saving the city and gave her the sword War marked the beginning of a new life. Amy emerged from the bayou on two legs and never went back. She had new purpose. A mission. She held on to it like a lifeline.

I smelled the brine in the air on the night she met Shadow, in the alley behind Snake Bite Tattoo. I sensed all the subtle and overt ways he wore her down. Built a path to her heart. Made a home for himself there, and a home for her in his. He saved her. She saved him.

And then Lucifer and the rest of us arrived to fuck it all up.

Didn't she deserve love? A life? A way to walk in the world and do good? Hadn't she suffered enough?

Each question hit me like a punch to the gut.

She refused to give in to War because that meant everything would change once again. Maybe Shadow would leave. Maybe she'd push him away. Or the world would end and it would be her fault.

I slid my magic over hers, through hers, weaving and winding in the small spaces between the streams of thought and emotion. Grounding the wild energies of dread and heartbreak. As I slowed my breathing, so did Amy. With every breath, the fear abated, washing away until the only thing left was the unbelievably powerful magic and tattered soul of a raven—haired girl who wanted to belong. Who wanted to be loved.

Red's magic flowed around us, covering that girl with love, letting her know she was seen and known and accepted for who she was, not what she could be or what she could give. It didn't matter whether she was human or fae, or possessed enough power to save the world. But she mattered, more than anything or anyone in this moment.

Her question echoed inside my mind. *You sure that's true?*

Red, Luna, and I answered as one. *Yes.*

But I know why you're here. What you want. I can't do it.

Luna stepped in front of us, meeting Amy magic—to—magic, heart—to—heart. *It won't be anything you expect. It'll be hard, and unlike me you'll have to fast—track things because we're running out of time. But you* can *do it. We need you.*

Amy trembled in the face of so much power pushing against her—the Horseman, the three of us. Waves of magic threatened to overwhelm her. She felt small, like a seawall against a hurricane's wind and surge. But she held firm.

It's different for me, Luna. It won't be like it was for you or Night, or even Famine. You don't know what you're asking me to give up.

Being alone inside your own head, Luna said. *Making decisions on your own. Living and loving on your own.*

It was more than that. We were asking Amy to be ready to forfeit her life.

Amy shook her head. *You have no idea.*

She risked her life every day. She threw herself into danger. Into fights against beings powerful enough to kill her. What we asked of her, even down to losing her life, was exactly the same.

Red reached for me through the heart link, flooding me with sudden doubt. Hesitation. He saw something I'd missed.

Amy, what is it?

She never got the chance to tell me.

CHAPTER 28

I N THE SEA of love Red had created, in the seat of Amy's magic, thunder rolled. It eclipsed the rhythmic rush of Amy's blood, the pressure and push of War pounding against the gates of her heart. Lightning flashed, the shocking strength of it stunning Luna, Red, and me too stillness. For a heartbeat, my magic froze. I couldn't speak. I couldn't move at all.

I'm here.

I recognized the voice. I knew it intimately. I'd heard it in my own heart and mind months ago, when Shadow had been the enemy. When he'd taken me over and used his unmaking power as the first Watcher to take me apart, one molecule at a time. He'd been after the Angel then, stripping away every part of me to get to my Horseman, words dripping with venom.

There was no poison in them now, only love—as different from Red's sacred heart as night was from day.

Shadow's love was as desperate and full of longing to belong as Amy's. He held on to her as tightly as she did him. Apart, they were broken. Together, their broken places fit together like pieces of a puzzle, scarred and seamed, but as whole as they could be.

Amy shook, this time like an earthquake. *If I do this—*

It's not forever, Shadow said.

You can't know that.

Trust me.

Amy was silent so long, the time seemed to stretch for days instead of moments. When she finally spoke, her voice was so rough with emotion, it stung.

If you're wrong, I swear to God I'll find a way back and take your head off.

Her words held no power, only fear and worry.

The desperation she felt, along with Red's doubt and Shadow's sudden appearance, boiled in the pit of my belly. Something was wrong here. No, worse than wrong.

What is it? I asked.

Amy took a deep breath and blew it out slowly. *If the Angel were with you, you would already know.*

But I couldn't touch the Angel. I couldn't let him out of his cage until the right moment. We needed all four Horsemen to put an end to this madness. Only with the other three working together could we hope to keep the Angel in line.

You know what will happen to you afterwards, she said.

I did. My human family hadn't yet put two and two together. When they did, all hell would break loose. *Not now.*

We're not going to be able to talk about it later, Night. There's not going to be a later for me.

You should listen to Shadow. He loves you.

Amy sighed. *Yes, he does. That's why he's telling me what I need to hear.*

Shadow put up a strong front, but I could feel his heart breaking behind it. And Red and Luna's demand to know what all this meant. If I allowed so much as a sliver of that information to saturate my thoughts, the rest would rise to the surface. They would know everything.

You owe it to them, Amy said.

I owed them a lot more than that. I owed it to them to show them my whole self—all the good and all the bad. That was what I promised to give them, even if I'd never told them that out loud. That was what loving them meant to me.

I let the thoughts rise. I didn't try to camouflage them or make them beautiful. They had razor edges. They'd draw blood, and I couldn't do anything about that.

My family had saved me from being trapped in stasis forever with the Angel. But there was still the question of what to do with both of us once we'd averted the Apocalypse.

The Angel would only start over, working to end the worlds in fire. Once he managed that, the next cycle would begin. And I would be right there with him, because we'd merged into one being. Because there was no way to separate from him.

I was his perfect vessel. With him inside of me, I couldn't die. I'd be with him for eternity. That was the endgame. It had always been the deal. I'd just been too busy trying to keep us all alive to let myself realize it.

All the things I'd told Luna about how a human influence could change Pestilence, how she could make a difference—I didn't want to believe it was bullshit. I hadn't lied to her. I'd told her the only truth I'd known at the time.

But things were different now. I knew better. I understood.

I felt Luna's dawning horror. How could I not? Her mind and magic were woven with mine. Red's panic swelled for a heartbeat before he clamped an industrial—strength lid on it. It would only be worse later, when we found time alone. *If* we found time alone.

The helplessness in my voice frightened me. *What can we do then?*

I felt her hands in mine, as if she'd taken them to reassure us both —or so we could grieve together.

She spoke with more confidence than she felt, pouring hopes and dreams into her words. *I trust you, Night.*

Then she *moved* with enormous speed, the shape of her heart shifting and changing, opening to the force of the Horseman who wanted her for his own. The rush of his martial energy knocked me out of her heart and mind, shoving my magic back into my own body.

Amy's scream took me to my knees. Luna hit the ground beside me.

Wetness stung my eyes. I wiped at my face. My hands came away red with blood.

Amy's soul rose, flowing out of her flesh and blood through the pores of her skin. It floated, a silvered mist above her body, before it dove for the ancient silver of the sword she held.

I lunged for her. I had no idea what to do, only that I had to do *something.* I couldn't let this happen to her.

Sunday wrapped her arms around my waist from behind. I dragged her forward two steps before she threw herself backwards and flipped us over, taking me the floor and pinning me there. She held down my shoulders with her hands, my hips with her knees.

A wail pierced to my depths. I could hardly draw breath against that keening.

Sunday focused on my face. "Look at me."

I shook my head.

"Look at me, goddamn it."

I refused. She grabbed hold of my gaze with her magic and turned it. The second my eyes met hers, my world went black.

I froze—will, mind, magic. And body. The keening stopped. It'd been coming from me.

Sunday shook me. "Night."

I swallowed and croaked out a single word. "Here."

She waited a beat before she let me go to make sure, and still she hovered.

Even if I'd wanted to fight, I didn't have a single ounce of emotional energy left. I didn't have a fucking clue what to do. So, I gave in. My muscles went limp, every breath a shudder on the way to more bloody tears.

Movement toward where Amy's body lay caught my attention. I couldn't left a finger, but I could let my head roll in that direction so I could witness Shadow kneel beside his lover, his body so tense he could explode. How did he hold himself together like that?

His hands trembled as he traced a finger along her lips before he placed a kiss there and on her brow. Then he removed the sword's hilt from her grip and took it from her. He held it with care and reverence, as if it might shatter.

He could shoot it into the sun and it wouldn't destruct. It contained Amy's soul and the Horseman, War. Like me, it would live forever.

Commotion behind my head dared me to move. I couldn't, not even an inch. But I didn't need to look to hear Lucifer and Dream negotiating how to lift Luna off the floor. Where to take her? How long until she woke up?

Sunday slipped from my line of sight. Red took her place, his salt—and—pepper hair shadowing his eyes. He reached for me through the heart link, his emotions mirroring mine.

"Will you help me?" he asked.

"Of course." Michael slid his arms underneath my shoulders and knees. For someone made of fire, his touch felt ice cold.

He carried me out of the circle and up the basement stairs. I was afraid to meet his gaze, to see the disappointment I knew had to be there. I listened to the creak of our weight on the steps and looked at the ceiling instead, marking years of dust against the white face of the paint and the sudden brightness of the naked bulb on the landing. Michael's golden hair brushed the pull—string, sending it swinging like a pendulum.

The air seemed to turn gray and fuzzy, color and edges blurring. The creak of the hall door was the last thing I heard before unconsciousness swallowed me.

CHAPTER 29

I WOKE IN THE DARK, held so tightly, I could barely stir. I lay on my left side, my arm half—asleep. Red slept, too, spooned behind me, his grass and earth a protective cocoon. Sunday lay in front of me, the curve of her hips tight against mine. Her chest rose and fell slow and deep, the vanilla scent of her hair a calming drug. But the rose gold of her halo glowed blood red, giving her away.

In that moment, her bearing changed. She knew I was awake.

A third voice filled the silence before she could speak.

"You couldn't have known."

Michael. In the chair beside the bed, long legs stretched in front of him. He'd damped the glow of his eyes to pinpricks of light.

I didn't want to hear sympathy. Or excuses. "I should have. All the clues were there."

"Some things are too big for any one person to track. It was too much. Too overwhelming. You did the best you could, Night."

"I'm not in it for the participation trophy."

"You want to win," he said.

"Amy didn't deserve what just happened to her."

"Since when has it ever been about what anyone deserves?" He shifted his weight, leaning forward to rest his elbows on his knees.

That was the right question, and it pissed me off. "Never."

"There you are," he said. "Your spark. Your fight."

Sunday cleared her throat. "Hey, Mike? You want to give us a minute here?"

He raised a brow.

"I appreciate your watching over us and all, but we need to talk about human shit now. You mind?"

He stood, meeting my gaze. I saw no recrimination in it. No disappointment. Only hope.

I didn't understand where he got that. How he could feel it at all.

He headed for the door. "I'll be right outside."

The thud of his footfalls on the rug and the hardwood. The squeal of door hinges. The sound of Sunday's breathing and the gathering force of her rage. Those things filled the world.

As soon as the door nicked shut behind Michael, she turned over to look at me, rocking the mattress. "You knew we were screwed and you didn't tell us."

"You're mad about the Angel and me."

"I'm furious about all of it, Night. Amy—"

"I thought she was shielding her heart against her Horseman. That he was trying to break in. But he was only creating a path for her soul to follow once she decided to give in. That fae sword—it bears his goddamn name. And here I am, thinking it was a coincidence. There's no such thing. We learned that early on in our training with the Order. How could I have forgotten?"

"You can't know everything."

"I have too. If I don't, what good am I?"

"Are you trying to make me stab you?"

She had every right to. "What did you want me to say? What can possibly say now to make it better? I can't fix any of it."

"You can. You will. You understand me?"

Her faith was admirable. And misplaced.

She placed a hand over my mouth. "Don't want to hear it. Not until you come up with a solid plan. There's always something we can do. Something we haven't thought of yet."

I searched her eyes. She really believed that, but how? "Not this time."

"Is that what you're going to tell Red when he wakes up? That what you're going to say to Faith?"

"I don't know what to say to any of you."

She held my gaze. "Do you love me?"

Since we were kids, in every way possible. "Always."

"Then don't let me down."

That was an impossible ask. I knew it, and Sunday did, too. I didn't want to make a promise I couldn't keep, so I didn't say anything out loud, only nodded.

She leaned in and planted a sweet kiss on my lips. "I'm going to leave you two alone. Try not to kill each other, 'kay?"

Her drawing away and planting her feet on the floor felt like an abandonment—and also a relief. Before I'd met her, I never in a million years thought I'd have a friend like her, who had my back no matter what. But she also saw too much and expected too much.

"The hell are you going, anyway?" I asked.

"Luna's room."

"Luna's?"

She set her hands on her hips. "What? It's the end of the world. I like her. She might like me."

I remembered the way she'd looked at Luna the other day, when we'd gone to Faery—me to answer Kevin's summons, Sunday to pick a fight. "She should like you, if she swings that way. You're awesome."

"I know." She winked at me and made her way out the door.

The room was silent except for the sound of Red's deep breathing. He seemed to be asleep, but the scent of his magic was too strong for that to be true.

"Penny for your thoughts," I said softly.

He sighed. "Darlin', you'd need a million pennies."

"You pissed at me, too?"

"Not mad at you. Just plain mad."

He was telling the truth. It should've made me feel better, but instead I only felt trepidation. I feared what he would say next.

"I'm not angry with you because I know who you are, Night. I understand why you do what you do. I expect nothing less. That's what scares me."

"That makes two of us. Scared, that is."

"You know me by now," he said. "Don't you?"

I turned over, propping my head on my hand so I could see his face. There wasn't a single worry line in his forehead. He looked serene, as if he'd made up his mind about something and let everything else go. "What?"

"I'm not Sunday. I'm not gonna be content with a half—assed nod when I ask you the important questions."

I didn't want to hear them. I didn't want anything to change between us. If I could fix it so that we could stay exactly here and now, this close, and shut out the world, I'd do it in a heartbeat. "Are these questions about Amy, and how she's not human or fae anymore? About how she's made of steel? How she can't speak or touch or fuck her lover, and how maybe that's forever?"

"Night—"

"Let me finish. Are the questions about how wrong we were when we did everything in our power to convince Luna we were right, that she could influence Pestilence, that she could have a meaningful life?"

"If she's amenable to Sunday's offer, she's having a meaningful life this minute."

I scowled.

"It's a good thing," he said.

It was more than good. It was life—affirming and it meant everything. "Are you thinking about what's gonna happen to Faith and Corey or Ben and Jess? About all the others? About innocent people who might get caught in the apocalyptic crossfire?"

He shook his head. "There's nothing we can do about any of that. None of it. Recriminations won't make it better. Second guess all you want, but the choices you made—my choices, too—they were the only ones."

I opened my mouth to argue. He narrowed his eyes, and I snapped it shut again.

"I'm not you," he said. "I don't have the fate of the worlds hanging over my head, and I can't tell you what to do about it, but I've thought about it from every angle I'm capable of, and I can honestly say the plan you and the others have come up with is solid. It's the only way to go."

He wasn't finished. I waited.

"But you know me by now, Night. You understand there are certain things I refuse to accept—and certain things I refuse to live without."

I pushed up on my elbow. "You are *not* telling me you refuse to live without me. That's not okay."

"I'm telling you not to shut me out."

Relief washed over me. "I won't, not if I have a choice."

He reached up to tip my chin with his thumb. "But you don't always."

I shook my head.

"Wherever you go, I'm coming with you."

That was a harder ask. I didn't know where I'd have to go, whether any human—or anyone at all—could follow. "I promise to reach for you, if I can."

He breathed in my words, and the love behind them. "I promise to reach back. If you fall, I'll catch you."

I exhaled, a stream of tension flowing out of my body. "Not if I catch you first."

He nodded, rising to kiss me. It was gentle and sweet, and not at all what I needed right now. He pulled back far enough that I could meet his gaze.

I saw fire in his eyes, barely contained. As I leaned into him, a sound traveled from upstairs—a moan of pleasure. I knew that sound like I knew my own nature. Sunday, in the throes of a climax.

Red's lips curved. "Wow."

A spark of joy lit my heart. "Sunday and Luna."

"Sunday called that one. What are the odds it lasts more than one night?"

A million to one, maybe. I didn't care whether their getting together was for tonight or forever. There was love between them, right here and now. "It doesn't matter."

"I guess not," he said. "I'm happy for them."

For a second, I allowed myself to feel hopeful. "If we play our cards right, they'll have more than this chance."

"I like hearing you say that."

I liked it, too.

"Sunday's right all around," he said. "It's the end of the goddamn world and all we have is each other."

No idea what tomorrow would bring—or if there would even *be* a tomorrow. But we had the room to ourselves. We had each other and whatever time the Powers granted.

I kissed him back, breathing him in like a lifeline. If I could draw that breath deep enough inside, I could make it part of me—of my heart, my soul, my magic. I could keep that piece of him, no matter what happened.

He reached for the hem of my shirt, shoving it up and over my head, fingertips brushing the curves of my hips, sliding up the hollow of my back to unhook my bra. He tore his mouth from mine, bending to lick and suck first one nipple, and then the other. I pressed my lips against the crown of his head, stifling a moan of pleasure that swept away my worry.

I needed to feel. To be with him. To memorize every line and curve, every scent and taste and sound.

His hands dropped to my waist, working the button and zipper of my jeans, peeling denim and cotton down my legs in one swift movement. He surrendered his shirt. I savored the view—the plane of his stomach, the rise and fall of his chest. The glow of the sacred heart. The shine of his own, just as bright.

How had I ever gotten so lucky to find him?

He grinned as he stepped forward. I reached for his belt buckle, but he brushed my hand aside and planted a knee between my feet, wrapping his hands around my ankles. He pulled me closer, trailing kisses along the inside of my thigh before he found my core. My breath caught at the slide of his tongue. The sweet rhythm of his fingers as they slipped inside me.

I needed more, now.

I fisted my hands in his hair. "Red—"

He lifted his head just long enough to meet my gaze. "Not yet."

"But—"

"We have time."

Time was exactly what we didn't have.

"I'm loving you, Night. Feel me loving you."

I let my let my head fall back against the mattress and gave him what he wanted. He took me so high, I saw stars. He paused just before I exploded, then drove me to the brink of ecstasy again. I grabbed hold of the sheets, every muscle tense and quivering, praying for this to end —and never end—until I couldn't stand one more heartbeat of waiting.

He whispered, his breath a caress. "Let go for me."

I held my breath.

I was afraid to let go. Scared to death that, if I did, I'd lose any control I had over what happened from this moment forward. Terrified that my surrender would be all the Angel needed to break free from his prison.

Fear had its place. I understood it intimately. It should flow through and then out, not hold on. Not gather and burn. Not like this.

My eyes felt suddenly wet. A second later, tears rolled from their corners into the tangle of my hair. My lungs heaved, forcing me to breathe out, to hitch in another breath, to give in to life.

Life and love and desire poured through me into the heart link. Life and love and desire roared back. I exploded, a star gone nova, light and heat filling every empty space inside and out, driving away the taste of ice cold death. It burned my fear to a cinder. Dried my tears.

This time, when I reached for Red, he let me pull him up and over me.

When he kissed me, I tasted my own salty sweetness and his grass and earth. He deepened the kiss as I made fast work of removing his jeans and boxers. The sound he made when I closed my hand around his cock vibrated through me, all the way to my marrow. I stroked him hard and took him in my mouth, drawing him into my throat, loving him as he'd loved me.

He let me, as long as he could stand it. Then he slid his body down the length of mine, skin on blessed skin, and I guided him home.

For a long moment, he didn't move at all, barely breathing. He looked at my face, and I looked at his, fixing every detail, before I met his gaze. He began to move in long, gentle strokes, each deeper than the last. I met every one in kind, tracing my fingertips across the small of his back to cup his ass. To pull him closer.

My magic slipped the edges of my skin, breaching his, connecting us mind—to—mind. I saw him as he saw me, tasted what he tasted. He felt what I felt.

His thought bloomed in my mind. *This is forever. This is always.*

Then he surged inside me, all thought of taking his time swept away. He whispered, his breath warm against my neck. "Night, I need—"

I kissed him. Bucked against him. Need took me into its iron grip, too, stripping everything but love and desire.

He moaned, quickening his rhythm, all conscious thought and carefulness gone.

He fell, and I fell with him.

The glow of his sacred heart grew brighter, lighting his face like an angel's, spreading along his skin and mine, taking us over, creating a bedrock of love so we could both let go. Then, there was nothing else but wild abandon, soul—deep need.

Wave after wave of love and desire, of ecstasy, flowed through us. We rode them toward the shore, falling together, heart to heart, eye to eye.

We were one body. One heart. One life.

Afterward, in the stillness, I became aware of the sound of his breathing and the quickness of his heartbeat, the weight of his body on top of mine. In the same moment, he rose up on his elbows and pressed a kiss on my brow.

"Better?" he asked.

I grinned, amusement zinging all the way to the bowl of my belly. "Better."

"We should probably sleep."

Who knew when we'd get the chance again?

I opened my mouth to reply, but a knock interrupted. I glanced toward the door.

Beth's muffled voice followed. "We have company."

I met Red's gaze again. "Who could it be? Everyone is already here."

"It's Famine," Beth said. "Before you panic and rush through the door naked to defend us all, the archangels and the boss man have her tied down tight. On the other hand, you might not want to take the slow boat because the boss man is also thinking of all the ways to torture the shit out of her in revenge for, you know, killing me."

I raised my head an inch in surprise and protest, then let it fall against the bed. "Damn."

Red rolled over, covering his eyes with the crook of his elbow. "Thought we'd have to hunt her down."

"I don't want to leave this room," I said.

"That's two of us." Our connection through the heart link pulsed, as if it had a heartbeat of its own. "You remember what we talked about. What we promised each other."

I turned to kiss his temple. "Forever and always."

He took my hand in his. "All right."

"All right, what?"

"I'm satisfied you have your priorities in order."

I usually did, but events had a way of taking over. "Time to save the world."

He laughed. "Again."

If I heard nerves underneath the surface of his good humor, I pretended not to notice. We'd done what we could to prepare.

Now, we had to weather the storm.

CHAPTER 30

WE FOUND FAMINE trussed up like a Thanksgiving turkey on the floor of the living room. She lay face—down on the jute rug between the twin sofas, where the coffee table had once been, a centerpiece of evil and doom whose big button eyes reflected the light and heat of the flames in the fireplace.

She'd been divested of her Mary Janes, and toes on each foot wiggled through holes in her tights—Addie didn't allow people to wear shoes in her house, in spite of the occasional Apocalypse—related exceptions. The hem of Famine's navy blue dress was ripped. Scratches and dried blood peppered her hands like mysterious Morse code, and the magic that held her wrists together dug into the skin.

The whole household formed a loose circle around her with the exception of those who wielded the strongest magic. Lucifer guarded the front door. Michael hovered near the kitchen, guarding the back. Malek perched on the arm of the sofa that faced Red and I, looming over Famine like the predator he was.

Famine had never been anyone's prey.

Luna leaned against the opposite sofa arm, her back to us. She wore Amy's sheath, a ribbon of leather down the length of her spine, with War—Amy—tucked inside. The sword's hilt seemed to lean forward over Luna's left shoulder. Listening. Watching. Waiting.

Sunday stood behind the sofa, at Luna's right flank. She braced one hand against the sofa's back. With the other, she played with the ends of Luna's hair. I couldn't help—and didn't hide—the smile that bloomed on my lips.

Sunday glanced over her shoulder at my approach. She looked happy.

"What took you so long?" she asked.

I didn't get a chance to answer.

Famine took a deep breath, her voice full of exasperation. "Oh, good. The boss is here."

I glanced at Beth, who, along with Stacy, had pulled out a couple of Addie's dining room chairs to sit on. "She just showed up?"

Beth straddled her seat, arms folded on top of the chair back. "Said she was drawn here and couldn't fight it, like something physically picked her up and transported her here from one of her hells. She'd just trapped someone and was all hopped up on their pain and fear, but we tore her away and she didn't get to finish feeding. She doesn't want to be here blah blah. She's not going to cooperate blah blah. We can all go fuck ourselves with something hot and sharp blah blah. That about sum it up?"

Famine snarled.

Beth nodded. "Yep, that's it."

Red gazed at Famine as if she were a dangerous animal. He was right to, because she was. A cornered, dangerous animal.

He took my hand in his and lifted it to his lips. "Do what you need to, Night."

I understood that he didn't just mean in this moment, with Famine. He meant from here on out. I pulled his hand toward me, mirroring his kiss before I let go.

While he took his place in the circle, I made my way toward Famine and squatted in front of her so she could meet my gaze. Her eyes blazed with rage and hate, both of which I expected. But something else glinted behind them. Something human. That surprised me.

"Why are you here?" I asked.

"She told you."

Uh—huh. "I don't believe a word of it. No one compels you. I'd wager not even the End could make you do something you don't want to."

She raised a brow. "Are you trying to flatter me? I really hope not. You should know better."

I scoffed. "Please."

"Then what?"

"I'm being practical. Going with what I know about you person-ally. What Beth has shared. I think I'm on the money." I leaned closer, lowering my voice. "What do you want?"

She didn't answer. "This is her fault."

Her, meaning Beth. "What'd she do to you?"

She deflected again. "You could force your way in to my mind. You could take that information. So, why ask?"

"You're right. I could."

"Why?" she demanded.

"I'll get the answer out of you one way or the other."

She flashed a half—grin, half—grimace of triumph.

"But if you don't give it freely, it doesn't mean a thing."

Her smile faltered, then her expression shifted so fast, I might think I'd imagined it. "I could tell you anything. I could make you believe anything."

That was her magic. What she did. She understood what people hungered for and gave it to them. I had no illusions that she could find a way to harm me, but I had a couple of things going for me that most of her victims didn't—extensive experience with mind magic, exten-sive experience with Horsemen of the Apocalypse, and a new, sting-ing, unflinching knowledge of my own strengths and challenges.

"You probably could," I said. "But I'm not easy to hold."

She came back as if each word hurt her to say. "I'm here because I'm supposed to be. Because there are four of us and we're supposed to be here together. We're supposed to do something, and I don't want to do it, but it's my goddamn purpose. It's the only reason I'm alive in this miserable goddamn world. So fuck you for existing and fuck the others, too."

Finally, an honest reason. "We need you, Famine."

"To take the Apocalypse forward."

"To stop it."

"And then what? We're just supposed to go on like we were before? More of the same?"

That was the hope, but the truth was more complicated. "I don't know."

"What's that mean?"

"Means whatever we do will change the course of destiny, or fate— whatever you want to call it."

She mulled that over. "So, whatever we end up with, it won't be the same as it is now."

"We can choose."

"Best we can." I watched thoughts flicker in her eyes, the glow and fade of possibility.

"You know I want the world—all the worlds—to end. You know you can't trust me."

"That doesn't change anything."

She stared at me in wonder. "You'd take that chance?"

We didn't have much choice if we wanted to keep the worlds from being destroyed in fire—that was my thinking, my family's thinking. Famine didn't operate with the same motivation. To her, letting the worlds burn was a real option. Taking a chance on her, trusting her even an inch farther than we could throw her, risked so much. If she were in our shoes, she would never consider it. She'd welcome the flames.

For the first time, I glanced up at Luna, her dark eyes rimmed with the bright green of her Horseman. She nodded.

A cacophony of whispering voices rose like a flood in my mind, coalescing into a single voice that was Amy's and not—Amy's. I looked at the hilt of the sword at Luna's shoulder. It seemed to meet my gaze, silver glinting.

I had their answers, and I knew my own. "Yes."

"Shit."

I waited for her to attack. To surrender.

She exhaled, the tension flowing out of her body as she stopped fighting the Malek's magical bonds.

I looked at him. "Let her go."

He raised a brow.

I held his gaze, steady and sure.

He licked his thumb, then rubbed it against a spot on Famine's arm —dissolving a drop of blood. The bonds faded, but Famine didn't— couldn't—move.

Malek signed. *It'll take a while to fade.*

"How long?" I asked.

Half an hour.

That would give us all time to get used to the idea of working together—or not. It would give us time to prepare the ritual to connect us.

If I could get away with asking Beth and Malek to take Famine to the basement, set her up so she was comfortable, and let her know what we were about to do, I'd ask in a heartbeat.

Instead, I sighed. "Creating the magical connection the way we need to means not just the usual suspects, but everyone assembled here, including Famine."

Rude whistled. "That puts all of us at serious risk."

Famine bristled. "What kind of connection is this?"

Beth answered. "The kind that allowed us to kick your ass before."

Stacy rose from her seat beside Beth, moving through the circle to join me in front of Famine. She knelt and sat back on her heels. Her blond curls shone in the firelight like a proverbial angel's halo.

"The witch," Famine said.

"The connection is my spell. It ties us together psychically, physi- cally, magically. We're still individuals, but we can also access each others thoughts, memories, feelings, skills, power. We're ourselves, but we're also one."

"Kumbaya." Famine smirked.

"Normally, you wouldn't get an invitation to the party. Normally, if Night so much as suggested this bananas bullshit plan, I'd have told her where and how to go fuck herself. But, since we're at the end of the road, I can't do that." Stacy flashed me the kind of side—eye that telegraphed every kind of bodily harm she wished on me before focusing again on Famine. "Still, I won't put my friends and family in harm's way if I don't have to."

"Spell it out, Witch."

"I'm giving everyone here the opportunity to lock you out if they feel like it's necessary."

"Do I get the same option?" Famine asked.

Stacy shook her head.

"That's rude."

"It's what you deserve—as far as I'm concerned, you're the enemy until you prove you're not. Self—preservation against an enemy is SOP. You'll get as much trust as any one of us wants to give you."

After a moment, Famine nodded.

Beth stood. "I'll take her downstairs."

"Not by yourself." Lucifer stepped forward.

Malek waved her off. *We've got this.*

Beth mouthed her thanks to Lucifer, then busied herself gathering Famine's immobile body into a moveable package. She and Malek took Famine downstairs the way I'd envisioned to begin with.

Leaving me at the head of a circle of magical power. All eyes were on me.

"Anybody have a problem with this?"

Kevin snorted, a very un—King—like sound. "Even if we did, it's a little late in the game to change course. What do y'all need from us?"

"Backup, the same as when Luna and I slipped into Amy's mind. We'll need a container, and we'll need as much juice and power as you can give us. Any knowledge or insights that come to you. Roads forward that might appear as we work—in case we need to change course."

"You really think you can appease God?" he asked.

"I haven't been thinking of it like that." I never did, actually. One, because I didn't believe in one God, I believed in many Powers. And, two, appeasement was a temporary solution to a permanent problem.

"If this being and all its followers are determined that this Apocalypse will happen, that's a lot of power to fight against."

I shook my head.

But it was Michael who spoke first. "I'm here with you. On your side."

Kevin nodded. "That's great, man. But what about Gabriel? What about the others?"

Luna shivered. She'd been a normal before Gabriel found her and gifted her with magic her body couldn't handle. He'd turned her entire existence inside out.

"Gabriel follows his own rules," Michael said. "He'll make his own choice, and so will all the others."

Kevin shot sarcasm like bullets from a gun. "We just have to hope they'll make the right choice."

Michael cocked his head. "You talk as if hope is a bad thing."

"It's a pipe dream."

"No."

The word reverberated so strongly, it shook the art on the walls, knocking family photos from the mantle behind me. The glass in the frames cracked as they struck the floor.

Michael continued. "Hope is what allows you to get out of bed in the morning. It's the lift you feel when you gaze at the sunrise, at blue sky, or at falling rain in the midst of a drought. It's the hand that reaches to help you up when you don't believe you can take one more breath, beat back one more assault, stand one more moment of heartbreak. Hope takes despair by the throat. Hope opens the door for love and connection. Hope is sacred. Holy. Mark my words, and never forget them."

Kevin blinked at the archangel. "Thank you, cousin."

Ben's deep voice filled the room. "Cousin?"

Kevin took a deep breath. "Faeries are the angels within the earth."

"And faeries are cousins to humans," Stacy said. "Our closest relations among magical beings."

Those words sparked a different kind of hope. Most of us spent a lot of time considering our differences, but not the ways we were related. We might be different from each other, with different priorities, motivations, and powers, but we weren't strangers to one another. We were family in every way that counted.

Michael looked at me, a question in his fiery eyes.

I asked it for him. "Are we together?"

Luna reached for my hand, twining her fingers with mine. One by one, the others followed suit, forming an unbroken chain.

Together, we were strong. Together, we had a chance.

CHAPTER 31

POWER HUMMED IN the walls. In the concrete underfoot. It reverberated through flesh and blood and bone, singing along my skin. The basement held our entire army, the protections strengthened by everyone present in the circle, bolstering the house spirit's magic and creating an unreachable container for our own.

The usual chill I felt down here had fled in the face of so much body heat, not to mention the raw, electric, air—bending energy Michael and Lucifer exuded. I breathed in for a four—count, tasting scorched air, and breathed out for a count of six. Slowing myself down inside took the edge off my nerves. It let me focus, listen, sense.

The basement was silent. Beneath the quiet, it was a goddamn cacophony of stray thought, worry, and dread.

In order to facilitate the spell Stacy was about to cast, I had to open my mind, blurring the boundaries between my thoughts and the others'. Married with the nuances of body language, facial expressions, and the shifting colors of halos, everyone in the room opened like a book before me.

I didn't want to know all the details I picked up. Too bad for me.

Red stood opposite me, on the other side of the circle. The heart link between us pulsed strong, a source of calm in the gathering storm. He'd meant every word he said to me in bed—he was hellbent on following me into the maelstrom, and he didn't care what it cost him. He watched me like a hawk, every sense tuned to me as I tuned to him. If I tried to ditch him—if I tried to do anything to keep him safe at my own expense—he'd know before I acted. He'd stop me. He'd stand with me.

Sunday leaned against him, poking a friendly elbow in to his ribs. "C'mon, Jenkins. Take a breath before you turn blue."

"Fuck off, Sloan."

She grinned at that, but the smile didn't reach her eyes. She was as brittle as Red, and as keyed up as before she and Luna went to bed. She wanted—no, needed—a fight. She felt torn between making sure she covered my six at all costs and making sure my daughter was safe.

So what if Faith carried a god? So what if she should be indestructible? She was still my kid. She'd always be that, no matter how powerful she became or how old she grew. If I worried about her, I couldn't focus on doing my job. The other Horsemen had parts to play, but as far as Sunday was concerned everything depended on me.

On Red's other side, Faith held hands with Corey, their grips so tight, their knuckles bleached white. Corey's bone—white halo blazed with inner fire. I could practically see the shadows of the dead all around her—around all of us—as she called them to guard us. More of them gathered around Faith than anyone else because Corey willed it so.

I met her solid gaze, nodding approval and sending her love and strength. Then I focused on Faith, slipping into her mind.

She didn't wait to hear what I meant to say. *You got this, Mom. The Awakened and I will do whatever we need to. We'll keep everyone safe, so don't worry.*

The Awakened might have other plans. If it did, it hadn't yet enlightened Faith. I'd have to trust it and her. And I'd have to respect that almost everyone in this circle held the others' safety as their priority. That was what we did for each other.

I love you, I said.

Love you, too. Do what you need to. I'm here.

I pulled away gently, bringing my awareness to the Horsewomen who stood beside me. Famine to my right, fidgeting like a small child on the last day of school. And, to her right, Luna and Pestilence, with the War sword that had swallowed Amy in its sheath on her back.

Famine whispered for our ears alone. "This had better work."

Luna smirked. "It'll work, or it'll blow up. Either way, we'll be all right."

I swallowed hard. "But the rest of the world—all the worlds— might not."

A ringing in my head, like bells on a clear, cold day, telegraphed Amy's agreement.

Famine shook her head to clear it. "If it doesn't work, I'm going to make all of you sorry."

"Eyes on the prize. You can plot your revenge later." Luna glanced at me from the corner of her eye.

On my left, Ben cleared his throat. "If you all are the saviors of the rest of us, we're screwed."

I looked at him, at his stone gray halo, the shock of dark hair that hid half his face, the mirth that shone in the one gray eye that I could see. "You always were the smart one."

Beside him, Jess rolled her eyes. Tendrils of hair had fallen loose from her bun. Every star in her halo pulsed. "I'm the smart one. He gets it from me."

Ben and Jess. Corey and Faith. They were all my kids. A few months and a million years ago, before Sunday and the Angel of Death came to town, they trusted me to coach them. Teach the how to be comfortable in their own skin, to be strong.

Ben slipped his hand into mine and squeezed.

The silence grew thicker. No one broke it.

Stacy took that as a signal, tucking her blond curls behind her ears, her blue eyes downcast and hidden by thick lashes. Addie handed her a broom from the corner of the basement, just an ordinary cleaning instrument. But in Stacy's hands, the wooden handle glowed.

She walked the circumference of our circle, sweeping away not dirt, but every bit of energy that might break our concentration or hold back the work. If it didn't serve right here and now, we would leave it behind. When she finished, she leaned the broom against the far wall and spoke a word of power that turned the broom straw to cinders.

Dot every I. Cross every T. Take no chances.

She made her way to the center of the circle, skirt rustling as she sank down, pressing her forehead against the floor. After a moment, she rose, stretching her arms toward the ceiling. Simple gestures, but I saw the power within them as she anchored all of us to this space and time, to the earth beneath the house and the sky above.

Malek, Michael, and Lucifer stepped into the center with her, the four of them joining hands and taking a long breath together. Stacy's indigo halo expanded, its edges shifting and changing, becoming deep blue flame as the angels passed power to her. Then Malek closed the small distance between himself and Stacy, grazing his bottom lip with his teeth hard enough to draw blood. He bent toward her, planting a red kiss on her forehead. The smear of blood soaked into her pale skin in a split second. She closed her eyes, rocking back and forth with the power of it. When she looked out again, the whites of her eyes had turned crimson.

She let go of the angels and Malek and made her way around the circle, beginning at my left, with Ben. Her witch's magic, augmented by the power shared with her, wove a web with every step, every touch, every word. Unlike those she'd crafted before, this one burned everything and everyone she touched.

She bound us Horsemen last. Luna. Amy. Me.

From the moment she drew me in to the web, I could not only hear the others' thoughts and feel what they felt, I could touch their magic and instinctively know how to channel it. All of that was familiar. What was different? The strength of the connection. It's depth. And the fact that, before, Stacy's connective spells had lasted a while before fading. This one wasn't meant to fade. I understood that in my gut and in my bones.

This one would last for always. Only death could sever it.

I shivered.

Stacy tied a knot in the web, a pulse point that could act as a both a connector and a block. If she or any one of us had to sever the web in this place, we could do it without adversely affecting the rest of the group.

Finally, Stacy, turned to Famine. "You agreed to this."

Famine nodded.

"You want this."

"Yes."

"I bind you to your word, Famine. I bind your vessel as well."

Famine furrowed her brow.

Stacy spoke a name I'd never heard. "Tate Rosen."

Famine's eyes widened. "Tate Rosen is dead."

"You're wearing her skin. You absorbed her soul. She's not dead. She lives inside you, however deeply buried."

"How can you know that?" Famine asked.

It wasn't a stretch, not with the assembled power and knowledge in the room, from the very young to beings who'd existed since the beginning of time. Someone here held that knowledge, and now the rest of us did, too.

It took a moment for Famine to come around to that realization on her own. She sighed. "Get on with it."

Stacy touched a finger to her forehead, smoothing the lines, bringing her in to the web.

Famine's jaw dropped. "Damn."

It was the last word I heard before the world around me turned fuzzy and gray. Before the floor seemed to tilt underfoot. Before I tipped forward, unable to raise my hands or arms to break the fall.

The silence erupted in voices and sounds—hands on my back and shoulders and wings, shouts and screams, the thud of feet.

The world inside me imploded. Magic rushed in, searching for adversaries. Hunting for traps. Healing energy built and built, because it had nowhere to go.

Feathers fluttered around my heart.

· · ·

THIRTY—TWO

I MET MALEK's GAZE. I READ THE QUESTION IN HIS EYES A heartbeat before the binding he'd used to trap the Angel unraveled.

It snaked and whipped like a cord under too much tension. It scarred every place it struck. It sank venom into my magic. My blood. My bones, skin, and heart.

My soul.

The world tilted again—someone turned my body over, onto my back. A kaleidoscope of blurry faces invaded my vision. Details sharpened, then faded. Hands touched me. I felt no connection to them.

The Angel's consciousness slammed into mine, overrunning and overwhelming. My heart stopped. My lungs seized.

Sparks rained down all around me. I tasted burnt fabric and burnt skin as air flowed across my tongue. I knew it had to be Faith and her god. Their magic, trying to break through to me.

I felt a pull in my blood. Michael, whose blood ran in my veins, trying to open a door in our shared DNA. Trying to reach me.

The heart link between Red and I drew taught. A flood of emotions washed over me. I could feel none of them. I couldn't even name them.

The center of my heart turned to ice.

That, I felt. The pins—and—needles tingle of blood—infused flesh sliding from quivering and alive to sluggish and choking. There was no oxygen. No spark.

Only death.

The killing ice spread like a wildfire, taking my entire heart, pouring into my veins. Building in my lungs. Stealing every breath of life and replacing it with the chill of the grave.

My body heat bled into the cold concrete. Every last speck of warmth fled. The cold settled in. Frost. Numbness.

Red tried again, reaching for me through the heart link. His touch seared. Scorched. My mouth opened wide.

Still, I grasped and slipped and staggered toward him through the link. I couldn't get close enough.

The heart link cracked like ice ripped away from its home, plunging into the freezing sea.

I tried to scream. I had no air. I made no sound.

Red fell. I couldn't see or hear him. I couldn't feel him. But I knew. I knew he'd given everything to hold on to me. He held nothing back. He'd emptied himself of all his love—and all his life force. And when he fell, he hit the concrete dead and gone.

The last warmth in my body clawed up my spine. Into my throat. It hissed into my mouth, a raw and bloody scream of anguish that made no sound at all.

A hole opened inside me. A bottomless pit of grief and despair and longing for heat and life and love. *La Muerte* needed what he could not have. What he could never have.

I understood then, because I had no choice but to wrap what remained of my mind around what he was.

He was the dark and cold. Breaker of the bond between body and soul. Reaper of souls.

He had a function in this and all the worlds. He'd been created to fulfill that function. Only to do that thing.

But he wanted more. He needed more.

Because all the billions of times he'd reaped the dead, he'd taken not only their souls to guide them to what came next, he'd taken on their hopes and dreams. Their loves and losses. Their unfulfilled purposes. Their wants. Their needs.

They'd become his, too. They'd become the bottomless longing inside him.

This Apocalypse—this destruction—was his chance to create a new world. New *worlds*. Where he could become something else. Something different. Where he could fill the aching need inside him.

That was what he was. That was what I'd been fighting all these months. What I'd taken inside myself, bit by bit. What I'd compromised with. Finally, what I'd joined with.

I thought I'd won every battle. That I'd grasped victory from the jaws of defeat. Saved my family's lives. Saved the world.

And I had. But I'd also lost, because there was no way in any world, any timeline, for me to fight this. To fight him, and win.

I'd thought he was on our side. My side. But he'd infected me, piece by piece. I'd taken control for granted. I'd hurt people. Done things I couldn't say I was sorry for or take back. I'd come around to the truth too late. I'd made us vulnerable.

Mi abuelita, as powerful and ancient as she was. Michael. Lucifer. Malek. My family. The other Horsemen.

The binding spell should have made us stronger together. It always had before. Now, it made us easy prey.

The Angel of Death used the bond Stacy had forged for us, the web of connection, to drag my family down. He drew them into himself. Gathered their consciousness. Their magic. Their skills. Their thoughts, hopes, dreams, and desires.

He left them as empty as he was. Cold. Needful.

One by one they fell.

My frozen heart cracked. I drew no breath. Physically, I felt nothing at all as the Angel moved my limbs. He raised us up on our elbows. Pushed us to standing. But my heart—

I blinked as my sight cleared.

The basement looked as if a magical bomb had detonated. The Angel and I were ground zero.

The rug and colorful pillows had been shredded, crimson fabric splattered all over the concrete like smeared blood and down feathers suspended in the air like snowflakes. Bodies lay everywhere—human, fae, elder, angel.

Chests rose and fell—except Red's.

My heart did more than crack—it shattered. Even as it broke into a thousand shards, the Angel wove it back together.

My legs buckled. The Angel refused to let me fall.

I stumbled toward Faith. Shoved the Angel out of the way just long enough to check for a pulse.

It was too fast and thready, but it was there. She breathed. Her heart beat. She lived. They all did—except my love.

My family wasn't dead and gone. Not yet. But they would be soon. No one could live for long the way we'd left them.

La Muerte didn't care. They were a means to his end, just as I was.

The house spirit pushed against us. I wanted to cry out for help, but what could it do for me?

I managed a single thought. A single prayer.

Help them.

Before I could speak another word, or feel guilt or shame or fear, the Angel took my voice. He wiped my emotions off the map. No feelings reached the center of my cold heart.

The Angel spread our wings with a sound like thunder and *moved* us through space and time towards our destiny.

CHAPTER 32

W E LANDED ON concrete. A familiar sidewalk, even in the dark. The ghosts of strong coffee and fresh bread mixed with the taste of cold rain that soaked us to the skin. Wind gusted from the east, carrying the memories of ice and snow from the Columbia River Gorge into the heart of the city, whipping our hair into a nest of snakes.

To our right, parked cars huddled against the curves of the neighborhood street. On our left, the traffic lights turned from red to green, the rain—slicked asphalt reflecting the color like a mirror—until a sparse, midnight wave of cars split the mirage.

We folded our wings tight against our back and pressed our hands against the glass door of Justice Gym, flexing scaps and lats, drawing shadows all around us, making us invisible to all but the most discerning eyes.

The paper sign taped to the door chilled me further. I hadn't thought that possible, but I was wrong.

Closed Due To Family Emergency

I knew what night this was. Which wee hours of the morning held us close.

I saw clearly. Our reflection in the glass. Skin, turned from warm brown to pale and frostbitten. Eyes, from brown to white. Hair, too—from black to the color of fresh snow. I looked like a Gorgon, like Medusa. Like a goddess with one purpose only—to turn every living, beating heart to stone.

The Angel had control. He pushed off the glass and opened the door. The rush of warm air from inside stung our skin. The outdoor scents gave way to rubber and cleaner and dirty socks and fear. One quick turn on our heels brought us face to face with someone who shouldn't have been here, because his body was back at Addie's house, in the basement with the others.

Ben sat on the sofa, his halo stony and fierce. A spell had him trapped. Motionless. But panic filled his gaze.

Deja vu washed over me so strongly, for a long moment the world seemed to be made of layers as thin as tissue paper. Then the feeling passed. The layers fluttered together and set as one, and I understood the look in Ben's eyes.

The Angel marched past him without another glance, turning toward the stairs and leading us down, past Red's office, into the well of the gym, where Addie and Sunday lay bound and as trapped in their bodies, as voiceless, as Ben. An Order operative lay dead beside them.

Faith stood stock still, facing the Night Sanchez of this timeline. This Night was quiet as death, a battle raging in her mind.

Deja vu struck again. This time, the world rearranged itself again in shorter order.

Nothing looked exactly the same as it had before, in my memory of this night. The night the Angel had taken over Faith, intending to make her his vessel, and I'd chosen a different path us all.

The Angel had brought us back to this moment, but not in the same timeline.

For a moment, confusion reigned, but then the differences became clear. I knew why he'd brought us here because he did. Even as I fought him for control—and lost—in every second, he couldn't hide that crucial information from me. We were one. That was a two—way street, no matter who took charge.

In this timeline, I wasn't as strong as in my own. In this timeline, the battle between *La Muerte* and I was closer. I still won. I still imprisoned him within my mind, as I had in every timeline. But here, the odds could be tipped in his favor. He only needed a push. A little extra edge. And we were here to give it to him.

The Night of this timeline didn't notice us. How could she? Every ounce of her will and magic focused on battling the Angel in her mind.

A strangled sound interrupted the silence. The Angel and I turned to glance over our shoulder and caught a glimpse of Red. His mouth hung open, eyes wide. The scent of grass and earth overpowered all others.

Corey wasn't with him this time. He stood alone.

I couldn't say a word. I could feel a thing. I could only think the progression of emotions that wanted to rise within me. Soul—deep relief. So much love, it overflowed every barrier that tried to hold it back. I needed Red to see those things in my eyes. But he couldn't, because the Angel had locked us down.

The sacred heart inked on Red's chest began to glow. He raised his hands to push that magic toward us.

La Muerte rifled through the magic we carried and constructed a hasty shield woven from Michael's protective fire and my mind magic. A pale precaution the Angel shouldn't need, but always better safe than sorry. Better to keep Red occupied while we entered the battle here and turned it into our victory.

Red shoved his power at us, the flood of compassion and warmth melting the edges of the Angel's ice.

La Muerte's turn to panic—because in our own timeline, Red's magic shouldn't have been able to touch his. The Red in this timeline shouldn't have been able to do any of this at all.

Red pushed harder, forcing the Angel to turn and face him. Giving him—and me—a full—on view of the power he wielded, the strength of his magic. The knowledge in his eyes.

I trembled inside, shaking in my depths as the Angel redirected his magic toward Red.

My Red.

Not just the one from this timeline, but the one from ours, their souls entwined, their magic more than doubled, two separate minds and hearts and wills, woven into one. He'd promised to follow me no matter what it took. Nothing would hold him from keeping that promise.

Not even death.

I heard his voice inside my head, part of the magical web. I shouldn't have been able to—he shouldn't have been able to beat the Angel's will. But he did.

I heard him, loud and clear.

If you fall, I'll catch you.

CHAPTER 33

THE ANGEL GATHERED his magic—and mine—to strike.

Red marked the change, backpedaling, sneakers catching on the black rubber mats underfoot. He stumbled, but caught his balance before he went over. The grass and earth scent of his magic grew stronger, the glow of the sacred heart on his chest brighter. He stepped back again, putting distance between the Angel and himself. And between the Angel and the people we loved—Faith, Sunday, Addie.

A loud thud shook the floor up on the landing. Ben had found a way to roll off the sofa. But he couldn't stand. Couldn't make his way down to help us.

I sensed him fighting—not just the Ben of this timeline, but the Ben from mine, waging war inside my head against the Angel. Giving it everything he had, ripping his goddamn spirit from his physical body in the process. Killing himself in the other timeline to bring all of himself right here. Right now.

I drew a shaky breath—an impossible breath—into frozen lungs that shouldn't be able to expand. But they did, because the Angel couldn't maintain complete control any longer.

Ben wasn't the only one who joined the battle. Who made the leap from the other timeline to this one.

One by one, they came. Faith and Corey. Jess and Addie. Beth and Malek. Kevin and Rude. Sunday and Dream. Michael and Lucifer.

Luna and Amy and even Famine.

The Angel staggered, taking us down to our knees. We struck the mat hard, sending shockwaves along our spine. The Angel snapped our wings

I dragged another breath into my lungs. My heart met that breath with a slow, single beat.

I tasted sand and salt and water. Heard *mi abuelita*'s voice as I'd heard Red's.

You're the only one who can do this, nena.

After hers, Faith's. *We trust you, Mom.*

And Sunday's. *Got your six.*

They gave their all so I could fight for them—for us all. I would give nothing less.

My magic rose against the Angel's will. I drew it forth like a whirl-wind from my icy pores, darkening the air behind us to midnight black, as thick and dark as any moonless night. I let it carry all of me —all my thoughts, feelings, experiences, skill, knowledge. Everything that made me who I was. I rode the darkness like an arrow, straight into the Night that belonged to this timeline.

I slipped into her mind on a sharp point and a prayer, shoring up her magic, filling in the holes behind her. Letting her know in no uncertain terms that I was on her side.

I felt familiar, but not the same as her. I knew what she didn't yet understand—what would come to pass. The decisions she'd make to save her people. The sacrifices. The risks.

The Angel in her mind, months younger than mine, marked my presence with alarm.

Night Sanchez—the one who'd only just come clean to Faith about the death of Faith's parents, who'd been forced to kill an Order opera-tive, who'd raced to the gym not knowing what awaited her—embraced me utterly.

She opened her magic to mine. Her consciousness to mine. Her will to mine. We wove together as if it were meant to be.

She shuddered as her power expanded. As her awareness grew.

The Angel in her mind tried to escape. To exit her mind.

We held him in.

He turned and ran through the corridors of her mind.

In my timeline, he'd dragged me kicking and screaming through dusty hallways, my shoes scraping on the concrete, to the door behind which I'd locked the one memory I feared most. In this timeline, we gave chase, because we knew he couldn't break us. Not like that.

We were faster together. Smarter.

When the Angel swung open the iron door that held our most haunting memory, he skidded short, stretching his wings to keep from plowing forward.

He'd expected the little girl with wide doe eyes, face ghostly pale, long, black hair pulled into a painfully tight braid that flowed to her waist. He expected her in pink pajama tank splashed with red hearts and little pink shorts, with finger—shaped bruises striping her skinny arms. He expected her bare feet to shrink from the cold stone floor of the dark room where she'd lived for endless years among dust and cobwebs.

Instead, he got us.

We filled the doorway, stronger than he could imagine.

He whispered a question. The words reverberated off the stone walls.

Who are you?

CHAPTER 34

S URRENDER, we said.

The Angel stepped back from the iron door. He exhaled frost, then met our gaze and held it. *You don't belong here.*

Neither do you.

He was the invader. He was the emptiness that could never be filled. He wanted to destroy the world as we knew it, to change it forever into something unrecognizable. We refused to allow that.

The tips of his wings scratched the corridor walls, dislodging dust and crumbling stone. He went still, and for a moment, we thought he might actually back down, but he seemed to grow taller and wider, as if he were a puzzle whose missing pieces finally found home.

The Night of this timeline sucked in a breath. *What—*

La Muerte had merged with his counterpart, the same as we had. *The Angel from my timeline is with him.*

She measured their strength against ours. We were closely matched again. Too close. We could fight. We might win. We might lose. And the balance of all the worlds was the prize.

I spared an anguished thought for my family—the ones this Night knew, and those she had yet to meet. My Angel had overpowered them. How badly were they hurt? Were they dead? What about Red?

I was the only one who could beat the Angel. They trusted me. They had my back. They counted on me. I'd fight until my light went out for good. I'd take the Angel with me. I didn't care whether he was impossible to kill. I'd met too many Powers, none of them invincible. If I couldn't lay the Angel low, I could break him. I had to, for my family. For all the families of blood and choice. For all the people. All the beings in all the worlds.

Rage rose in me, a hard, cold fire. It threatened to sweep every other thought and feeling away. To take over. I wanted to let it, because that fire would carry us through. It was the only way to be sure.

My twin pulled me just back from the brink. *Can we do this again? Jump timelines? Find another Night to join with?*

Every instinct in her cried out to do just that. To build on what we had. She wasn't ready to give up her life—not if it could be saved. She could make different choices, now that she knew where my road had led. She'd do it better. She'd succeed where I'd failed.

Except for one crystal clear fact: as many Nights as we joined with, as many different circumstances, skills, experiences, and gifts as we accumulated, the Angel would follow suit. We had no idea how many timelines existed, or how many our actions here or elsewhere might birth into being. We could fight forever. We could win in one reality and lose in another.

If we wanted to keep our world, we needed to finish this here.

What if we can't? Keep our world?

What if any one choice we made now changed everything else forever? That was the question. Because it would. There was no way around that. We couldn't know what our actions would create. We could only do our best—just like we'd done every single time until this moment—and deal the cards fate dealt us.

I thought of Dream. Our memories of her. All the bad, and all the good. As much as the Order had raised us, she had, too. The choices we'd made to walk away, to save Faith, to make a stand with the people who mattered to us—those decisions had been borne of who we were, down deep at our core. The family we'd built. The love we carried inside us.

Those were a thousand times more powerful than rage. A million times more meaningful than any revenge we could take.

We learned our lesson, Night said.

We'd taken to the Order because it offered us vengeance for the lot life had forced on us. For the magic. For the deaths of our parents. For the shame and horror we'd endured. In the end, it'd destroyed us.

We'd broken apart. We should've died. Instead, the souls of our victims had put us back together. Granted us the second chance that allowed us to love. They'd thought we were worth that risk.

I took a deep breath and blew it out slowly. *It's our job to pay their gift forward.*

What do you mean?

I started to answer, but in the end didn't need to. She followed my thoughts. She understood every word—and she began to shake from the inside out.

Not that. Please.

She was afraid. She had every right to be.

I can't ask you to do this with me, I said. And I meant it. If I had to do it on my own, I would. I'd find a way. I always did.

I waited.

You're not me, she said. *You have no right. This is my life. Mine.*

She held the high ground. Nothing I could say would make this okay.

You took me over, just like the Angel wants to.

I couldn't argue the point. I'd done what was needed, nothing less and nothing more.

It's not fair.

It'd never been. Never would be. Bargaining wouldn't change that.

I could kill you.

She could try. And while we fought, the Angel would emerge victorious. I couldn't help my Faith—not any of my family, not anymore. But I could help hers, and all the others out there.

She closed her eyes, shutting me out for a long moment. I felt the movement of her thoughts. The sway of her emotions. She encompassed my intention. Looked for every possible way out. She was methodical. Professional. Practical. She searched high and low. Found no other choice that made sense.

Without sorrow for the future lost—but no hesitation—she steeled her spine and her will.

I'll follow your lead.

It was more than I'd hoped for. And more than anyone should have to give.

CHAPTER 35

MAGIC FLOODED US, aching against the boundaries of our skin. The air around the Angel froze as he prepared to fight. The battlefield was set. Each of us meant the first strike to be the last.

The Angel lunged forward, drawing his wings close as he sailed across the threshold, then snapping them wide as he barreled toward us. The rush of ice he pushed before him frosted our lashes. Our skin. It sank deep, burrowing into our flesh and blood.

He tackled us to the stone floor. Stole our breath. He wrapped his wings around us, plunging us all in to darkness.

Feathers turned to stone, locking us in. Silence descended. We were alone with the Angel of Death. There was no way out—not for us, and not for him.

We sent out a call. Slippery magic. Assassin's magic. The kind of power that slid between the bars of guarded gates, searching for the smallest weakness. This time, we looked for the mirror reflection of ourselves—no, myself.

Not Red or Faith or Sunday. Not those we held dearest.

We called to the other Horsemen.

If only I could beat the Angel, only the four of us could stop the Apocalypse.

La Muerte knew exactly what we did. He sent tendrils of ice and death after our magic. Hunting it down. Cornering it. Smashing what he could. Always, the smallest signal escaped, showering sparks of light into his shadows. Hooking into his deepest fears. Following them to the one iron door he didn't want us to find.

He pushed hard, demanding with every fiber of his being that it remain closed. We pulled, digging into cracks and crevices, fingers coming away smashed and bloody. Still, we dug.

On the other side of the door, my sisters put their shoulders—and their magic—into the game. They shoved and carved and fought and slammed over and over again into the door of their prison until the hinges squealed and the iron moved.

They needed only an inch to take it all. We gave them that.

They poured out of the cage and turned to stand with us. Luna, with the sword War no longer in its sheath, but in her hand. It silver blade gleamed in the darkness of the Angel's mind, the light coming from inside.

Famine shifted her weight from one Mary Jane to the other, unsure whether to hold or run. If I gave her a choice, she'd take option two. She'd leave us to fend for ourselves. She'd leave us to lose. To die.

We met her gaze. *If you don't help us now, you'll be a prisoner forever.*

It was that simple.

Her mouth twisted, but she stuck.

What's the play?

I didn't want to trust her with the knowledge, but refusing to tell her—refusing to take that chance—put everything we were about to do at risk.

He either takes what we have to offer, or we send him on his way. He can have peace, or he can have more millennia of suffering.

Luna kept her gaze trained on the Angel, but she spoke to us. *Night, you can't.*

We could and we would. But we needed something in return from her. From Amy. From Famine.

Stay, afterwards. Help us put things back together.

Luna nodded. The sword shone.

We turned to Famine.

What's in it for me?

Possibilities, we said. *Something new. It's up to you.*

Her eyes widened.

We turned to *La Muerte*. After all this time—after everything we'd been through—he struggled. He could still win, if he bided his time. Even if biding meant centuries upon centuries of waiting in misery, of unfulfilled longing, of new battles whose outcome couldn't be known.

Or he could lose. He could surrender, not knowing whether what we planned would be enough. Not knowing what the future held, or what it would mean.

He'd used me. He'd convinced me he was on my side. He'd kept my body and my family alive. He'd made me trust him. And then he'd betrayed me and mine. Why would I consent to do this for him? He didn't deserve it.

I couldn't speak for the Night of this timeline, but I knew in my heart that I hadn't deserved that chance. But then, it wasn't about what I deserved, was it? I'd needed it, and they'd given it. I couldn't ask for anything more than what grace had allowed me to receive. If it all had to come to an end now, so be it.

The Angel bowed his head.

Famine twined her fingers with mine. She placed a hand on Luna's back, behind her heart.

I reached out to Night, and she to me—but it was more than that. As our hearts beat, so did the hearts of all the Nights in all the worlds. As we breathed in, so did they. As we gathered our magic, as we concentrated it in the depths of our hearts—in the place that reflected all of who we were—so did they.

It was far more than I meant to have. I hadn't asked, but they consented. We felt it across every timeline. In our souls, and in every soul that mirrored our own.

There was no word of power to speak. No magic spell to weave. There was only our wish and our will, and none had ever been stronger.

We were the four Horsemen.

We were every Night. All of the darkness. All of the stars in the night sky, reflected on the calm surface of the sea. We belonged to ourselves, and to one another.

We held each other close across space and time.

Every Night—all of us—wished.

Our souls shattered.

A billion shards of light and life, remade and redeemed, streamed into the Angel of Death. They filled the cold with warmth. They banished shadows. They turned an unquenchable light on the feelings inside him that had known only darkness from the beginning of time.

The world—all the worlds—began to shift.

As the last of our light bled into *La Muerte*, what remained of his darkness rose up to meet us.

CHAPTER 36

I WOKE ON THE FLOOR, curled in the fetal position, black mats cushioning my weight, the perfume of the rubber in my nose and on the back of my tongue. I inhaled a shaky breath and exhaled shakier. My body ached like it never had before—not even after the worst of the beatings I'd taken in the name of saving lives or worlds. But my arms and legs answered the call to move, and I pushed myself to sitting, hands braced behind me.

My twin knelt at my side. She swept her gaze over my face, measuring both my expression and the strength of my halo. I knew not because I had a door into her thoughts, but because I knew the look.

"Your color's back," she said.

"No more white?"

She shook her head. "Everything's good and brown."

Thank all the Powers. "Your people?"

"They're all right. They're just"—she glanced over my head, toward the upstairs landing—"trying to get a handle on what happened. People don't drop in from other timelines every day. They're kind of freaked out."

"I would be, too."

Not would be, really—I was. I was just afraid to give those feelings free reign. If I did, I might never get them back under control.

She met my gaze. "The Angel of Death—he's still inside you, isn't he?"

I didn't feel him—not like I had before. But feathers fluttered around my heart. I nodded.

"Is it okay?"

"You mean, is he done trying to bring the Apocalypse?"

She waited.

I asked the question inside my mind, half—expecting an answer, and half—expecting only silence.

It's done, he said.

That was all.

"I think we're safe for a while."

She sighed, her relief a palpable thing.

I tried to stand on my own, but she wouldn't allow it. She helped me up and kept a hand at the small of my back until we were both sure my legs would hold. The gym—climbing ropes and kettlebells, racks and barbells and medicine balls—spun for a hot minute before the room settled again.

I was in no shape to travel between timelines. Between worlds. That didn't matter. "I need to get back."

"I know." She inclined her head toward the landing, her expression pained. "Addie's waiting for you to be ready. She said she can help."

"She doesn't like you."

"She thinks I'm better off dead."

"If things go the way they did for me—" I snapped my mouth shut.

"What?"

"Things won't go the way they did for me, because the worlds are different."

"But in your timeline, before, we worked it out?"

"Yeah." I looked at her, at her dark halo. At the reflection of my own face in her eyes. "Thank you."

"No need."

"There's every need."

"We did what needed to be done." She closed the sentence like closing a door.

Even if I felt I had more to say, I respected that. There was one other thing I had to ask.

She didn't give me the chance—just cocked a thumb over her shoulder. "Red's there."

I turned carefully in the direction she pointed to find Red leaning against the wall outside his office, arms folded across his chest. He looked at me as if I was a lifeline. I raised a hand to my heart, realizing belatedly that there was no link between us. Not with him. Not with my Red. The link was just…gone.

Night laid a hand on my shoulder. "You should talk to him. And you should know he asked to go back with you. Not to stay—at least not all of him. But there's a part of him that's yours that needs to return to your timeline. I'm good with that."

"You're sure?"

"I know what he means to you." She turned on her heel and marched past him, up the stairs.

I made my way to Red, surprised when he held out his hands for mine. I gave them to him, and he drew me close, burying his face in my shoulder. I wrapped my arms around him, pulling him so tight, he groaned.

He spoke low, for only me to hear. "You scared the shit out of me."

"I did? You fucking died." And he was still dead in our timeline. I could barely breathe at the thought of what I'd find when I returned. No, when *we* returned.

"We all did, but I don't think we have to stay that way."

I pulled away, framing his face with my hands. "I have all of you. The Angel and I."

He nodded. "How do you feel?"

"I'm afraid to feel."

"You're afraid to look at what you are now. You don't need to be. I can see it."

"But you're not gonna tell me."

His mouth quirked in a half—smile.

I closed my eyes, dropping my hands to his chest so I could feel his heartbeat. It steadied me, as did the burst of grass and earth that followed.

My power rose instantly, at the bare thought of magic. I let it wind its way toward my heart, staying one step behind, trying to match hope with fear. To stay balanced. To remain calm so that I could see what was true.

The center of my heart, the seat of my magic and the core of who I was, was not empty at all.

Fear fell away, and hope surged.

There was something new there, something raw and fragile and strong as hell all at once.

"What is that?" I asked.

"A new soul."

"Where did it come from?"

Red planted a kiss on my brow. "I have no idea. But we've got friends in high places. Maybe one of them did the deed."

"For all of us?"

"For all of you."

"I love you," I said.

"I love you, Night. Never doubt it."

"Never." My voice trembled. "We can go home now?"

He called over my shoulder. "Addie, we're ready."

She descended the stairs like a combination of cop and queen—exactly who and what she was. She came to a stop in front of us, resplendent in her purple velvet tunic and black leggings. She wore black riding boots and a halo so full of stars, I felt awe.

"I don't know you—not this version of you, anyway," she said. "But you've got to promise me something."

I stared at her.

"If things are well enough, leave well enough alone."

"That, I can do."

"Don't come back here to visit. One of you is plenty."

"That's two things," I said.

"So it is." She raised a brow.

"I can do that, too."

"All right, then. Mr. Jennings, hold her hand. Angel of Death?"

Another flutter of feathers around my heart signaled his attention. I spoke for him. "Present."

"Good. I want a cup of coffee and a piece of pie in my own damn kitchen. Let's get this done."

CHAPTER 37

THE ANGEL AND I spent the next three nights searching out the souls of our family and bringing them back into the bodies the house spirit had kept alive. The basement became a triage center, a familiar place for the newly returned to reacclimatize to being among the living once more.

Addie set up a mini—kitchen—coffee pot, snacks, a card table and chairs—and used her magic to heal hearts and minds. She helped open the way for the Angel and I to bring back Red, good as new, and to send the other one home to his own time and his own Night.

I thought people would start to head home once they got their feet under them, but every one of them stayed for the last piece of magic—even Famine.

The remains of the red rug and colored pillows had been swept up and tossed, so the basement was nothing but bare concrete and protective enchantments, the comforting scent of fabric softener and the soft tumble of towels in the dryer the best music.

We stood in the same order, in the same circle as before. The moment we joined hands, the web Stacy's magic had built between us reconnected, although this time more gently. We weren't here for war.

We were here for peace. If we were unlucky, for thousands of years. If luck stuck with us, forever.

Famine, Luna, War, and I created a second circle in the center, the human—bodied among us holding hands, with Luna and me grasping the hilt of the sword.

Before we could speak a word of release, the Angel's voice bloomed in my mind.

I owe you.

I shook my head. *We're square.*

Without you—what you did—we wouldn't be here.

Alive, healthy, happy. *You can't pay me back.*

There was no way to repay a second chance like the one the other Nights and I had been given so many years ago, or the one we'd given him.

I can pay it forward.

Yes. You'll know who, and how, and when. I had faith in that. And, surprisingly, in him.

If you need me—

I'll call.

I'll come.

I heard no lie there, only truth. And then nothing, because there was nothing left to say.

The release took us all to the floor, bodies shifting and changing, feathers molting and muscles smoothing themselves back into human shapes and sizes. War clattered to the concrete floor, sparking a burst of flame that resolved into a human shape as well—Amy, naked as the day she was born, but whole and hale. I thanked all the Powers for that.

I wrapped her in my arms for a brief moment, before Shadow rushed in and pulled her close.

One by one, the others drifted out of the protections and upstairs. We slept under the same roof that night—those of us who slept, or could sleep.

But not me. Wrapped I a blanket, I wandered in to the kitchen after midnight and poured myself a cup of coffee to take out to the front porch. I settled by myself in the rocking chair, blanket tight against the summer night chill.

The scents of lavender and rosemary found me, and the blinking yellow—green eyes of Addie's tomcat. I rocked, porch boards creaking softly under my weight. I hardly knew what to do with myself.

No wings. No Angel. No second voice in my head or around my heart. I was still filled with magic, but I was human, and that was all I wanted to be. Humanity was what had held me together. My humanity—in all the worlds and all the times—had saved the day.

No one had fessed up to giving me a new soul. Not *mi abuelita*. Not Michael. Maybe neither of them had done it. Maybe both of them had. I wasn't sure it mattered.

Hinges squeaked behind me as the door opened, then nicked shut again. Sunday perched on the arm of my chair, pinning it in place.

She shivered in her tank top and pajama pants. Kittens, of all things. Kittens in Santa hats. She didn't say a word.

"You don't need to talk?" I asked.

"Nope."

"You want to fight?"

"Nope."

"Why aren't you with Luna?"

"Too keyed up."

"There's ways to handle that."

She rolled her eyes. "Sanchez, I just want to sit here with my best friend and wonder what in the wide world out there is different now. What did we change, when the news is still the same old trash fire and half the world is in a hand basket on its way to one of Famine's hells?"

"You watched the news?"

"I couldn't help it. I had to know. Now, answer the question."

I looked up at her. "You mean that?"

She nodded.

"We stopped the Apocalypse."

She smacked me in the back of the head.

I scowled at her, but couldn't hold on to irritation at the sight of her grin. And the real question in her eyes. She wanted to know we'd made a difference. And we had. We still could.

"Each of us has a chance now to make choices about what we want to be. Who we want to be."

"That's a little simplistic, don't you think?"

"I'm not a wordsmith, but I know what I'm talking about here."

"Me, too," she said.

I raised a brow.

"Hope."

The door creaked open again. This time, the opener didn't close it. Instead, he leaned against the doorjamb in nothing but a pair of jeans, his salt—and—pepper hair blowing in the gentle breeze and his green eyes locked on me.

"You coming to bed, Night?"

"She's to keyed up," Sunday said.

He sighed. "There's ways to handle that."

Sunday rose and dragged me to my feet alongside. "Get."

She didn't have to ask me twice. I reached for Red's hand as she slipped past us.

"What am I gonna do with you two?" he asked softly.

"Live with us."

"Now, there's a thought." He started inside. "You coming?"

"In a sec."

"No longer than that, Night."

"No."

He flashed a grin that promised love beyond my wildest dreams before he vanished inside.

I took another long look around. At the peaceful street, lights out and sleep filled with dreams. At the night sky, the moon bright and the stars stretched out across the velvet black. I thought about what Sunday had said. The word she'd used.

I tried it out, rolling it across my tongue. Tasting it like a delicacy. Like everything I'd ever wanted. It echoed in the night before it fell away to stillness.

I left it there, crossing the threshold in to the house. Into old love. Into new life.

Into hope.

255

REVIEWS

If you enjoyed this book, please consider leaving a review. It doesn't have to be long—even a few words will be very appreciated.

Reviews make it possible for an author to continue writing books in a series. They make a big difference in helping to get the word out about a book or a series. And reviews can make the all difference in the world when a reader wants to take a chance on a new author, but isn't sure whether they will like the book.

Thank you for taking hours out of your busy life to read. I hope this book brought you time to escape into a story, and that it brought you joy.

ABOUT THE AUTHOR

Since the age of seven, Leslie Claire Walker has wanted to be Princess Leia—wise and brave and never afraid of a fight, no matter the odds.

Leslie hails from the concrete and steel canyons and lush bayous of southeast Texas—a long way from Alderaan. Now, she lives in the rain-drenched Pacific Northwest with a cast of spectacular characters, including cats, harps, fantastic pieces of art that may or may not be doorways to other realms, and too many fantasy novels to count.

She is the author of **The Faery Chronicles** and **Soul Forge** series, two complete series of urban fantasy novels, novellas, and stories filled with found family, angels, assassins, faeries, and demons.

Connect with Leslie
leslieclairewalker.com
leslie@leslieclairewalker.com

ALSO BY LESLIE CLAIRE WALKER

THE AWAKENED MAGIC SAGA

THE SOUL FORGE

(The Complete Series)

Angel Hunts

Angel Rises

Angel Falls

Angel Strikes

Angel Roars

Angel Burns

THE FAERY CHRONICLES

(The Complete Series)

Faery Novice

Faery Prophet

Faery Sovereign

SHORT STORY COLLECTIONS

Ink & Blood

Ink & Stars

Ink & Sword

COPYRIGHT INFORMATION

www.ingramcontent.com/pod-product-compliance
Lightning Source LLC
Chambersburg PA
CBHW051144190726
48290CB00006B/1985